MY BEFORE

AND

AFTER LIFE

ALSO BY RISA MILLER

Welcome to Heavenly Heights

MY BEFORE

AND

AFTER LIFE

Risa Miller

St. Martin's Press

New York

MY BEFORE AND AFTER LIFE. Copyright © 2009 by Risa Miller. All rights reserved. Printed in the United States of America. For information, address St. Martin's Press, 175 Fifth Avenue, New York, N.Y. 10010.

www.stmartins.com

Library of Congress Cataloging-in-Publication Data

Miller, Risa.
  My before and after life / Risa Miller.—1st ed.
      p.   cm.
  ISBN 978-0-312-36013-9
  1. Fathers and daughters—Fiction.   2. Americans—Israel—Fiction.
3. Jewish converts—Fiction.   4. Israel—Fiction.   I. Title.
  PS3613.I5524M9 2010
  813'.6—dc22

2009033517

First Edition: January 2010

10 9 8 7 6 5 4 3 2 1

For Debbie Goldhair

acknowledgments

My deepest gratitude to: Elinor Lipman for her generosity; my esteemed and patient first readers, Jessica Keener, Joan Millman, Jessica Shattuck, and Rosie Sultan; my very wise and witty agent, Lisa Bankoff; my most astute editor, Dori Weintraub, who saw deep into the material and out again and brought me to the finish line, always with the *bon mot*. And to my parents, Dr. Melvin and Shirley Bulmash; my husband, Harry Miller; and children, Leah and Saul Feldman, Sara and Tsvi Zilberstein, Ari and Adina Miller, Miriam and Moshe Davidson, Eli Miller, and all those little ones, with much love.

BOOK I

one

WHEN OUR DEAR WIDOWED AND REMARRIED FATHER landed in Jerusalem and became a *born-again* Jew, he let us know in no uncertain terms that we should prepare to enter the Great Hall because this world is only a corridor. He let us know that when you stack seventy or eighty human years against the promise of eternity then all the playing rules in the here-and-now have got to be different.

Which is all I manage to write before Dad pops through my kitchen door on the way to my basement storage room, balancing a pair of white plastic milk crates. "Remember these? I found them deep in the recesses of my bedroom closet," he says.

"Those crates are like ghosts," I say.

"Well—maybe not ghosts. But I found some things," he says, sliding both of them onto the kitchen table.

"That's scary." I mean the word *things,* and the fact that for the first time in my life Dad won't be a five-minute walk away. His little sojourn in Jerusalem has a new permanence since he and his wife, Evelyn, have rented out their condo around the corner to a tenant who wants nothing less than a year's lease.

On the other hand, *scary* might also mean the response I know is coming. When he bends over and sees what I've typed, the phrase *born-again* sets him off on a soapbox.

"If you're so bent on writing the truth, say it correctly," Dad says. "Use the word *ba'al teshuvah*, 'returnee'—or just the proper translation: 'master of repentance.'" He drops one milk crate to the floor and begins to sort the contents. "Honey, you of all people, the haranguer for truth and justice, you should flee from distortion. *Born-again* makes it sound like some white-hot hallelujah moment." He pauses—but only to flick away a dazed and frozen spider with the back of his hand. "You know as well as I do that it's a process. And my particular take on the phrase *ba'al teshuvah*? It's that my eternal soul was always there and I returned to find it."

I can't help but notice how plaster dust salts his already salt and pepper hair.

"Hey! I wanted to show you something and now I can't find it," he says, pawing through the crate on the table. "I'll be right back." He turns out the kitchen door.

I find myself fiddling on the corner of the crate, like a blind person reading exit instructions with her fingertips. I haven't seen these fake milk crates since college, when they were the perfect size for my already antique LP records and my cousin's hand-me-down Whole Earth catalogs. It's there, bottom right corner, the curly script of my name, Honey Black, in blue glitter nail polish from one fuzzy rum and Coke college freshman night.

Dad's back. "I knew I'd seen them. They'd fallen off the top—I found them in the driveway." He's waving something—a stack of my summer camp letters.

Who knows if I'd saved them or Dad—or even Mom—but I know he means the adolescent elegy I wrote about fear not getting the best of me when the loons took over the camp lake at night and traded their grieving ululations. "And look what else I found." Under his arm is a shallow Filene's department store box, the kind which contained Mom's monogrammed linen. Once and long ago the linen was pearl pink and propitious, not meant to age in a cardboard box.

But the linen, the letter—they're props. Or an attempt to salve his aggressive piety, or the way his aggressive piety popped open old scabs and made the freshest of wounds. Or the way my foundation cracked, and our infrastructure crumbled and wanted to be put back together again—but only his way. Soon enough when he's out of sight it will be easier to write: Eight months ago Dad and Evelyn were visiting Jerusalem and he got tapped on the shoulder while standing at the Western Wall, and they were invited to a Sabbath meal. In warp time they became observant, orthodox. Religious. And we were, to put it mildly, shocked—and provoked.

Our reaction had its rhyme and reason. My dad had been no regular dad. Twenty-five years ago, when my dear mother died of breast cancer and I was twelve and my sister, Susan, was eight, Dad made one of those movie-script declarations that as long as he was around it would be as if we had never lost our mother, that he was good enough to be both parents. He was good for his word: through graduations, prom. College. Law school. My wedding. It didn't change when Dad got married to Evelyn, ten years ago. We never lived more than a two-block radius from each other, and I took for granted the lifestyle and love continuums in family—especially ours. They were the biggest comfort we had.

Then, suddenly, Dad pulls. Just in case we need more proof how serious he is, his version of events includes a broad statement of revelation: like the way you'd feel when a lightning bolt hits the path while you're lost in the woods at night and you see, suddenly clearly and specifically, where it is you're going. My version? Loss, more fresh loss just when I thought it couldn't happen. I mean, twelve months after Mom died I had to look at photographs if I wanted to remember her face. But, after all these years without Mom, when Dad broke his promise to be close, and to be our progenitor, all I felt was how the loss of Mom came bounding out of some old account ledger like I had some kind of interest due.

THE FIRST TIME I saw Dad after he was born again was in Jerusalem, where Susan and I went to go bring him home. My husband, Allan, had sat us down: We must intervene and talk sense into Dad the same way you do when a family member has an addiction. Next thing we knew, Allan said, Dad would try to convert us too, and weren't we fine the way we were? So, Susan and I got last-minute tickets on a Swiss flight with a stopover in Zurich on, of all days, December 25, which I hoped was some kind of good karma. I couldn't tell about the karma, but the stewards and stewardess were cheery and celebratory, serving sandwich cookie treats and shot-glass servings of chocolate ice cream every couple of hours.

We were cheery too, snug in our blasphemy and irreverence. Plus, I had my personal chimera, Mr. Uber-Jew, a dusty, bulging-eyed, black-frocked alien with side curls and rumpled pancake of a fedora. Unmistakable, spot-him-at-a-mile Uber-Jew, an alien on home soil.

Then, not that I needed another reason to go see him and get him back, but there was something else: Might there be, possibly, something wrong with Dad, physically wrong, like a fatal illness with a ticking clock, and the religion was his in-the-trenches reaction? Which was how I finally spooked Susan into going with me, though, sick or well, evangelist or alien, our agenda was the same: We were going to deprogram Dad from his brainwashing cult, bring him home, and sick or well, evangelist or alien, we were going to save him from saving his soul and revert to who we were, revert to order.

It was our first trip to Israel. Susan and I sat in a row of three, which we shared with a frequent Israel traveler, a Boston woman not ten years older than I, who said she had married children living in Jerusalem and yonder, and that she had Israeli grandchildren numbering in the double digits. When she asked us where Dad lived in Jerusalem and Susan dug out her address book and read, phonetically, "Re-cha-vee-ah," the woman hymned and hummed and haed, impressed.

I understood the response when the cabdriver out of the airport deposited us at the elegant, deciduous entrance of a four-story building, with an elevator and—the way they had terraced the interior hall—a garden entrance for each apartment. The inside-outside ambience, the views and windows and afterthought little extra porches were design hallmarks of what was indeed a fancy building in, as it turned out, an upscale, gentrified neighborhood. Dad and Evelyn lived on the second floor. But, beyond the elegant entrance, the apartment was compact, five small rooms. You walked directly into the living room, there was no hall closet, and the entire space was half the size they were used to. In his brainwashed and maybe sick condition, Dad had neglected to mention that they'd traded down their gallant concierge and health club condo in Brookline for a little Lego house.

I would have gone directly on to the offensive, to my planned and calculated deprogramming, except, a scant hour later, sitting deliciously and distractingly alone with Dad out on his little balcony, I found myself resisting: first of all, the inveiglement of dry, warm springtime air in the middle of winter; then the flickers and sparks of affection and connection coming from deep inside me. (Nothing Allan's directive had prepared me for.) Susan was napping off her jet lag on a living room sofa, and Evelyn had asked if we minded but set off anyhow to a prayer class which had a come-hither pop-song

name like Heart and Soul. I couldn't remember the last time Dad
and I were alone, just the two of us. Which was a dangerous, di-
verting thought. Especially since—was I really surprised?—Dad's
eyes weren't bulging; he looked healthy all right, pink cheeked and
a little fattened up, and he wasn't dusty or wearing a frock coat or a
black fedora. He wore his old gray Levi's, sneakers, and a sports
jacket. Only his yarmulke was a serious statement of identity: a
high, black, puffy velveteen affair.

The porch chairs were familiar; they were the same ones Allan
and I bought for our deck last spring on one of the Home Depot
Sundays we drag our boys to before we get them sushi and ice cream.
The chairs were, in fact, exactly the same: white Adirondack style,
thickly cushioned. And, above us, the round winter sun rolled
across the sky, right to left; was it possibly the opposite direction of
movement from where we live, in Brookline, Massachusetts? Questions of time, space, structure, weight-bearing properties were the
usual fare that showed what heroic capacity Susan and I had always
held Dad in. Dad was a powerful and smart man, who in his real
life built and owned and managed the biggest scaffolding company
in New England.

I was glad to be sitting. The task was big and I took a deep cleans-
ing breath and I fronted some small talk about the sweet, springlike
weather in December. I knew how to soften Dad up by summoning a
long-standing joke to say he'd special-ordered a good day just for us.

"Not so special and not so sweet," he said. To my surprise: Didn't
he remember the joke?

"The weather isn't supposed to be dry and warm like this in December," he said. "It means we Jews are doing something wrong. *Darn*
it. If people are doing what they should, the rains and all the right
weather come in the right time." His features softened into his face
familiarly, but he was all worked up.

A shot of hard energy raced down my lower back, and I screwed my legs firmly on the balcony floor. This was it: Dad's phone calls and e-mails were full of the same cosmic talk, and I'd come to wave my saber. "Dad, your *darn it* makes you sound like a Boy Scout who's stubbed his toe," I said.

"Well, I can say *darn* if I want. What? You want me to say *damn*?"

"It would be better." I meant, of course, better to have unearthed the real him, the unpious, less cosmic him.

Dad looked at me and shook his head as if I wasn't so funny and he'd just figured out why I was sitting there with him in Jerusalem. "You're wrong about this. It's not what you think." Then he changed the subject, abruptly. "I installed the railing myself," he said, standing up and pointing to the whorlly iron around the balcony.

So now, a beat too late, he was going to remember and play to our history: He knew that the old daughter-me wouldn't have blanched if he said he installed the round winter sun himself. It was only slightly easier to picture Dad kneeling his back into a C, dabbing a carpenter's level against the tall scrolled posts.

"I planted those bushes too," he added, wagging his forefinger to a spot below the balcony, to a small grassless playground where a dozen kids of all ages turned up dust in a space the size of my backyard. There, rows of small shrubs, crawling like dry pachysandra, were scotched with neon pink flowers. He paid for the drip irrigation, he was installing a water fountain.

Oh, he was handling me; he knew what he was doing: If I paid too close attention to the details—the flowers, the water—the slowdown would suck the focus right out of me.

I jumped back to business. "Come home, Dad. How can you do this, to our family?"

"Do what to the family?" Dad said. "I haven't murdered anyone."

"Oh, Dad—"

"What do you mean, 'Oh, Dad'? I'm sitting here content. With some perspective on life—and death, I might add. Which might affect you if you'd care to listen. You've always been a smart one. Can't you at least say you're happy because I am?"

"You're *too* happy." Quick rejoinders are my specialty, but it wasn't the last moment on that trip that my mouth opened and sounded smart, but I didn't believe what I said.

"Don't worry."

"I am worried." I guessed I'd hit a nerve, judging from the lines which began to crawl across his forehead. Time to raise the pressure and be all-inclusive. "You're sitting here—you've turned your back on every*thing* and every*body* you've ever known."

"You're exaggerating."

"I wish you were wrong. You left. You walked out of our lives. That's what it feels like to us. To Susan and to me."

His forehead flattened out. Though not in remorse or conciliation. So I pulled back. "Okay. Look at you. The way you're sitting there. It doesn't bother you that we feel that way?"

"Okay. You want bother? You want bother? What bothers me is having spent my whole adult life in total ignorance, where I've been, where I'm going."

We both knew that wasn't the bother I meant, but in spite of himself he'd given me an opening. "You see. How you've turned away from us? All your e-mails, your phone conversations: They're all about your heritage, your soul, your afterlife. What about this world, this life? You're—you're hyperfocused." I nudged the insult. "You're giddy—no, not quite giddy, you're . . ." I scrambled for the perfect words, *the rapture state*—something. If Susan were awake, she'd have had the perfect observing classification. "Beatific!" is what finally popped in my head.

"Beatific?" He looked puzzled. "Am I too beatific or not beatific enough for your idea of why this is all wrong?" He didn't wait for my answer. "Okay—I won't be beatific. Here's a real complaint," Dad said. "There's so many kids here—and the noise outside my windows is unstoppable." He sat back, whooshing loud air out of his seat cushion.

"Now you're playing me," I said. "You're trumping up a complaint for the benefit of proof. The noise doesn't really bother you. You *are* beatific."

"Yes, I'm full of joy and rapture, if that's what *beatific* means. And, yes—I'm also trumping—just so you won't call me on the carpet for all the other extremes—televangelist, freak, alien from Mars— one or the other," he said. "I don't have to be a genius to guess your agenda, something straight out of a deprogramming manual."

Okay, so he was on to me, but at least I could see the battle line. From where I sat in my life, with my husband and family, why would anyone in his right mind self-impose a life of limitations such as orthodox *anything*? And, didn't he get it? We were always good people before this, he—we—didn't need this, so why all of a sudden . . . "So then, what *about* obeisance to rules and regulations?" I hammered on. "Or financial exploitation? Or exploitation, period? Clarify for me: Did you mean you dug the hole for the bushes and put them in the ground, or did you pay for the planting?"

"The works," he said, backing his chair away.

My facial muscles went slack in frustration. He couldn't help but notice; his voice softened.

"No, really," he said. "I'm not saying it to put you off. It didn't amount to much shovel work or much money. Stop straining so hard. Why are you hacking at me for the truth if you don't want to hear it?"

I ignored the comment. I had that last, perverse thought. "Dad, is this some end-of-life, what's-it-all-about thing?"

"You mean like repent before I die, or something like that?"

That's what I meant. He leaned out of his porch chair and grabbed me by the arm with a little force. He was serious. "Yes, actually it is all about end of life. I am finally, finally, *finally* paying attention to my eternal soul, and I am well. Never more well than in my whole life. As far as I can tell, I am not dying tomorrow, but I plan to be prepared if I do."

What could I have said? What could anyone have said?

We were saved from our awkward standoff by a loud, strained squeal on the street beneath the balcony: a delivery truck working its way through what they called streets in that neighborhood (which would be called alleys anywhere else in the world). And the tapered flatbed, narrow and flexible as a caterpillar, was clearly evolutionized for native terrain. The truck stopped, and the driver jumped out in front of Dad's building, hoisting red and blue crates onto his back. Behind us, back in the apartment, came the loud, steady buzz of the doorbell, and Dad beelined off the balcony to answer it. Not before an uncharacteristic sprinkle of irony: "Eternal souls have to eat while they are in this world."

The doorbell woke Susan up. Dazed and disarrayed from her heavy travel sleep, she walked into the kitchen, standing next to me at the doorway as we watched the delivery boy, who knew his way into the kitchen. He passed Dad a cardboard flat of white eggs, emptied the food onto the kitchen table, the chairs, the bookshelves under the telephone, next to the Mr. Coffee. He shoved flimsy cellophane boxes of grapes, white, bulbous vegetables, and yellowed tomatoes on top of the microwave. After he left, Dad moved about deliberately. I watched him tuck the boxes and cans into cabinets, under counters. "I save the fruit for last," he said.

Dad was telegraphing, and we got the message. This putting away, the domesticity, was routine, and his job, not Evelyn's. Even half awake, Susan raised her eyebrows; her eyes met mine as we turned our gaze to Dad. In a second, anyone could have known: Didn't we three belong together?—our muscular bodies, big foreheads, wide-set, expressive green eyes. Even the delivery boy had to know Dad was us, Dad was ours. We watched how Dad laid out the food, just like scaffolding, in ladders and flats: He pulled out the fruit drawer in the refrigerator to arrange and stack the produce, laying the crushables in their containers around the edges, laddering them in the center, tucking extant apples and pears in between a pallet of cello boxes. Susan laid her hand on my arm. He looked so much like the Dad we knew; maybe this religion stuff was some temporary madness, like a sickness from drinking the wrong potion.

"Okay. Okay. We get it. In spite of it all," Susan said, "you're still building. You want to tell us you're exactly the same."

"No, there's nothing to be in spite of, and I want to tell you I'm *not* the same," Dad answered. "I'm not building *things* anymore. I'm building a soul." With that, he turned his face away, an old habit of faux modesty that reminded me: Right or wrong, he was never one to restrain himself. Then he spun his yarmulke, a very new and uncharacteristically nervous gesture that, yes, in spite of everything he said, made my heart tilt, allowed us to hope that all—he—wasn't lost.

two

BROOKLINE, MASSACHUSETTS, THE PLACE DAD LEFT, IS THE place where I grew up, the place where I live and practice law; it's the place where my sister, Susan, is the day manager of Beacon Seafood, her husband's family's famous restaurant. Brookline is the place where Susan lives and renovates her Victorian house on the historic register. Actually, she renovates the restaurant as well as her house, both facts which put her in *Boston* magazine or *The Boston Globe Magazine* every other year.

Brookline is a town in its own right, with evolved, liberal self-governance, and I of all people should look over my shoulder when I say this, but in spite of its reality as a town—elected officials, town police, et cetera—Brookline is best described as a bedroom community to the city of Boston. When I'm traveling and meet new people, to streamline the conversation I often say I live in Boston, though technically that's a lie; my mortgage documents say, for example, Brookline is a town in Norfolk County. Not a mention of Boston proper.

Brookline is especially proud of its clean and safe mass transportation, a vast park system with special off-leash dog hours, excellent public schools, endless ethnic culinary opportunity; and, for the record, it's enlightened, intelligent, and tolerant, an urban paradigm of the melting pot, including orthodox Jews who've staked out their turf here or the handful of monks who turn up in the bank or the supermarket in full robe and rope regalia. If this were a year ago, and the story weren't happening to me, I could have imagined a Brookline family picture of perfect multiculturalism, a tidy scene straight off a little Colorforms board: a yarmulked dad walks alongside a secular and blue-jeaned daughter, and they smile and exchange the props they have in common, like yellow rain hats and umbrellas with curly handles. But life never works so smoothly when it's off the prop board.

I hear Dad slam the hatchback on his car, and he comes through the kitchen door. This last box from this last carload has finally made him break out into a sweat and roll his shirtsleeves back on his still strong forearms. He roots himself in front of me; he's holding out a slim children's picture book with his free hand. Mom grew up in Brookline too, he wants to remind me. I can see from the cover the book is about some Jewish folk hero or superhero. Dad says his name, Bar Kochba, which he translates for me as "Son of a Star." Inside, the title page bears an inscription: "To Rachel Mandelbaum, for General Excellence, Beth Aharon Hebrew School, third grade, June 1958."

Dad is making a point. Okay, so Mom had background. Jewish religious background. She knew about all the religion stuff Dad is up to because she went to a religious Sunday school. I don't have to be reminded. Mom's own parents were small twigs from broken branches of two orthodox religious families, the Briskers and the Mandelbaums, family names recognized anywhere around the Jewish world, like the Barrymores might be in Hollywood or the Kennedys in D.C., except their signature traits were piety and scholarship. And Mom's family was known as the red-haired Mandelbaums, which from our experience skipped generations and gave brown-haired people like me red-haired children like mine. And for the record, Mom—more than Dad—had that small residual of religious identity: She never ate a cheeseburger (the forbidden: a calf boiled in its mother's milk), and I knew to never eat one in front of her. She never took us to restaurants like Steve's family's, now Susan's, for crab cakes and lobster tails (the forbidden: bottom-feeding crustaceans with no fins and scales). Mom never served bacon with our eggs, or glasses of milk with our lamb chops, but in the end nothing set us apart from our neighbors. Dad asks if I want to keep the Bar Kochba book upstairs, and even though it's speckled with mold, black and blue as a bruise, and I have no desire to read about heroes—especially Jewish ones—of course I must say yes. He trots that last box down to the basement, and I keep writing.

DAD AND EVELYN'S ROOTS trip last year was the beginning of it all, and the basic facts already sounded straight out of a drama. Maybe *King Lear*, Susan said. "Or 'King of the Road,'" I said. "Mom used to like that song." (Which, because of our difference in ages, Susan didn't remember.)

I like to think ROOTS was an adventure Mom would have chosen, but who knows? Her sickness and struggle sapped all the life out of her even before she died. The ROOTS idea was brought about by survivors, from survivors, for survivors: Evelyn's gaggle of breast cancer survivors (her included) and the walkathon and marathon friends from whose orbit Dad and Evelyn were fixed up. The survivor travel agent advertised the trip in big pink letters. ROOTS: a positive and personalized visit back in history. No matter two cities or four or eight, a city per grandparent, the tour cost the same. Plus, 10 percent of ROOTS tour profits went to breast cancer research.

Just for the record, Susan and I have worked hard to be grateful

Dad married Evelyn, for all his reasons, but from our point of view the plus side is significant: Evelyn is Dad's age, a little overweight—dumpy really—no trophy chippie, no betrayal of Mom, as if all the time he was caretaking he'd been biding his time and the man in him wanted something hotly different, hotly alive. Plus, for second-wife business, the outlet for healthy humor is priceless, a gift really. Our family name is Black, and before Evelyn was married her name was White. What's black and white and red all over? It went something like that.

On their pink ROOTS ticket, Dad and Evelyn flew to Budapest and traveled eastward to her grandmother's Prague with an automaton golem figure, part Gumby, part ghost. The hocus-pocus stuff charmed Evelyn. And Dad, equally charmed by Evelyn, actually did what she said, kept packing, touring, packing up again. He kept in touch with us with phone calls and e-mails. Had we ever heard of the Golem of Prague? When was the last time he took so much time off? Dad and Evelyn scheduled a half dozen places, east and west of Ukraine, from Kiev to dot-on-the-map Volochisk on the Polish border, and then something happened along the way. Two weeks into the trip, they went to Israel. Evelyn had a grandfather who'd gone to the Holy Land directly from eastern Europe in 1898, drained a swamp, laid cornerstones for a half dozen municipal buildings until he was ambushed and dismembered by local tribesmen who coveted his fine black horse. His family didn't get the letters until two years after he died. The grandfather's hut was long razed and gone, but they found his grave.

A week later we got an e-mail that they liked the weather. That they rented a hotel-apartment suite in the little resort city of Netanya by the Mediterranean Sea. And they never said they were extending their vacation, but they weren't rushing back either. This was no longer a ROOTS trip but recreation. On the beach, in a sun spot. The apart-hotel provided cleaning help and twenty-four-hour room service and an English-language newspaper at the door every morning. Okay. Dad and Evelyn knew how to enjoy themselves. And then they booked an Elderhostel excursion up to Jerusalem and took that fateful trip to the Western Wall.

You know, I never found out who tapped Dad on the shoulder, but when I close my eyes, I picture him like in *Spy vs. Spy* in an old MAD magazine, an illusory figure, face shadowed by a wide-brimmed hat, hand creeping out of a draping sleeve. Everything sneaky and bad I can attribute to the picture, I do. Maybe because of the shock. Maybe because of the suddenness. Most likely because of the primal fear of separation and "otherness" which struck in my gut when I opened that first declaratory e-mail.

I was home alone, downstairs in my office. Slipping on my reading glasses, slouching behind my desk. Maybe, the moment also struck terror because I knew that when Dad sent the e-mail he could picture me, exactly; he was the one who drew out my office design to make it exactly like his own home office; he was the one who showed me how we could build into the main basement room by moving the furnace and the hot-water heater and how to set a bow window behind the desk just like he had where there's enough afternoon sun to keep the flowering plants alive.

The e-mail came with a title in all caps:

RE: FROM HERE TO ETERNITY
From: dan@buildascaffold.com
Fiduciary@vistanet.com (Honey)
cc: SP @ BeaconSeafood.com (Susan),

Hi girls: Our trip has turned into a journey. A life journey. We're renting an apartment in Jerusalem and we're going to religion classes. Getting religion—I've seen the light, am saving my soul—no, just kidding, no—not kidding. We bought a gorgeous painting and I'm learning Talmud and the Books of Moses with orthodox rabbis here who are really not bad the way you might think. So we're enjoying the Sabbath, staying and learning all sorts of things mostly about when you stack 70 or 80 human years against the promise of eternity how the human playing rules have got to be different. Even if they make you different. Anyhow, did you know that a giraffe is kosher (if only they could figure out which part of the neck to slaughter)? Will call you girls—you *women* (Evelyn is correcting over my shoulder)—with details, our overall plan here, what seems to be the overall plan being handed to us. Love, Dad & Evelyn

I read it a second time, and all I could think of was that he'd gone crazy.

I scrolled down a third time, looking for a punch line which didn't exist, and then I called Susan on her triptych of numbers. Home, restaurant, cell—where I found her in her decorator's car, creeping through a rush-hour travel circle in East Boston. On their way to the Decorators Showroom in search of an embossed tin ceiling for the restaurant foyer.

"I just saw it on my BlackBerry," she said. "I thought it was a joke."

"A joke? It would have to be a pretty sick joke," I said.

I heard her decorator, Carnie Goldstein, her unmistakable voice, smooth as glass, tinkling out a laugh. I could tell from Susan's playfulness she was in one of her empowerment moods, one of her search-and-seizure highs. When she was on the hunt, when she was in the middle of renovating, designing, planning, or decorating or choosing, the rest of the world fell away. She always came back to earth, but sometimes she needed a prompt.

"You have to take this seriously," I said.

"Look, I have my own high standards to uphold—here—first." That comment was for Carnie's benefit, but no doubt Carnie knew the drill, the holy grail of Susan's decorating success: Susan's best inspired visionary contribution to the restaurant, which was the wallpaper she'd purchased the same month she married into the business, when she marched herself off to the Decorators Showroom in East Boston, flora and fauna in mind. Browns to nurture, greens to relax, red to stimulate appetites. How, in five minutes, she'd scored an all-in-one, a dense Victorian pastiche of brown melons held up by green curlicue vines held up by red cabbage roses. And the local restaurant Old Favorites Restaurant Review said, "Bravo, keep it coming." Carnie tinkled another laugh in the background.

"Susan—concentrate. I need you," I said.

She would be back at Beacon Seafood in an hour. She hung up with a promise to call me after the lunch crowd.

As far as my life, then and now, what was and hasn't changed in fact is that I'm a wife and a mother of two redheaded boys: Richard, twelve, and Ronnie, eight (resonant ages for Susan and me). I'm also a social action attorney with a master's in city planning. I fight buildings and neighborhood development; I fight coercion, monoliths, attitudes, and institutions which crush individual need and identity, which could have meant religion but up until recently never did. I champion the right and the good and the true. But what has changed everything in fact is that when that e-mail came from Dad I had just taken on a big case. Big not because of the numbers or size of the project but because—even without Dad lining up with the other side—I knew I would flap wings, make waves, whatever metaphors you have for turning the town into a dodgeball game. A case of a neighborhood association against the expansion, or in our opinion the neighborhood usurpation, of Brookline Hebrew Day

School, an orthodox Jewish school, chief plaintiffs being a neighborhood task force led by Rae Stark, an old family friend and my husband, Allan's first cousin.

Up until recently, when it wasn't such a sensitive joke, Allan would say that my religion was cause-baiting, fist-raising do-gooding. Allan is the picture of the so-called rational man who only believes in what he can see in front of his eyes or, more accurately, believes that what he can see with his eyes is the only reality. He's also a lawyer, though the quieter type; he specializes in intellectual property litigation, whose battle is to keep the lines of the mind clean and tidy (most recently, for example, protecting municipal solar energy trash-compacting machines from cheap Asian-made imitations). He works on the thirty-sixth floor in an office tower next to the State House.

My home office is closer to my clients, who are, in fact, mostly neighbors. In the same year, I might redesign two U-turns on Beacon Street, less convenient for the chain supermarket but safer for the day-care center; wangle pedestrian crossing guards near the assisted-living home; keep a Barnes & Noble from buying a home for disabled children or building a four-story emporium across from a Borders bookstore.

Until that first heralding e-mail, we were normal people, with a normal sense of who lined up on what side of truth and consequences.

Oh, sometimes I wish that I were less honest, that my pursuit of truth didn't lead me down paths I never wanted. It would be awfully convenient now to say that when I got the first complaint against the orthodox school from Rae Stark, I felt the flutter of trepidation in my chest, a moment of self-consciousness, a moment of what-if? regarding the metaphysical consequences of taking on religion.

And it's not as if I never thought about what would have been so bad if, instead of pursuing truth, I'd made coffee cakes for a business, like Rae and her husband, who turned a tired family bakery into mail-order gourmet. Or if I'd joined the Build-a-Scaffold team one of the hundred times Dad asked me to. But until this year the answer was always clear. Scaffold building wasn't enough do-gooding for me. As a teenager, I used to make fun of Dad's—would I call them pedestrian?—aspirations. I was barely five years old when our great-grandfather's dairy farm in Millis whittled itself down to a barn and some generational serfs and Dad bought a truckload of scaffolding and decided to rent it out. A small beginning, but by the time I was a teenager there wasn't a building in northern New England that didn't have his name on it. I, daughter know-it-all, urging some more socially large or at least esoteric pursuits, tried to convince him to at least use a more evolved name—Higher Highs— which he hasn't reminded me of yet. But I'm waiting.

three

THAT FIRST NIGHT IN JERUSALEM, IN SPITE OF THE SPIKY moments, Dad and I parted at bedtime with hugs and kisses. We still had our relationship, and I had five more days to dispute his little cache of bother and beatifics and soul-searching. Of course, I hadn't counted on my turbulent subconscious, which got very busy the minute I sank into my bed, whisking up—of all things, of all the reactions!—images of Mom. The little things she did and what she said, which even at the time I understood as Jewish; that is, Jewish meaning not the same as my neighbors Tammy Nolan and Karin Sullivan. And Jewish not like Rae Stark's mother, Molly Stark, who was Jewish but a study in white-bread expression. For example, if we heard not the best report from the doctor, Mom's first response sounded as if she'd been punched in the stomach: "oy!" Molly Stark, on the other hand, said "my goodness" or "oh my" or once I heard her say "good grief."

And then there was Mom's excessive response when I complained about the food at summer camp. When we didn't like what they served breakfast, lunch, or dinner, we could eat peanut butter on white bread or bologna and cheese. Do not eat the bologna and cheese, Mom said. Do not eat milk and meat together. How could

I not eat bologna and cheese if everyone else was eating it? But she meant it, the way Tammy Nolan's mother admonished her to brush her teeth or not wear white shoes before Memorial Day or after Labor Day. Of course I ate milk and meat together anyhow, though I still heard Mom's voice—years later, when I ate hamburgers in my college dining hall, spooning melted Velveeta cheese from the vat onto my burger. I was doing something wrong. Wrong to whom? To what? Why should I have been the one who stood out? In the end, those little Jewishisms didn't create a Judaism—not anything passed forward or distinguishing us—they were just what we knew of Mom. Like bits of personality, like that she'd been a naturally early riser or that purple was her favorite color. All these years later, as I ponder Mom's "religion," it's like holding a handful of puzzle pieces when I'm missing the picture on the top of the box.

THAT FIRST MORNING in Jerusalem, struggling to nurse my poor focus into concentration, I stood in the living room in Dad's new apartment, smack inside a Middle Eastern winter sunbeam wide and dry as a searchlight, all this Jewish and not on my mind. It reminds me now as I write of the stupidest joke I'd heard as a kid but never understood until this minute: the searchlight joke where a kid comes across his friend scrounging for his watch and when the first one asks the scrounger where he lost it, the scrounger says, "Over there," pointing away, and when the first one asks why, then, is he looking over here, the guy says, "This is where the light is." The point my subconscious had been pounding at was whether there was something right about all this, whether Mom might have minded Dad in this incarnation. Would she have argued with him? Not minded? Partnered with him?

I checked my watch, which I'd reset on the plane, a funny little travesty, considering it was Mom's gold flex-band Baume & Mercier, which I'd worn since she didn't wear it anymore. I walked into the kitchen, found the phone under a clean and empty Mr. Coffee. I'd planned to call Allan; 6:45 A.M. Israel time meant 11:45 P.M. Boston time, and if he was sleeping, I'd hang up. So I picked out the small-print instructions on my calling card and Allan answered with loud, sleazy music in the background. "Hi," he said, sounding wide awake. "I'm watching *Goldfinger* on TV. It's just starting. But how's it going?"

He would have to pull himself away from *Goldfinger* if he wanted to hear the real answer, that I'd sniffed out the situation in a day, that I was beginning to wonder if I was going to let him down because Dad had already played the intractable hand. So it wasn't the truth when I said I didn't want to disturb him, and so he didn't read my mind and turn down the sound, but I managed to hear that he signed for a FedEx delivery of a set of Brookline Hebrew Day revised building plans. The school was serious and relentless; this was the third set of revised plans, coming as fast as we asked for them. All that by-the-books approval seeking, that too eager response to all our requests raised the goodwill stakes, in its own way just as disconcerting as acrimony. They'd flooded us back with so much paper that when I left Boston I'd walked out on a bloated stack of accordion files, which could have held up my credenza and not the other way around.

In my defense, even now I'll say it, I wouldn't have signed on the case and agreed to be chief counsel for *Neighborhood Association vs. Brookline Hebrew Day School* if I didn't wholly believe that a single-usage group such as the school mustn't appropriate a neighborhood. Period.

I'd sat in Rae's living room, in her musky old Tudor with high, small windows, which had for years anyhow reminded me of lookouts or arrow slits in castle walls, to see what she meant. At 7:45 A.M. a rattly fifteen-passenger van came clogging up the road, releasing a dozen skinny, yelping children from each door. In non-legal terms, I couldn't quite put my finger on it beyond that look of otherness: The plump and pretty teacher-mother-driver had stiff, maybe what you would call bobbed, honey-colored hair; translucent skin, which made her face dewy and pure; and from below the knees, anyway, stork-thin legs and tiny ankles, each of which looked to be the size of a marble. She parked the van down in the dead-end circle in front of Rae's house, by all accounts legal parking, as long as it conformed to the town's two-hour residential parking limit. But was that smugness as the sidewalk morphed into *her* turf when she burdened along with her travel coffee mug looped through her thumb and rolled poster board—the day's lesson—under her arm?

A half dozen teachers and mothers came just like that: vans, kids. And boom, from Rae's house to the end of the street, every inch parked up. *Appropriated*—Rae's word. Even before she hired me, she began calling the Brookline Police. They knew her, of course, from her organization of antiwar rallies, PETA rallies, and her company's antihunger initiative, called Let Them Eat More Than Cake. The point was, the town listened when she said the school employees parked cars over two hours on her residential street and there was no reason to be lax or generous, the way the police usually were. Some teachers got a fresh parking ticket every two hours. In legal terms, well, the letter of the law.

The wanging *Goldfinger* theme song brought me back to the conversation, with Allan, in Dad and Evelyn's bright, sunlit Jerusalem kitchen. "Well, I'll let you get back to your movie. I was just checking in," I said, as the not very sunny but very obvious thought occurred to me: If Dad were back in Brookline, his new alignments and associations would land him firmly on the other side of the school case, the side against Rae and me. If Dad got one whiff of the case before I brought him back, what I had to do first in Jerusalem would backfire. Allan caught my tremble.

"You sound shaken . . . or is it stirred? Are you okay?"

"Very funny. But it should be obvious. If Dad hears about the school case before I get him back, he won't see that he and the school are two separate things; he'll just use it against me and my arguments to get him home. That all I'm about is antireligion."

"Well, turf issues often become social agenda. And vice versa. That's nothing new."

"But turf wars break up families. He'll never talk to me again. Or Rae. Or you. It's so complicated."

The more I thought about it, the more complicated it got: Rae and the Starks, and Allan and Dad and I went way back before the school case, before religion, before anything. Mom and Rae Stark's mother—who was Allan's aunt—had breast cancer together. The first club on their block before people talked support groups. Infrabuddies, they used to call themselves, best hospital friends, and they infraed together through their whole series of treatments until, true buddies, they both lost the same month. Mom died first. For years we and the Stark family got together for rite-of-passage occasions, Bar Mitzvahs, graduations—less social and more like signal beacons— the dot-dash-dot of the living where attendance blinked assurance, that we'd gotten on with life too.

Allan came in the picture after one tedious Bar Mitzvah one spring Saturday. The rest of us were busy stoking our famous long, slow good-byes, to Rae's family, to Dad, to Moses Stark (Dad's peer in loss), to each other. The first to leave was a defector, usually to no reward. I slunk out the door, blowing a kiss in their general direction,

and my double take on Allan was a double surprise. I knew Allan—
we all knew Allan—even spoke to him a dozen times over the years,
at the interfamily affairs.

I've only told him the next part once, because it's silly: There he
stood across the median at the trolley stop, light bouncing off him
through the heavy arms of full, leafy trees, and something inside
me lurched—actually, physically lurched in his direction as he fleeced
himself of a berry blue yarmulke (a party favor) and there he stood
figuring out what to do with the yarmulke. I watched him peer into
the public trash barrel, start to drop the yarmulke in, then stick it in
his jacket pocket.

As I've known Allan, built my life with him, had children with
him, I've come to understand that, just in case I was wondering, his
keep-that-yarmulke gesture was more environmental than indica-
tive of any incipient spirituality. So when Allan signed off the phone
call, he used some football charge, something like "Go get 'em."

Which would have been a fine thing to say back in Brookline.
But I was in Jerusalem having all kinds of bouncing and crazy reactions. Standing in Dad and Evelyn's new kitchen: When I heard
the rumbling noise in the master bedroom just on the other side
of the kitchen wall, my stomach fluttered. Drawers opening and
shutting, some talking—the privacy and repartee of a couple, the
hint of goings-on behind a closed bedroom door, shouldn't have
embarrassed me; I was an adult, Dad and Evelyn were a couple. But
Evelyn walked into the kitchen, alone, snapping shut her cell phone.
"Cellcom to Cellcom is free. Your dad has been out for an hour.
He's at the Kosel," she said.

"Where is Dad exactly?" I asked.

"He's *davening* at the Kosel," Evelyn said. *He*, of course, meant
Dad. I didn't understand where he was any better for the repetition.
I could hold steady against the foreign-word onslaught. I didn't

have to know what the Kosel was. "You've been a busy bee," I said
instead, pointing to the vegetable assembly on the counter, and the
trash can full to the brim with peelings. I didn't have to be a foodie
like Susan to notice the smug look to the kitchen, being used full-
force gale and all cleaned up at the same time. Except for the single
unprocessed object on the counter, which was a cellophane tub of
dirty mushrooms.

"We get up early. I cook more than ever, and your dad makes the
mushroom salad for Shabbos."

The definitive irked me: *the* mushroom salad. And her insider
words were a stomach punch: *Shabbos* raised my hackles back to yesterday's alert. And since when did Dad *do* mushroom salad? Anyhow, was this the evidence of mind control I'd been looking for?
Maybe Evelyn was the problem, but the thought rang false, like an
easy way out. Though, to her credit, Evelyn pulled a jar of Nescafé
instant from the refrigerator, nodded in the direction of a plug-in
teakettle, and ticked the plug into the wall.

For a single regressed moment what I really wanted to ask was,
why wasn't Dad home? What was Dad doing that was so important
it competed with our visit? But my mission to bring Dad home was
larger than being his daughter, even if being his daughter was something strong and protected, like basking under a wing. I twisted
myself back to priorities, my caustic, evaluating eye a proper offensive tool, more what I'd expect from Susan than from me. Beyond
Evelyn's head, the truncated kitchen was a victim of hyperdesign:
the kitchen cabinets so high against the ceiling you'd have to wear
stilts to reach them, a half-width stove with a flip-down lid that
doubled as counter space, the regular-width refrigerator with nowhere to go but half way out on what they called the laundry porch.
And, I didn't know what and I didn't know why, but Evelyn had
taken to wearing something on her head: yesterday a pink Red Sox

cap, today a denim-colored sack the likes of which I'd last seen on one of the Seven Dwarfs. I didn't mind the feminist symmetry with Dad's yarmulke, if that's what it was. (Not that I was going to ask and pop open some other dam.) She looked like herself, more or less. Her forehead was high and smooth, her eyes puffy with morning, her mind working behind them, brooking no ill will. Until she began to talk again.

"Your dad is *davening* to make the rain come," Evelyn said.

The foreign word wasn't what got to me that time. It was the sudden mental image of a rain dance. I must have groaned out loud.

This, Evelyn got. "Oh—*davening* is praying." That said, she rattled out a couple of plates and cups, front-loading questions as if she were firing a cannon: Did I want milk for my coffee? Was I hungry? Was I finding Dad difficult what with all the changes and all?

Before she married Dad, and for many years afterward, Evelyn had been a middle school guidance counselor, and it was easy to slip into her orbit, since she often began a conversation with a little reconnoiter, like how was I feeling about something. On the other hand, who wanted to drive to the core of every conversation? Did she really want to hear that Dad's changes made me fresh with Mom's loss or that I felt as if I'd been abandoned on the roadside? But I was stuck with our strategic planning if Susan and I were going to influence him and bring them home. I motioned for the coffee, and we sat down at the kitchen table, a glass circle big enough for two in comfort, three with touching knees and elbows. Séance ready, if the offer came up. I held my tongue till the coffee put me back in form. Evelyn offered me a poppy seed roll from a white paper bag and held up a plastic tub of soft cheese.

That's when Susan tumbled in and broke the caustic spell I'd tried so hard to create. There are two sides to Susan, the deco-warrior I lose patience with for her aggressive shallowness, and the woman

behind the scenes who annoys me with her soft, stretchy adaptive-
ness. She might have gotten off the plane as the first Susan, but now
she was the other, wearing an unmatched brown T-shirt and blue
flannel pants drawn tight into a wedgie, rifling through a stack of
mail next to the Mr. Coffee—an at-home gesture if there ever was
one. She pulled out the third chair and sat. "The place here is nice.
Strange but nice," she said, as she sat down. "You know, Evelyn, the
things are you and Dad, but the decor isn't you and Dad. It's like
home–not home."

"We're trying," Evelyn said. Her face brightened, off the hot spot
for my unspoken list of offenses, which allowed her to express herself. "But truth be told, the furniture isn't our first choice. Not at
all. We rented it furnished." She paused, about to talk about something else that wasn't first choice, then changed her mind. "But the
food's ours, the atmosphere." She took her own roll gingerly, sliced
through it with a knife, and swiped soft cheese on it, barely losing a
poppy to the turn of her hand. Then she took a tiny, pyramid-shaped
shaker, sprinkled green spices onto the cheese, and walked back to
the sink and washed her hands.

Meanwhile, I tried to head off Susan's pleasantries and bland
equivocations, which were bound to blur the lines in the sand.
We were not there to relate, be polite, accommodate. To no avail:
Susan lifted the spice pyramid, turning it round and round in her
hand. "What is this stuff?"

Back at the table, Evelyn shook her head silently and wagged two
pinched fingers in the air. After she'd sat and swallowed a bite of
bread, she answered. "A local-yokel spice. Called *za'atar*. Oregano.
Sesame. And a blend of other stuff I can't read on the label."

Susan tapped some spice on her finger. Tasted. Smiled. Smiled
big. Even if she was "off," she didn't have to be that enthusiastic at
the risk of subverting our goals with her flattery and interested

questions, which she would defend to me later as needing a cup of coffee, being disoriented, jet-lagged. Evelyn laid out a coffee cup for Susan, and to Susan's credit, she read my face and stopped talking. But Evelyn's chatter took up the empty space like some law of conversational physics.

"Anyhow," Evelyn said, "you know what our neighbors did, our neighbors upstairs." She took a bite of her bread, unaware of the drumroll in my brain. One day into our mission, and I was already trigger sensitive to the heralds of change; my bare feet burned against the cold stone floor. Out of the sunlight the stone was cold enough to confuse my sensations.

"It's not like there's a real reason, except that it's a neat cultural adjustment," Evelyn continued. "Our upstairs neighbors changed their name from Gold to Zahav. The Hebrew. Down the street there's a little square near the playground named for an artist whose European name was Weiss, which is a translation of White, like my maiden name. He's famous; he changed it to Levanon. The Hebrew. In Hebrew, Black is *Shachor*." She pronounced the central consonant with a guttural *ch*, the same way insiders say *Chanukah*, not *Hanukkah* with an *H*. "What's Levanon and Shachor and red all over?"

Susan and I looked at each other. We never knew she knew our jokes. My chest flapped, and time froze. I heard a wooden chair leg rubbing the floor, whose?

Evelyn laughed, bit into her roll again. Susan, more wakeful, rolled her eyes and then caught mine. We'd had the conversation for years, how once in a while Evelyn's openness to others had worn down her censoring devices; it was a workplace casualty like black lung on a miner.

Even so, Susan's nicey-nice impulse reared its smiling head, nodding into Evelyn's interior logic.

"Can you just *do* that? Just change your name?"

Evelyn tilted her head into a thoughtful answer. "It's a little much. Even I agree. After all the other changes."

WE WERE JUST about finished with our rolls and coffee when the man who prayed for rain in Jerusalem came home. Under his arm Dad carried a box of cellophane-wrapped minicroissants, and hanging off his right hand were two large bakery bags. The fresh-baked goods smelled as if a whole bakery had walked in the door; his sense of our appetites was touchingly off scale, as if we were still teenagers who could eat half gallons of ice cream and empty pantries in a single midnight raid. "The Angel bakery," he said, "bakes all night and all day. Except Shabbos." He heaped the bags on the kitchen counter.

"Angel is a great name for a Jerusalem bakery," Susan said, waving and wobbling her hands in imitation of airborne cupids.

"No, Susan, no, Honey." Dad laughed. "It's not angels like some Valentine's Day card. Angel is an old Jewish-Italian family name. This was the same bakery which opened its grain stores to feed the entire city in the siege of Jerusalem."

If this had been a normal visit of loved ones to a new country, the cultural fill-in-the-blanks would have worked. We would have asked: "What siege? What grain stores?" and he would have given us the history. I clamped my mouth shut and found Susan's foot with my own. Enough engaging him.

But Dad used our silence as an opening. He hadn't planned on asking, but did we want to visit the bakery? Susan wagged her head into a broad yes and squeezed her chair around the circle table so Dad could move in a fourth chair. A welcoming and kind of accepting and totally off-agenda gesture, especially as I'd been the front man, so to speak. I was going to have to talk to Susan, keep her in line. Did she think that I didn't have the same childish impulse to make him like me? Did she think I wouldn't be drawn to all the samenesses, like how you couldn't miss the way Dad still looked tight and athletic in his Levi's, like the fact that his forever buzz cut had transcended all the changes. (He hadn't yet grown the jaw-length sideburns that he wears today—the businessman version of religious side locks).

"We'll go to see the bakery this afternoon, while you're here," he said. "Evelyn, we'll *daven mincha* at the Kosel."

This time, for a moment, Susan and I realigned and met eyes. In an instant with all that gibberish, the man we thought we were talking to like normal people turned back into Soul Man. I had nothing to say as he went to the sink to ritually wash his hands, as Evelyn had, with a supersize two-handled cup. They were always washing hands with that big cup; I could hear Allan making some comment about regular faucets not being good enough. Dad sat down and dug into his bakery rolls. We didn't ask him to explain, and I'd never seen him eat soft cheese on bread, but then I'd never known him to go to the bakery either. I made a mental note of stray adjectives to pass on to Allan: *domestic, oddly content.* The adjectives that undermined our goals.

Then Dad pushed back his chair and crumpled his napkin into his plate, and Evelyn asked if there was any change outside. "You know. I mean . . . the weather."

Which got Dad all worked up again. About the rain, or the lack of it. And finally, now, it was officially a drought. What he meant was that Israel had few natural bodies of water, that it depended on rain in its right time to fill the reservoirs, and there was some cosmic tie-in to reward and punishment. If we were good, the rain came; if we were not, there was none. So when the rain didn't come, everyone was concerned. "There are signs all over," he said.

"You mean some mammoth finger wagging out from a cloud? With the booming warnings of grave repercussions?" I had no intention to be shy about my healthy and well-grounded skepticism.

"I don't mean signs and wonders," Dad said. Laughed. Laughed at what turned out to be my overreaction. "This isn't the movies with special effects." He meant *signs*. Plain old signs, the kind that hung on the walls and gates and storefronts and kiosks. Announcing prayer, self-improvement initiatives. "This is the real thing. Something you do with your mind. Work on yourself to change the world."

He was saying that to *me*? "I work to change the world. That's my calling card," I said.

"I said work on yourself to change the world. On yourself—your insides. That and special additions to the daily prayers. Then a proclamation for special public sessions."

With that, Dad walked up to the sink, turning his back to us. I watched his shoulders butterfly and hunch as he turned on the faucet and poured water the regular way, doused the cellophane tub of mushrooms with dish soap, and set the whole thing to soak on the side of the sink. Just the fact that Dad patronized me like that could prove he was gone, not gone, plain gone but pulled in another direction and pulled by something real, a fact pattern of existence beyond my thinking. My chest began to tingle; the tingle turned into a tight grip down the breastbone, focusing me on my exhalation as if I were a wind instrument.

four

I'D BEGUN TO THINK IT WAS A MISTAKE TO HAVE SUSAN COME along.

"We're saving Dad from saving his soul and all you can do is ask interested questions," I said. That was the nice version of the complaint I'd ruminated on till we had this first moment alone. I sat on my bed in the guest room, half propped on one of those corduroy arm pillows my friends used to call a husband.

Susan didn't break stride as she raked through her suitcase to find her sunglasses. "Got 'em," she said, heaving herself back on the opposite bed. The fresh air lifted the blinds in small bursts, making its treacly, spring-in-the-middle-of-December point.

"You didn't respond to what I said. What's with all the interested comments? The lead-ins that derail our little mission here?"

"It's just conversation. I'm just being polite." She'd slipped on her sunglasses. They were the hip kind that wrapped around her face like ski goggles (as if she didn't already see only what she wanted).

"You wouldn't be so polite if you heard Dad say that the good weather means we are bad Jews." Subtly off with my paraphrase, I had a point to make.

"Dad's said a lot of things. The way I look at it—"

"You always start 'looking at things' when I'm in the middle of talking about something else."

Susan looped her gaze out the window, proving me right.

"Stop being literal. Just stop giving him openings to pontificate and monger his worldview to us."

"What do you expect me to do? I mean, he says, 'Do you want to do some sightseeing?' and I'm supposed to say, 'Dad, come home.' He says we're going to the Kosel and you kick me when I ask what the Kosel is."

"We're not here to tour. We're here to dislodge Dad."

"What are you so afraid of? That you'll catch what he's got?"

"Not for a minute." Not for a second, I thought.

"Anyhow, did you expect any less from Dad? Think about it. If we were in London, he'd take us to see the queen. Or if we were at SeaWorld—when we went to SeaWorld, you were fourteen, I was ten, remember? He took us to see Flipper the dolphin."

BACK IN THE kitchen, Susan solved the problem, just the way I'd asked her not to. "I know the Kosel is a wall, but what kind of wall is it anyhow?" she asked Evelyn.

"The Kosel is the last remnant of the wall surrounding the second Jewish Temple," Evelyn said.

Dad wasn't about to be left out of that explanation. "It's on the same ordained site as the First Temple of Solomon. Holiest place in the world, last remnant of the Shechinah, the Divine presence. You girls know what I'm talking about, right?"

"Of course we do," I said. Actually, I had no idea what he was talking about, but, with or without Susan, I intended to stop the flow where it started. The next good trick was turning it back on him. "Susan and I aren't *that* ignorant." In our lifetime as Jews we had seen many pictures of the Kosel aka Western Wall on calendars or holiday greeting cards or someone's Bat Mitzvah invitation or the front page of the *Globe* when there was some excitement: the big, uneven stones, the visitors dwarfed by magnificence.

FORTY-FIVE MINUTES LATER, on the way to the Kosel, our small white taxicab crept through heavy city traffic, generating a huge discussion between Dad, Evelyn, and the driver about whether we could have walked in half or even a third of the time. Finally, finally, the cab turned up a ramp, a ramp which looked like a castle moat, especially the way it was surrounded by a stories-high stone buttress. And then inside, a wide-open commercial area was filled with MONEY CHANGE HERE signs and competing pushcarts hung with round brown breads. We drove directly into a crowd of pedestrians, who obeyed some local law by flattening themselves against the stone walls without a look over their shoulders. Past one busy parking lot, past one majestic view of hills, valleys, and hovels, we curved downhill; and then we stopped, abruptly, at a small clearing across from a circular driveway, a driveway filled with puffing buses and a thicket of passengers climbing on and off.

We waited for Dad while he paid the taxi driver. By that time the buses were pulling away, and the entrance—except for some small potted trees—looked more like an airport security check-in than an outdoor site. Metal bars, police—or, who knew, soldiers?—in oversize vests, behind Plexiglas shields. Is this safe? I asked. Dad and Evelyn ignored me. Or didn't hear me as we crossed the driveway, joining a small group of visitors narrowing to single-file lines in front of a pair of security booths. There, without a blink, Evelyn laid her pocketbook on a table and walked through a body scan. The guard unzipped her pocketbook, raked his fingers through it, zipped it up, and handed it back. Same with my bag. Same with Susan's. He was a black man, spongy haired and fine featured, wearing a knit yarmulke—Ethiopian, Evelyn whispered. Then leapt to valorize, "Just wait till you see what's around the bend."

Just a few steps ahead, Dad motioned us to hurry, hurry. "It's the nerve center. That's what it is."

A few steps later, we landed on a wide stone plaza, walled and floored by pink and beige light-reflecting stone; surrounded by pink and beige stone, multitiered buildings; overlooked by pink and beige stone; squared off by pink and beige stone. The big Wall was down to the right, with hundreds of people jiggering around. It was just that I hated the sudden freeze in my organs, my joints, even my brain, not knowing what to do until I got further instructions. Less disoriented, or in a place I could classify, I might have come out swinging. Now, with pitifully small heroics recognizable only to myself, I boomed a question: "So now what do we do?"

"Experience . . . ," Dad said.

"Ex-per-i-ence?" I drew out the word into flat, ironic syllables. It wouldn't hurt him to know how my insides boxed up, the same way they do before a deposition or a hearing.

Dad ignored me and repeated himself, "Experience . . ." He shook his left hand into an A-OK loop, as if he'd made a point at the end of an argument.

"Dan, that isn't fair," Evelyn said. My heart sang at her full stop, the way she moderated Dad's aggressive pious moment. But if I thought it was for our sake, I was wrong. "We schlepped them here," Evelyn continued. "We've got to tell them *what* to do. Or *how* to do." She turned to Susan and me. "People write little notes, mostly requests and wishes. And they put them in the cracks of the Wall."

She set her purse down on a low stone divider and rummaged for a pen and paper.

"What happens to the notes?" Susan asked.

"They go to *Hashem*," Dad said, dipping his voice. I never heard that word, but it was obvious Who he meant. Then, his eyes swept the ground and he bowed a little. Not to us, it turned out; not to what should have been abashment over all his esoterica, but to let a woman pass, a woman in what was best described as a bonnet, with that unlined purity of face of someone who would wear a bonnet, pushing a stroller with a link of small children on either side. Whose placid, sweet, satisfied face reminded me of that Brookline Hebrew Day teacher with the marble-size ankles.

The sight brought out the worst in me: "Notes? Notes like 'Dear Santa Claus, North Pole: I want a new eighteen-speed bike'?"

Dad's head bobbed back, surprised, a little offended. "The notes aren't so trivial. And the line of communication isn't fake. Anyhow, the notes get cleaned out once in a while and buried—disposed of properly, like holy books, like Torah scrolls. They do that with anything that has holy names on it."

Holy. Holy. Holy. Had I heard the word *holy* a hundred times that day, or did I just feel as if I had? Did I hear the word *holy* ever spoken anyhow? Maybe on the news: holy war, or holy battle. Holy moly. Anyhow, I already knew what to write if I was going to write anything: "Dear Lord," or in Dad's lingo, "Dear *Hashem*, Make Dad normal and bring him home. Any way possible."

"Here—give me," Susan said, taking the pen, leaning against the stone wall, thinking hard, and focusing out in the distance. I followed her line of vision past a pair of looming construction cranes to a cemetery with tumbledown headstones. Susan wrote. Scratched out. Wrote again. "What's the big deal? I'll get some divine assistance with my renovations," she said as she handed me the pen.

I couldn't tell if she was joking. I could tell by the way his forehead lifted and peaked that neither could Dad. But he calmed his forehead and waited politely, until the moment I capped the pen and he looked at his watch. "I'll meet you back here in—what—fifteen minutes?" Then he sprinted off across the plaza to the men's side, and we followed Evelyn down an incline into a dense crowd of women and then the Wall itself.

Later on, Susan said that seeing the Wall reminded her of when Vice President Cheney and Winona Ryder came into Beacon Seafood the same week and she recognized them and Winona Ryder had skin like a piece of silk and Cheney did not and she was so utterly familiar yet Susan surprised herself that she still had room to make judgments and observations.

My reaction? I touched the stone—creamy smooth and worn, like sea glass. I hadn't thought for a minute that I'd feel magic jolts, and I was right. It was a stone wall. So then what? I remembered my note, which I'd stuffed back into my purse. I fished it out and rolled it tight and small as could be, and stuffed it into a popular Wall crack overflowing with other notes. My direct push shot several of those others out of the crack onto the ground. A bad moment—being responsible for someone else's belief, hopes, wishes. I quickly scooped them up before someone saw or scolded me. Tempted as I was to open one and read, I behaved myself and fit them back in the crack, one by one.

I didn't know whether to laugh or feel sorry for myself. Evelyn and Susan were still in my peripheral vision, and I didn't know whether to laugh at Susan or figure it served her right for being so accommodating when she was out of deco mode. Susan stood, sandwiched between Evelyn, who was moving her lips as she looked into an open prayer book, and a cadaverous, toothless woman crying fresh tears and making deep chest noises. Susan took on a reflective moment herself, twirling her sunglasses in her hand and laying her head on her arm, leaning into the Wall, eyes closed, tracking lines to her wishes, dreams, aspirations, renovations of the material kind.

A quick jerk on my pocketbook strap brought me back. On big-city instinct, I jammed my pocketbook closer to my side. But it was only a teenage girl shoving past me, hair pulled back so tightly it made her eyes bobble as she looked me up and down and then straight in the eyes as if she recognized me, as if—as if she was going to invite me to a Shabbos meal, I amused myself—evoking tribal irony even I didn't know I had: Was it Groucho Marx or Woody Allen or my Allan who asked why he would want to be a member of any club which would accept him?

Even with all my circumlocutions, when Dad met us back on the central plaza after exactly fifteen minutes, I did have an aha moment, my perceptions unnaturally clear and cleared up because, the way mountain air and high altitude had you see distances, I saw little truths, though the truths had to do with them, not me: First of all, there were so many people there who looked exactly like yarmulke Dad and hat-on-the-head Evelyn. With all that bulk, a mass delusion could look like the real thing and make you wonder.

Second, what I hadn't been able to put my finger on earlier, especially from back in Brookline, especially in spite of my resistance, was what I saw clearly now: Not only did Dad's face look lighter but everything about him looked lighter—as if he were backlit. Not that it changed my thoughts about being born-again, but it was just a little insight into how I could feel so bad when Dad was feeling so fine. I mean, I was the one who always said that if you made a pie chart of Dad's innards and my innards you'd see 20 percent shaded in black and that's what Mom left for us, partners in loss, partners in that shadow and darkness. And now, with everything else going on, Dad had a new formula, a new look on the pie chart. As if he'd finally pushed loss aside and I was the surviving—surviving and oddly fresh—mourner. Maybe that's what I was fighting; and it wasn't fair.

I stopped the free association. At least that time.

We tramped out of the plaza single file behind Dad, not the way we came in but through a revolving security gate where bars lined up horizontally across my body, neck to knees, the kind I'd only seen going to my safe-deposit box at the bank. We began to climb a set of stone steps.

"Oh," Evelyn said, looking up. She didn't have to say any more. Coming down the steps on the other side, with a bevy of gowned maidens, was a young bearded man, Fabio hair, wearing flowing white garments and summer leather sandals. He could have been anyone's vision of a prophet, and he strummed a lyre, or some vaguely ancient string instrument. The women, equally flowing, shimmered their tambourines into light, plinking notes.

"That's the third prophet I've seen this week," Dad said.

Except for the flowing garments exchanged for the Levi's and sports jacket, wasn't this like the pot calling the kettle black? But Dad and Evelyn had a name for this version.

"Jerusalem syndrome," Evelyn said. "It's a real phenomenon. The jiggling loose of the psyche. All religions, actually. Go look it up. You get these Norwegian tourists in a church group, and all of a sudden the mild-mannered electrician thinks he's St. Paul."

"Or the Messiah. And having delusions," Dad said.

I looked at him. Considering the opening he'd given me, it came out milder than I planned. "Delusions? Dad—just what I've been thinking—what we should be talking about," I said. (Though, truth was, we'd been talking plenty. Just not the way I wanted.)

"You don't seem to understand." Dad rolled his eyes. Then the way he climbed the steps in twos made me wonder if I'd hit a nerve. I scrambled up the steps behind him. Maybe I had an opening.

We landed in a small commercial plaza and settled ourselves at a small round table outside a small food kiosk called, thematically and correctly, Holy Bagel. For now, big topics were dropped, and we ordered four tuna-on-everything bagels. We waited while the friendly counterman with a Yankees cap slabbed our sandwiches together. If the Fabio guy or I had unnerved him, I couldn't tell, because Dad got busy with the table, which didn't have a chance for balance on the uneven stone floor. Dad marched back to the counterman, asked for some napkins (cached behind the counter, he explained, for economic and ecological reasons), and took a couple of patient minutes to wedge first one, then two, then three under the short table leg. Now, at least on the surface, we sat, we were balanced, on an even keel. Across the cobbled way, a storekeeper unloaded a cardboard tray of sweet buns from the window. We watched as he manually cranked down his metal shutters and hung a sign: SHABBAT SHALOM.

"That storefront reminds me of a diorama," Susan said. "You know, when you're a kid and you take shoe boxes and turn them on their sides and build little rooms inside." So much for Susan putting the kibosh on her observations and conversation openers.

"Those stores aren't usually much bigger than shoe boxes," Dad said. "All the products are stored up the wall."

"Or up to the ceiling," Evelyn said. "When we got here, one of the first words I had to learn was *reach*, as in 'I can't reach the paper towels.'"

"Evelyn, did you know—I meant to tell you—it came up in my prayer class how, just like in English, you can use the word *reach* figuratively as in 'I can't reach the next level of understanding.'"

"Too sophisticated for me," Evelyn said. "I'm still working on my Hebrew modals: *I want*, *I need*. Then I don't need to conjugate the verbs afterward. But then I even forget them and usually end up pointing and grunting. Oh well—in our neighborhood they're used to people like me, people who—"

"The Messiahs?" I pounced—this was my opening, now that Jerusalem syndrome had a name.

Then I could have killed Susan for helping them ignore me. "What about them?" she asked, pointing to a couple with a Rockettes line of children swaying to catch up on either side. The children were dressed in party clothes, and each of the older children wheeled and bumped a tall, handled suitcase. Each parent held a leather box and pushed a stroller.

"My guess? They live here in the Old City," Dad said. "But going someplace for Shabbos. The high box is a wig, the flatter box is a hatbox."

"There's a kind of a rush before Shabbos," Evelyn said. "Like squeezing time out of a bottle before time gets pushed aside. How did my teacher put it?" She asked the question to Dad, who was more interested in his interpretation of foot traffic.

"See those nice young men?" he asked, pointing to a half dozen college-age boys in jeans and white shirts, brightly colored yarmulkes big as rimless baseball caps. "The coming, the going. Students bus in to spend Shabbos in the Old City. Neophytes, like we'd been, ingathering on some gut or ancient siren call, without an idea of Shabbos finery at all."

"Maybe they're prophets," I said, adjusting my strategy. I was someone with a serious comment but making it airy and light.

"Let go of the messiah guy already. He's nuts. We're not," Dad said. "Let me put that idea to rest."

Oh, I was glad our sandwiches were ready. We ate them without forks or paper plates, directly on the white wrapping paper, using our fingers to stuff back the popping lettuce and tomato. Meanwhile, a trio of skeletal cats suddenly found us very interesting, spinning themselves between the legs of our chairs. I dropped a hunk of tuna to one, who ate heartily and ran, not—as I expected—begging for more or calling over his buddies. Maybe the sudden food was some kind of systemic shock. Now that was a clear psychological projection if I'd ever had one: I was the one in systemic shock.

Dad took his sandwich down in a half dozen bites and began observing again. I wasn't sure what had wound him up, but at least this time his talk was the familiar kind, building maven stuff: "All that stone? All that pink and beige stone you see. It's the law. The name of the law," he said playfully. "The municipal requirements have everything in Jerusalem built from this same stone. You won't see any wood or brick houses for fifty miles."

"That's strange," I said. "Just try that in Brookline." Brookline talk felt like a blast of fresh, familiar air. Air from our world. But delicate, its own balance as long as we stayed away from the school case, which I hoped I could trust Susan with.

"It's not as strange as you might think," Dad said. "You remember when we used to go to New Seabury on Cape Cod? You had to build all the houses there in the same cedar siding that weathered, uniformly, a dappled gray. Other towns on the Cape have the same regulations."

In spite of all the tension, my heart sang when Dad meandered on the Cape and our old lives. But Susan. Oh, what was she doing? She didn't play out our hand about the school case—maybe worse in a way; she hooked him back to Jerusalem. "Dad, how was the Wall made—how many thousands of years ago? Where did those huge stones come from?" She took a large bite of her tuna bagel and looked delicate as she managed to keep the tuna from squeezing out. She ignored my kick under the table.

"There's a quarry," Dad said. "Just north of Jerusalem. Some builders found it a couple of years ago when they were laying a foundation for a new school building."

"So how did they bring the stones here? And set them up—without Build-a-Scaffold?" Susan asked. Of all questions, integrating his old life and his new one. With half a sandwich to go, she was done, folding the paper around, her eyes scanning for the cats. Moving her chair over. This time I couldn't reach her to kick her under the table.

"They had to bring the stones downhill," Dad answered. "And you're talking about ten-ton stones. Gravity, first. Strong oxen second. But the real question is, how was the stone cut once it got down to the Temple area? They weren't allowed to build with metal. So there's this worm called a *shamir*, a worm that was created just for that purpose at twilight on the sixth day of creation."

Susan couldn't get over it. "A worm? Really?"

"Or Bigfoot—Dad!" I said. I am, I was, I will be the reality monger.

Evelyn and I were in agreement on that one. "Don't tell them the strange stuff. Stick with the normal things," she said. "Oh, here they are."

She meant the cats, and she took Susan's sandwich and, sparing the bagel, shook out the tuna onto the paper and laid it under the table. The cats ignored her. And it. In spite of what we thought they needed. I had to admit it: Dad and Evelyn didn't have Jerusalem syndrome. As a matter of fact, for a minute there I liked Evelyn very much, the way she managed to unloop our imaginations and interest, the way she put the kibosh on the weird stuff. On the other hand, maybe their normalcy was a little too showy.

Maybe that was it: not crazy, but normal. And wasn't normalcy a classic strategy of the religious, like the smooth-talking convert mongers who come to the door, clean cut, airbrushed, suited, and boy-next-doorish, Scriptures behind their backs, asking if the owner of the house is home.

five

Back at the apartment, I took the handset out to the balcony and called Allan, venting frustration in spite of the colorful winter flowers and the soft, warm, not too sunny air. With Susan and Dad off to Angel bakery, and Evelyn ensconced in the kitchen, I should have been free to tour and tell. When I had spoken to Allan last, the other day—night?—I hadn't really filled him in. But committing deep guts to words never came easy to me, and since when did you have to watch your back from normal people? I described the Fabio guy and how, to be fair, Dad wasn't Fabio.

"No tambourines or harps?"

"Just us golden maidens. But seriously, I can't put my finger on it. He's happy—content and excited. And crazed but not crazy. Normal—I hate to use that word. It would be easier if he were crazy. We're working against *some*thing here. Unlike Susan, I know something's wrong. Very wrong."

"No robotics—'take me to your leader.' That kind of thing?"

"You would think. But I haven't cracked it yet. The normal I'm talking about is like a more focused version of himself. For example, he used to take an afternoon catnap, but when we got back from the

Wall he made a big deal out of napping in the middle of the afternoon for Shabbos."

"You mean he only gets to stay up late if he naps?"

"You go figure. Every time I think I understand where he's coming from, he pulls away. It's like I'm at the bottom of the hill in an
uphill battle and the hill keeps running away. And then there's Susan, who's practically useless. She's like a sea creature that's come up
on land and grown feet." Now, expunged and expunged again, I
lifted my chin to a tiny breeze, which hummed across my face.

"Sounds like your father's the sea creature, too."

Was that what he said? Because that wasn't what I meant. The
breeze hummed again, this time gimcracking the phone line. "Anyhow, the point is, I won't be able to speak to you for a day and a half
because I can't use the phone on Shabbos."

"What?" he said.

"What? Shabbos!" I shouted. Was he hearing me? "Shabbos—no
phone. What do you need? Closed-captioning?"

"Why are you taking it out on me?"

"I'm not. I'm just not making seismic strides over here."

"You might still. Stop distracting yourself with Susan."

"Why do you keep saying things like that?"

"So I'll hang up, then." He didn't. And I rebounded to Allan
quickly: Whatever Shabbos amounted to, and for whatever I thought
Allan wasn't "getting," Shabbos was probably subject to the same
human rules as not going to bed angry or yelling at my husband
when he was six thousand miles away for something I didn't understand either. Beneath me, the playground lay in full view, ghost
town quiet, eerie, not wildly after-schoolish, something to do with
Shabbos, I was sure, like the quiet before the rainstorm Dad was
praying for.

"I'm sorry for yelling," I said, leaning over the railing Dad installed. "Really sorry. I'm a little tense. Not on track. I shouldn't have called you in this kind of mood except that it's almost Shabbos and I won't be able to call you—not because I don't want to but because I'm not allowed to use the phone here on Shabbos. Not only that, Dad says I shouldn't be calling you until Shabbos is over American time, which is in the wee hours my time, which means I'll speak to you Sunday morning your time."

"I *get* it," he said. "I'll be incommunicado too. We're going out to Gillette Stadium on Sunday afternoon." But he was clipping off his consonants.

To be fair, my disorientation had to be a wild card for him; Allan could count my rubber-legs moments on one hand, and those had real reasons. Like when we took our newborn Richard, a red-headed Winston Churchill look-alike, home from Beth Israel Hospital, and all the personnel on the nursery floor, from broom pushers to the neonatal physicians who had no clue, asked me, where did that red hair come from? When I cried for my mother on the way home, I made it sound all postpartum by blaming it on the complexity of the car seat, all those straps and clips.

"Hey, get this straight," I said. "It's not the same incommunicado. I can't call you, come hell or high water. It's not *convenient* for you to call: you might wake me up if you call when you're on the way out the door. But I *can't* call, I'm not allowed to call."

"Sounds like you're the one all wound up in the rules and regulations you've come to do battle with."

"No I'm not. That's what we have here: Dad's Soul Man routine, the impenetrable wall." For a second I had the feeling that my mouth was moving, and the words coming out, but the bubble over my head might belong to another character.

In the background, a phone buzzed in Allan's office. "Hold on—" he said, and I heard him speak into his other line: to tell them he'd be there in a minute. "I have to go. But you can do this. You can. Talk to him. Have a big talk with him. A B-I-G T-A-L-K."

"What do you think I've been trying to do?" But I liked the way he said it: a Big Talk, a Big Talk to Dad—a Big Talk at Dad—a Big Talk, not this arguing and convincing I'd been hacking at. A Big Talk the way a teenager gets a dressing-down for coming home past curfew. The very phrase blew some life into me.

I didn't see Dad, but back in the kitchen, Evelyn was busy levitating a flat metal tray over the burners of the stove. That done, she fussed with the oven knobs, adjusting the gas flame underneath the tray; then she set a large soup pot on the middle of the tray. Then she changed her mind about something, moved the pot over to the edge of the tray, then back again, halfway to the middle, and explained herself without turning around. "A little guesswork here. We don't warm up the food on Shabbos, but we can *keep* it warm, and it's hard to figure out what's enough heat or what's not enough. Or what's too much."

The rules again. The phone, the stove, now the soup. "Okay," I said, a toss-off *okay* that Evelyn could interpret as she wished. The stove and the soup were another symbol of the great monolith, normal or not, that I was up against, and unlike Susan I refused to be derailed by natural curiosity and ask a what or why. The Big Talk was going to be on my terms.

But not quite yet. Evelyn bent over the stove again, and caught me off guard. "You and Susan should be showering for Shabbos now."

"Shower?" I said. I couldn't remember the last time anyone told me to take a shower, much less take a shower in the middle of the afternoon. But I wasn't going to ask.

Evelyn made a half explanation anyhow. "That's what you do before Shabbos. Think of it like you're going to a party or something."

"What you do. What you do," I repeated to myself. My Big Talk was accruing ballast fast: The rules were now a sociology. On the other hand, I couldn't think quickly enough of a reason—or a way—to say no to the shower. I stalked off to the little bedroom hallway, to the linen closet, which looked about the size of a CD rack, another one of those Lego house adjustments which might have been a red flag when I arrived but, as I'd begun to understand, were not the point. The towels and sheets were rolled into tight tubes and log stacked, requiring the dexterity of a game like pickup sticks.

I contemplated too long. Susan swooped in behind me, and, reaching over my shoulder, she popped out a towel from the center. "Kind of like popping the first pickle out of a jar," she said, walking into the bathroom. "I have first dibs on the shower," she added.

Now, the last shower fight I'd seen was between my kids, Richard and Ronnie, who for some reason since last winter, since their twelfth and eighth birthdays, all of a sudden wrestle over the basement shower in my office bathroom. It's a jerry-built affair, aluminum, held in place by nothing, and I don't understand why their upstairs shower isn't good enough, but I suspect that it has something to do with the way they can play their voices with metallic echo, like microphone feedback. "Whuuuump, whuuuump."

But when I ask them what they are doing or whumping about, they act as if I live on another planet, as if I'm the one who has done something weird. Considering my cut-off roots, considering the fact that Susan and I didn't have a regular childhood, I hate being on the other end of dissonance. The very reason I was in Jerusalem to get Dad back was that, in my mind, parents and their children should be like geometrical progressions—always moving out, away from the core, exactly like the core. Maybe something evocative would have happened anyhow when my kids reached the ages Susan and I were when we lost Mom, but when it came to my own family, I felt like the core with no core. In any case, thoughts like that put more weight on losing Dad, and I couldn't help but feel sandwiched, excluded, on both ends.

"Don't drench the floor. Don't use up the shampoo," I called out as Susan shut the bathroom door in my face. I couldn't believe I'd been pushed to such pettiness, but the source was obvious.

So, obedient polite guest, annoyed and accommodating older sister, confused and wannabe hostile daughter, unable to communicate wife, and aching mother, I found myself sitting on the edge of the bed in a little two-by-four bedroom waiting for my turn in the bathroom. The window was open, and the air noiseless and fresh, and I didn't have to be a meteorologist to predict dry weather and say it was pleasant and I was going to tell Dad that it didn't feel like a curse to me. All of which feelings were not exactly juicing me up for a Big Talk. What would I say anyhow? That all this religious stuff was a sidebar, a distraction when he was making it his point? That he didn't seem, well, balanced? That Allan and I thought—what?

Ten minutes later, making noise about hurrying for my sake, Susan reentered the room in a wave of fruity soap smells, printing the rug with her wet feet. "Shower's all yours," she said, slipping on underwear dorm style by turning her back and making her towel into a tent.

She'd left the bathroom hanging with steam from mirror to toilet to tub. The shower stall, three-quarters size, was too wet, and the shower spray trickled weakly. I adjusted a lever. And adjusted again to another dribble. Turned it to the left. All the way over to the right.

Now, the same dribble. Worse, if anything. A couple of trickles. Lousy water pressure.

The water pressure: That was it. The Talk. The Talk Allan thought I should have.

I wasn't much cleaner, but I was suddenly a lot smarter. Maybe Dad was normal for his setting here but not normal the way we knew him. Water always helped me think. There was my opening!

The water pressure. Before Dad made proclamations about the meaning of life as related to the meaning of death, or about rainfall as a reward or punishment, Dad made proclamations about things. Real estate, for example. And his litmus test for a decent home had everything to do with the water pressure: When Allan and I were shopping for our first home, Dad's primary advice was to march straight into the bathroom, turn on the shower, and see if it lathered up the bar of soap in my hand. I jumped out of the bathroom, into the bedroom, not quite towel dry. I twisted on a skirt and sweater set. I had the entry point to jiggle out the Dad I knew, the Dad I would bring home.

I found him standing in the hallway, wearing a navy V-neck sweater, a white dress shirt, and a tie. It was 3:30 P.M. "Good-bye. Good Shabbos," he said, directing the last salutation to the kitchen, where Evelyn was stacking tinfoiled squares on top of the metal tray on top of the stove, pushing them around as she tipped a forefinger to the tray. "Oh, Good Shabbos."

"Wait, Dad," I said, revved up for a confrontation. I grabbed his sweater sleeve and held it. "What's this with the water pressure? Worst shower I ever had."

"What—I'm sorry," Dad said, pulling away and brushing the pinch out of the wool. "I feel terrible—sorry. But my shower wasn't so bad."

"Dad!" I stopped him in his tracks. "We have to talk."

"I know *that*." The way he emphasized the last word, I knew he meant he had to talk to me.

"No, I have to talk to *you*."

"That too."

"Dad—no . . . You broke your own rules. Your own shower rules. You might be normal for here but not for us. You're not supposed to break the rules."

"And are you, even all grown up, are you supposed to chastise your father?"

With that single right question, he punctured my Big Talk, though not comfortably: He stretched his tie around his neck with his forefinger and this time actually popped his eyes, like a sweating stand-up comedian. The nervous gesture turned into a real one, and he whipped his tie off in one motion, calling out to Evelyn in the kitchen. "I'm the only one at services who wears a tie. It makes me look—so—*American*."

"You *are* American, Dad," Susan said, walking into the foyer, wearing a red, arrow-patterned jilebba, which made her look like a hippie. Or a Middle East mama. I hadn't seen the jilebba until that minute. She must have picked it up when she was out with Dad earlier. I could have killed her for buttering the moment with her feel-good vibe. Later she would defend herself by evoking the good cop–bad cop strategy, but I felt undermined—pinned to the wall as Dad and Evelyn continued the conversation over our heads.

"I know I'm American," Dad said. "But when in Rome . . ."

I knew I'd lost, but I couldn't help myself. "What, take bad showers?" I said.

He opened the front door, and I body-blocked the exit. "Dad, you always said that a place with bad water pressure isn't worth the weight of the front door."

"I guess I did say that, didn't I?" Dad said, smiling weakly, distracted, a late-for-something tension chasing his eyes and furrowing his forehead.

"Bye, Honey. Bye, Susan and Evelyn. Good Shabbos." He kissed me and ran out the door.

I jumped over to the street-facing window intending to double-check his expression. Let Evelyn—even Susan—interpret the window watching as they wished—soft or sentimental or angry. Outside, Dad joined the foot traffic, matching steps with a little boy in a white shirt and dark pants, and jabbing his finger in the air asking or explaining something. I could see as far as the intersection where they joined a group of men waiting for the walk sign to blink. A city bus tore downhill, fast and blind, as if it was doing something wrong. The men jumped back and then crossed after the bus puffed out of sight. Was the Big Talk even relevant? I drummed up a list of observations to share with Susan later in private, if she'd be able to hear me: Dad was elusive, lying to himself, not facing reality, scared of confrontation. Most of which, if I'd only thought about it, applied to me too.

six

WITH DAD OUT THE DOOR TO SERVICES, EVELYN STOOD in the kitchen and erupted with a string of metaphors to describe the sudden transition from the workaday week into the transcendence of Shabbos. "Lighting the Shabbos candles makes me feel as if my insides were a balloon and they've popped. Or as if a set of bellows has sucked the air right out of me." She said she always went to lie down till Dad came home for the Friday-night meal.

Left alone in the living room, Susan and I arranged ourselves awkwardly, the way you perch in a doctor's waiting room, sensitive to the voice that calls your name, prey to authority. The Berber love seats were a matched set. In the square, downsized room they felt oversize and plump and made the coffee table too hard to walk around, and I had the feeling that by the end of Shabbos I would knock my knees on the coffee table one too many times. That, or knock Dad's neat stack of reading—English newspapers, two large, brick-red books in Hebrew and English, and a half a dozen English books I swear all had the word *soul* in the title—to the floor. Instead of peace and inner tranquillity, the word made me feel lonely, and my ear trained on an even-paced mechanical tick from the wall behind

the love seat. I twisted back to look. An electric timer held the reins
to the pair of hurricane lamps routed back to either side of the love
seat.

Susan knew I was already annoyed with her, but it didn't stop
her from explaining away. "While you were in the shower," she said,
"while Evelyn was fixing the heat on the stove, Dad set these up.
They turn the light off after the meal when we're asleep, on again in
the morning."

"It can do it by itself. But we can't?" I said.

"Now you're being flippant. It's not necessary. Stop it," Susan
said.

"Seriously. It's like you've fallen under their spell. What would
happen if I tripped over a cord and knocked the light off?"

"I guess we'd live in the dark while we're in their house," Susan
said. "That's just being—decent."

I looked at her. "Decent is passive, polite, good guest behavior
defined by rules that everyone agrees on. So what does decent have
to do with this? What would hurt if I turned on the light in our
room? Who would know? What would it matter?"

"Is that like the tree that falls in the forest with no one to hear
it?" Susan asked.

"Yeah—right." I could tell by the sad freeze on her face that I'd
unhooked her too, at least for a minute. When we were girls, that
was our kind of philosophic discussion many a night. A discussion
which had our personal variation: If a woman dies with no children, is it still the same sad?

"Come on," Susan said, recovering. Sadness, acrimony—she dis-
dained them both. She twisted her face as if she were wearing pince-
nez, mimicking social horror, the same look as for when the fish
sauce was too mayonaissey, when the printer spelled *bouillabaisse*
with one *s* or a waiter pronounced the *l*'s when he said ratatouille.

"Ratta-tou-*ly*?" she asked—reminded me of our old laugh, fishing out my smile. "Look. If you were in a Japanese home, you'd take off your shoes. Rae Stark's husband is from Montreal. Canadians take off their shoes when they walk into someone's house in the winter. I do the same thing at his house. It's polite. What we do."

I didn't have a quick answer, except I thought of how sure Allan was when I headed off to battle in a world that—from back in Brookline—we thought we could predict and conquer. I fixed my eyes on the opposite wall, where in New England there would be a fireplace and the fireplace mantel would hold a pair of lamps and knickknacks. At mantel height was that painting Dad had e-mailed us about: a couple sitting at a table set with two challah loaves, and the couple looked curiously full and satiated though the blue, high-ceilinged room was lonely and stark. Or maybe the point-of-view angles were off, the way you'd see it from a fish-eye lens, which flattened the table to the front of the canvas.

Then I noticed the two little paper-bound notebooks on the coffee table, the size of those blue books you took law school exams on. Inside each cover was Dad's name, then Evelyn's, then Hebrew, presumably their names again. "What's this?" I asked Susan.

"Their question books. Didn't he show you? He showed me." She realized she'd made some kind of mistake as soon as the words were out of her mouth.

"What, am I not spiritual enough? Not the same material?" If I'd been annoyed with the religion business for trying to include me, now I was annoyed by exclusion, the opposite. What was wrong with me?

"The conversation came up organically, after we got back from the bakery—you were on the phone with Allan—when I asked him what it meant on a sign that something was baked with flour from wheat harvested after the spring. He had the same question too. He showed me. He keeps lists of questions from the sublime to the ri-diculous. Here, let me show you." She picked up his notebook. "I don't think he'll mind. He showed me. Look . . ." She opened the first page and read. "'If they say that people get reincarnated, then when the people come back alive after the redemption, in which body, which person, do they come alive?' Or how's this?: 'Why do we boil at least three eggs or an uneven number of eggs in a pot?'"

"Does it have answers?"

"Penciled in as he gets them. Here." She read, "'In the Holy sources they say reincarnation . . .'"

"I don't want to hear it. Enough of that stuff," I said. We'd al-ready established that Dad wasn't dying. That he was normal, in some setting. Didn't she get it that the notebooks could finally de-bunk the standby, the cult theory? Cults didn't let you ask questions.

My brain felt like a large knot, and I was too tired to pull the ends of the strings; I should have been relieved when we drifted into a discussion about water pressure, except that Susan said she never remembered Dad having any adages about water pressure.

Susan didn't remember a lot of things, and usually there was no reason to argue about it. For example, when we talk about it now, Susan remembers in her Age of Aquarius style that the entry of Shabbos smelled like calm, out of the aerosol can, rainbow scented, end of the summer storm calm. *I* remember the audio effects: how at dinner with the balmy weather and the balcony slider open to other open balcony sliders of other apartments, other buildings, as if we sat inside a surround-sound system, we heard clinking of sil-verware against plates, table noise, short bursts of song, as if the whole neighborhood was eating dinner at the same time.

Their dining room table was a perfect square, and Dad and Ev-elyn executed a stiff rumba of ritual and hosting. First things first, Dad and Evelyn sang with little prayer books in their hands.

"*Shalom Aleichem*," they said when they hit the chorus. "The angels have followed me home from services," Dad explained after the last set of repeats. Then he sang a second song, this one by himself: "*Aishes Chayil*, A Woman of Valor."

"A tribute to the Jewish woman," Evelyn whispered. "A tribute to her solid spirituality. He's singing from a transliteration."

Next, he filled his silver wine cup literally to the brim, and held it in the flat of his hand. Evelyn held the prayer book up for him. Transliteration or not, I recognized the first part. "*Ba-rook-a-ta . . .*" Dad began the blessing over the wine and went on a little longer than I expected. He drank and passed around little silver cups. Evelyn unwrapped braided challah breads from their plastic bakery bags, and they looked at each other for a small congratulatory nod. Or a go-ahead: They brought us into the kitchen for ritual hand washing with that big, two-handled cup.

The meal itself, more natural, smoothed them out. Evelyn served baked salmon for a first course with Dad's mushroom salad, and Dad attempted to keep things friendly. Brookliney: When he'd left Brookline, there'd been a big hoo-ha about the disproportion of franchise stores in our downtown area, Coolidge Corner.

"So what about it? Are they wrestling down the franchise to private business ratio?"

"Getting there," I answered succinctly, apparently too succinctly.

Dad looked puzzled; I knew what he was thinking. The Brookline talk was for me, my vernacular. Why the stonewall?

He turned to Susan instead: Had Beacon Seafood gotten the extra parking approved? Had they spoken to the Zoning Board of Appeals?

I dug into my salmon and the mushroom salad. Now Susan had better watch herself. No way we could get talking about town building and then have one thing lead to another and next thing I know

I tell him all about Brookline Hebrew Day School and I've played out what looked like my antireligion hand.

Fortunately, he had another ritual. A good one this time. Dad turned back to the cabinet behind him and picked a bottle of Macallan single-malt scotch off the shelf. He pulled four stemmed tumbler glasses out of a small cabinet door.

"I approve," Susan said. "Both the scotch and the tumblers. Aficionado scotch glasses."

"Nevertheless, we'll still call it a shot of scotch. A must," he said. "Really—we have a palate cleanser between fish and the rest of the meal, and it doesn't have to be scotch, but it is if you like it."

"I'm not arguing," Susan said.

Neither was I. In two shots the back-and-forth about Brookline was run through, and I'd successfully held my tongue. Only then, once again we were stuck, *experiencing*: The food, the sitting, and a bottle of Chardonnay and then a second half bottle of some local nonvarietal white combined to make 8:00 P.M. feel like midnight, and Dad, who made neutral small talk until the soup bowls were cleared, began to toss phrases at us. "Some people call Shabbos the Day of Rest, but I prefer what I've been learning about: Shabbos, like the World to Come. The place the soul yearns for, connects to."

"I don't know about the World to Come, but the Day of Rest already has me confused." I meant to be ironic, and I pushed away my plate, slightly enough for an ambivalent read, finished food or finished patience. "Serving large multicourse meals like this, isn't that a lot of work? Not exactly a rest?" This was, after all, Susan's vocation. I had to keep her on her toes. And how was it that turning on a light switch, which took a millionth of the energy of food prep, was considered work?

"*Work,*" Dad began. I detected a smile. And a backfire; he was about to be pleased with himself. "*Work* is the wrong translation of the concept. What we're not supposed to do is what I do—what I've done, building scaffolds, making new things in the physical world. Shabbos is more like making scaffolds in time."

"That's the simple answer," Evelyn said, going on to explain that a light switch creates an electrical current, which changes the essential nature of something. And the food—prep, serving, and all—had restrictions actually, many of them, but all in all it was a service to some higher goal.

"It's not just that; it's not just filling empty stomachs, not just stimulating taste buds, not just . . ." Dad held up his hands to emend the list of negatives. "It's a way of feeding the soul," he said.

"Dad, you've said that already," Susan said. As I expected—and hoped—he'd pushed *her* wrong button. The restaurant, all that filling of empty stomachs and stimulating taste buds, was her life.

But instead of making it worse for Susan, he made it worse for me, and who knew when it would get better? "It's like the world is the body and Hashem is the soul of the world."

I stopped chewing midsentence. By now the wine was all in my upper head, either opening my brain to great depths or reducing my brain to thoughts no more than an inch deep. I'd never heard anything like that before.

"Hashem animates the world the way the soul animates the body." Was that what Dad said next?

Susan took the comment like conversational bait, not logic, not something that could affect her. "Dad, why is it that you need to bring your Hashem or any kind of godly figure into this?"

"Look, girls, it's not emotional or irrational. Everything makes sense, perfect intellectual, rational sense. It's not that I'm trying to sway you or convince you . . . you can see for yourself."

Evelyn threw him a look. "Well, girls, that's *his* version of trying not to convince." With that she held out her hand for a pass of dirty plates, starting with Dad at the head of the table. They scraped and sent the accruing stack leftward silently, until she added, "It's just that we're fresh with the idea, animated ourselves, really. Hashem's commandments—the way to live out the idea that this world is the journey and the next world, the world of souls, is the destination. It doesn't strip the journey part of meaning and substance."

"Or good food," Dad said.

"But, Dad, it's like a cult." I had to say it.

"Sweetie—maybe. But the point is it's the oldest cult in the world. And it's your cult too."

"You don't have to put it like that," Evelyn said. For a minute I thought she was talking to Dad and that she'd come to my defense. But my use of the word *cult* had offended her, and, with a slight pitch and stomp, she waved away our help as she took the stack of plates into the kitchen. A minute later she returned with even footsteps, a small tray balanced on the flat of her palm. On the tray stood four parfait glasses, lemon-striped swirls heaped with whipped cream. Dad lifted two parfaits off opposite edges of the tray. Then he took the other two and passed them around.

The worst part was that, soulful or not, Dad's gestures were maddeningly the same—there, Boston, anywhere: all about balance, equal weight, symmetry. The same way he'd spent his life tackling space and then restraining it—himself—willfully.

Back in the guest room, with Susan gloating that she knew the house rules and had laid her pajamas out on the bed hours ago, I tore through my suitcase in the dark to find mine. With scant street light trickling through the window, I managed to find both top and bottom and finally stretched out in bed, my throbbing head calmed—and grateful that Susan didn't ask me why, in the end, if I felt the way I did, I didn't just turn on the room light.

The problem was, I wasn't sure if I felt the way I said I did. I'd been certain the water pressure was a gateway reconversion opener, the Big Talk, the symbolic reality a bridge between Dad's former outer life and his present inner one. I was sure that Shabbos was a day to relax and retreat, not aspire to something, not food for the thing he called the soul. It wasn't that we were weak or not smart enough for this mission of ours, but what we were up against was the biggest monolith I'd ever come across, and with the ability to ask questions, the strangest monolith I'd ever come across. And if we were to take Dad's nervy inferences, our strange monolith too.

FOR ALL THE venting, I could only sleep in a fetal position, even then waking every hour to the same fizzling picture in my mind's eye: a tornado-twister of aroma, straight out of a Popeye cartoon where Wimpy followed his nose to hamburger heaven. The food smell was real, acute, the Sabbath stew that Evelyn simmered over-night on the hot tray on the stove but said was not her culinary invention. Cholent: meat and fat and legumes. In Susan's restaurant vocabulary, a real cassoulet.

I'd come all this way to save Dad and bring him home, and the real reason I couldn't sleep was that I was thinking about what he'd said when he said that Hashem animates the world like the soul animates the body. To make that comparison, to understand that comparison, you had to think about a soul first. So what was my problem? Didn't I know what he meant by a soul? Did he think he was the only one who wanted there to be something called a soul?

Unless someone told me there was an eternal soul, this was how I understood it. Anyone could get crying from the idea. When we were little girls, Susan and I would lie in our twin beds with the matching Amish quilts and I could get Susan crying in an instant with a rhyme: "*Dead.* Die. You will die and so will I."

My bed was tucked against the interior wall of the bedroom, Susan's wedged against the single window where we'd set plastic jack-'o-lanterns on the sill. Mine was still brimming with candy, and Susan's was emptied, snickering with borrowed backlight from the moon and the streetlamps. "When you end, when you stop, the world goes on and on. Dead, die. You will die and so will I," I hissed, pure, double-edged torture, hewn from the collective unconscious of older siblings, the rights and obligations of older siblings. Then I added the kicker: "The world will go on to eternity. Forever—and you won't."

"What's eternity?" Susan asked.

I must have heard the word somewhere. My eyes flashed on the globe of the world set next to the Britannica in an attempt to distract us from Barbies—and I saw it, spinning—forever. The sibling torture turned inward: I knew I was being mean, I knew I had to be lying, I wanted to be lying. I wanted to say okay, my physical self was limited, but that wasn't that the real me anyhow. What was inside me was the real me, but then how did I find it? And then what did I do with it? Mom already slept heavily with her round-the-clock drugs; Dad already siphoned off half his energy with caretaking, and they concentrated their parenting on the list of essentials, like bedtimes and meals, that didn't account for states of existential panic. Where would she be?

I didn't get to finish: Good sibling torture ended with exaggerated kindness. I called for Dad, and he came into the room. He sat on Susan's bed and tucked the blankets around her face and gave me a gentle what-for. "Honey, your job is to take care of your sister. And, maybe you don't know where you'll be," he said to both of us. "But I'll always know where I am. And I'll let you know."

That night in Jerusalem in Dad's apartment with my world swirling around me, I looked over at Susan, sleeping with her face tilted
to the open window, her mouth open, gulping the fresh, dry air.
What was going on here couldn't have been more obvious: No question, Dad had let us know.

seven

Dad has popped back into my kitchen. Two days ago he finished moving his storage boxes into my basement, so, in the general theme of being useful and encouraging, he's been working in the attic, where he's taken it upon himself to reset the skylight and install a pop-out window, all because he's seen Richard has set up a workout bench there and brought up the weights we bought him for his last birthday.

"There's dust on your hair. And spiderweb on your back," I say to Dad.

He wags his head in an exaggerated motion, imitating a slo-mo of a dog paddling himself out of a pond. "I have to go back to Home Depot because I got the wrong flashing," he says, bending over my laptop. "What part of the trip are you up to?"

I turn down the laptop cover. I don't want him to read it, but I don't mind telling him. "Shabbos. Shabbos in Jerusalem."

"That was a big event for us; we were so nervous to make it just right for you."

He must see how my eyebrows pull up my forehead. I still get surprised when I find out he's not beyond self-consciousness about how he's put down an anchor and built his world around it.

"Don't get me wrong," he adds. "Not right like my-boss-was-coming-for-dinner right. But right for you so that you wouldn't think Evelyn and I were crazy. So you could get a fair glimpse of what we were so hot to trot about."

NOT THAT I understood it in real time, but the minute Shabbos was over, what wasn't permitted was suddenly okay, just like that. We'd been under a spell. All that thinking about life related to the needs of the soul was like a hocus-pocus spell. And the moment Shabbos was over, when I turned on all the lights in my room, I realized I didn't want to be there anymore. Whatever had bloomed on Shabbos was going to chase and get me if I didn't watch out. It wasn't just Dad's search for meaning; what if it was my own sometime search for meaning that felt like a stone tied to my abdomen, ready to sink me?

If someone had suggested that after Shabbos we go out drinking and dancing—with strangers, with abandon—I would have jumped at the chance; it was a little scary how ravenous I was to detonate the experience.

No dancing and drinking, but Dad asked if we wanted to take a walk and do an errand and then get some frozen yogurt.

"Yes!" I practically shouted.

"Wait. Give me five minutes," Susan said. She wanted to look something up on the computer. But—where was the computer?

Evelyn marched out of the kitchen, where she'd been cleaning up, wearing a pink bibbed apron with KOSHER KARMA written in large slanted letters across the bodice. Hands wet with dishwater, she whipped a small white tablecloth off the desk—and there was the computer, also subject to Shabbos nay-saying. Apparently they covered it during Shabbos, so as not to distract the eye and the mind.

Susan sat and opened a search page. "How do you spell *cholent*?" Evelyn called from the kitchen, and Susan typed out loud. "C-h-o-l-e-n-t." She clicked, read. "Hungarian. Beans simmered in goose fat?" She turned to Evelyn, who'd come out of the kitchen again, this time with no apron and with dry hands, murmuring. "No. Or maybe yes. But not only Hungarian. There are as many cholents as there are Jewish communities."

"I can keep searching." Susan scrolled. *"Hamin. Adafina."* With her foodie foreign-language skill, she curled the words around the vowels authentically as she read them out loud. "The Spanish dish *cocido.* Hey, did you know that the poet Heinrich Heine compared cholent to ambrosia? Or a way to assuage assimilation? Huh?"

"The big deal is to eat hot food that was heated before Shabbos," Evelyn said. "Something about being able to tell the difference between the Sadducees and the Pharisees."

"Or the men and the boys," I said. "The Hatfields and the Mc-Coys. The Cabots and the Lodges." Free from Shabbos, I got very playful.

"Or Rae Stark and Brookline Hebrew Day School," Susan said. Clearly stepping out of bounds.

What was her problem? I had to get out of there. "Come on. Shabbos is over. Let's go. Go!" I tried to pull her from the computer.

"One minute," Susan said. "Can't you just get the flavor of cholent? Or use it on fish or seafood? I'm thinking about the restaurant," she said.

"The flavor is Shabbos, and you can't bottle Shabbos like it's some Cajun spice," Dad said, straightening the collar of a green cashmere sweater I'd got him for his birthday the year I started working. When had he changed clothes? My heart fluttered: what a nice signal of old Dad. And then he made the moment even better.

"Cholent makes the house smell . . . wicked good." Now that was a New England eruption if there ever was one.

But the little culture blends made Evelyn nervous. "*Wicked* isn't exactly one of our words these days, and Shabbos isn't all about the recipes. Shabbos makes the recipes."

IN HIS OWN way, Saturday night, after the Shabbos spell, made Dad playful too: himself, his old self, which Evelyn groaned at and whose glibness went over Susan's head. My heart soared with hope and possibility when he said, "Before we get fro-yo, we're going to my favorite art gallery."

"More like *his* art gallery. What he's spent there already." Evelyn didn't mean malice. She was proud, not show-offy proud, but tsk-tsking her rapscallion husband proud. "What he means," Evelyn said, "is that he's hankering after this painting and he wants to try to charm the gallery owner—once again."

"Dad's full of charm," I said.

Dad smiled at me; I smiled back; for the first moment the entire trip we were in sync, in what we were for and who we were against.

Out on the street, something about Saturday night, something about the switch back filled up the air like a nor'easter: if we'd been on some kind of a journey, an inward journey on Shabbos, the world was turned upside down on Saturday night, and the people on the street all looked as if they had somewhere real to get to.

"See that newsstand," Dad said, pointing over his left shoulder, "just before the playground? When we go past, take a look at the guy's face. He's always smiling. His face is made into a smile."

"Remember my cat Sheba who used to smile?" I caught up with him. Evelyn and Susan walked a few paces behind; this was our conversation, and my spirit soared again, especially when we drifted to regular normal things.

"That's what you used to say."

"Mom used to say Sheba smiled."

"Mom used to say a lot of things." His voice trailed.

I thought for one moment of the bologna and cheese sandwiches and tied my own tongue.

Dad scooted ahead, just to have us bunch up at a street crossing a moment later. He held us back with his arm like a crossing guard, and when the walk light blinked on, he relaxed, signaling us to cross in safety.

Susan and Evelyn walked ahead, and he caught up alongside me again, this time showcasing his literacy of his new neighborhood with the constant feed of his observations, the kind a person has when he's arrived someplace and has acquired the place, absorbed it into his psyche. We passed by the American Consulate, which was as much official presence as the American government allowed, short of the embassy move to Jerusalem, which, as Dad put it, might cause World War III. It was a small compound with serious-looking black cars in front and serious-looking, suited men on guard, ear sets in place, talking into their hands. Maybe because I was liking Dad that moment, his normalcy didn't seem fake or too studied.

Dad continued. To our right, the buildings used to be called No-Man's-Land, the bullet-pocked buildings on the city dividing line after the War of Independence. But the renovators came, finally, a couple of years ago. They'd preserved the façades and built inward. The four of us bunched up at another corner.

"This is the hottest part of the city right here, right now," Dad said.

"'Cause you're here," Susan said.

She didn't need to affirm him if I had already. I shot her a look,

which she couldn't see. We continued uphill, single file, next to a
construction wall where the sidewalks were cordoned off from resting bulldozers and cranes. There, when the light turned green, we
dashed across a pair of small streets.

"The galleries are up here." Evelyn pointed forward. "Past that
fancy hotel. Where we stayed on our tour, not the first time but the
second time in Jerusalem." Her long-ago-and-faraway tone wasn't
exactly accurate. I might have reminded her that they'd been tourists only some few months back. I knew I should be picking my
battles and didn't interrupt as Evelyn continued. "It used to be a
Hilton. The night before we got there, a terrorist stabbed a tourist
right out there in the driveway."

"Evelyn, you'll scare them away," Dad said.

"Oh, the tourist didn't die," Evelyn said.

I wasn't worried. I'd been so preoccupied with Dad I hadn't paid
any attention to other terrors of the night, which I realized when I
got back and Allan plied me with questions about whether I felt
safe or not walking around Jerusalem. The truth—and now the
problem—was that Dad would always and forever be my scout guide,
my tour guide, my life guide. My TV guide—Dad used to know
the end of every *Brady Bunch* episode, the end of any TV show,
without ever seeing a rerun. I didn't know that all fathers weren't
like that until one night in the Starks' green linen and mahogany
den we were watching a very tense slice-and-dice TV movie and I
was climbing the sofa arms and backs with fear. I couldn't take the
tension anymore and insisted Moe Stark tell me how the movie
ended. He reddened in all of a second and growled: I should hold
my horses. How was he to know? He hadn't seen it before either. I
grew up thinking that all fathers knew how things worked, how es-
sentially they worked.

In short seconds we landed on a very civilized street, storefronts with bright lights behind them, a touristy heartland with signs I could read: AVIS, HERTZ, BUDGET.

Susan came to a sudden stop at the next storefront. She grabbed me by the purse, Evelyn by the arm. "Look at this jewelry."

"Jewelry is a big business in Israel," Evelyn said. "The jewelry designers start here. Like couture clothes in Paris." She didn't need to point. In the low, well-placed lights, the large colored stones and yellow gold smiled at me, just like Dad's kiosk man. The commerce, the gold, the classy lights, the doormen, even a limousine which had us freeze at the crosswalk as it pulled out of a circular drive. The sign for luxury condos being built across the street.

"This is it," Dad said. Two doors past the jewelry store he stopped in front of a double display window set with great care: a single sculpture of a Moses-type man hugging a set of arched tablets, and a door-size oil, a painting more intimate than you'd ever want to see close up of a large goat head in black and white. Red all over the background too, which, if I were in the mood for a black and white joke, I would have pointed out to Susan. Dad pressed the doorbell, and a tall man with a chrome-colored beard and a black yarmulke exactly like Dad's waved through the glass and buzzed us in.

"Mr. Marciano, yes, like the jeans," said the man as he shook Dad's hand and bowed to Evelyn, Susan, and me and said something else in Hebrew.

"Saturday-night greetings," Dad translated.

In spite of his warm greeting, it was clear that Mr. Marciano knew why Dad had come and that he wished Dad was an easier customer. His gestures were more passive-aggressive than cap-in-hand, not the way you'd expect for a proprietor and his only business for the night. Slowly he raised the dimmer switch, and very slowly he walked to a back room and spent several minutes there before he returned with an oil painting, which he hung on the blank show wall near the picture windows. He reached up to adjust one spotlight, then a second, and Dad sighed. It was a picture I would best describe as a synagogue front, a door and blue columns with a kind of Jewish star. Identifiable but abstract shapes, the way they might look if you were dreaming the scene and then woke up and the picture had just begun to melt down.

Mr. Marciano sighed too. "I had a man in here from Dallas on Friday. Also interested."

"Also bargaining?" Dad asked.

"My business," Mr. Marciano said. His weak smile revealed it all: As a businessman he couldn't tell all the truth, as a religious man he could not tell a lie. That's when I knew the picture would be Dad's. I took a step back. Okay, in the real world, there was no accounting for taste. I backed away, my buoyant mood from a half hour earlier all but turned off. Which Mr. Marciano interpreted as boredom. "If you want, go in the back. Look around there," he said. He leaned over to his desk and pressed some buttons, and a series of lights went on to reveal a nest of back rooms filled with stacked and hanging oils, lithographs, and watercolors.

I wove through the small rooms. Piece after piece was a large-ticket item, shekel prices in the tens of thousands. What was Dad doing with himself and now his money? And now his aesthetics? When I walked back into the front room, Mr. Marciano had a thinking look on his face and Evelyn was smiling and saying something to Susan in a low voice, like a polite murmur during an opera solo.

Dad had concluded some negotiation, and I crashed. My interior light turned off. What had I been thinking? Dad's life, his focus, his food, his talk, his money. It wasn't just taste and aesthetics. Like the kosher food, his soul infusion, it was a new twist on pleasure. In his eyes, some kind of elevation; another notch in his born-again psyche. Which meant his whole new life was interiorized and his old life gone, all gone.

Maybe until that moment I couldn't admit it to myself; or maybe I'd underestimated the depth of his changes. I had no idea how right I was when I'd called him Soul Man. I attempted to catch Susan's eye above Dad's head, but she and Evelyn were bent over a stack of miniature photographs, sand-colored desert scenes full of dusty pilgrims. Okay, so maybe this wasn't a cult, but maybe it was worse. The changes were more substantial. In this religion, the physical world wasn't wicked—Evelyn's point. But there was a path to pleasure that was mindful, elevated—and soulful.

How I was beginning to hate that word.

eight

To make it worse, neither Allan nor Susan nor I understood how elusive Dad and Evelyn had become, the way they followed their noses on the trail of their own pursuits. In this case, rain. Quarter of five Sunday morning, I woke up to the sound of them whispering as they closed their front door, off for sunrise prayers for rain at the Western Wall. They'd left a note on the dining room table, where, overnight and coincidentally, had also sprouted a half dozen Torah Lights pamphlets for our elucidation. The first one, glossy and triangular, looked like a fortune cookie, and I snapped it open to large, lionhearted statements, the kind Dad wrote in his notebook.

"Living up to the Truth" (written in agitated blood red). "The controversy over Living up to the Truth." The word *truth* leapt forward in nervous, fuzzy lines.

A second glossy cookie had pull tabs identifying a different Torah Lights class for each day of the week, in boldfaced text columned out to mimic scriptural verse.

"Soul Food—Jewish Dietary Laws"

"When Seth becomes Shmuel." "When Jennifer becomes Chana. Changing past the fear of change"

Susan was also wide awake, wearing her new jilebba and pacing at the kitchen phone to a set of staccato adjectives. "Georgian. Victorian. Nouveau?" Hard to tell if she was talking to Steve or to Carnie Goldstein. Either one was a likely receptacle for her passion for Naughahyde seat covers for their back booths renovation. It wouldn't be the last time I thought this: Between her Victorian town house and the restaurant, Susan's zest for renovation sounded like Dad's when he talked about Shabbos and the World to Come and building his soul. I didn't have to comment, but I did. "Your real religion. Cult renovation?" is what I said out loud when she hung up.

"Bad choice of sneering comment," she said as she dialed one more call. This time to Carnie; so she *had* been speaking to Steve.

"I don't know how you can concentrate on anything else when we're saving a life over here," I said to her when she hung up the second time. "And notice I didn't say 'saving a soul.'"

Susan's jilebba might have given her an ethereal flow, and her mind's eye might have been fixed on colors and shapes of back booth and backsplash renovations, but I'd underestimated her. "Stop jumping all over me. You didn't hear the first part of my conversation with Steve. I told him Dad was happy."

"That's not an explanation, or an excuse. That's the problem. That's why we're here. If anything, he's too happy." Of course I fixed Dad back into our old family time. Shabbos might have left some afterimage for me, like a stain on the retina, but if anything, I'd come to see that the fight to get Dad back was a fight against *something* more concrete—and more up my alley. "He's going to lose us."

And then, maybe Susan believed what came out of her mouth. The only good thing I can say is that sometimes I underestimate her. "That's not so fair," she said. "We can't take him out of context. With us or with Mom. In another year he'll be married to Evelyn as long as he was married to Mom. Married to Mom viably,

I mean. Like any time that Mom was a companion. A partner. Why shouldn't he take all means available to move on? To keep on moving on?"

Her level of objectivity threw me, more worthy of a stranger, not a sister, and certainly not a daughter. I'd heard her say things before that sounded right: for example, how her own commitment to family dinners, restaurant Sundays at 5:00 P.M., was a knee-jerk response to our childhood. All those five years Mom was sick when we saw meals at our friends' houses, plated food or passing bowls served parent to child, like it or not. Our mother stayed in her sickbed and we ate sugar for a thrill, or a sleeve of Oreos for appetizers or canned soups for a main course, those memorable quivering cylinder curds we whacked down the side of a two-quart pot.

"Don't think I'm saying that Mom wasn't the viable partner. I'm just not like you. You don't scratch my surface and find loss . . . this loss, or *this* loss . . ." She waved around the apartment. But that's where she stopped, which was going to make it worse before it got better, and I couldn't help see how, for people unrelated, her loosened, overdirect tongue was exactly like Evelyn's.

"It's just that, from what I know, what I see, maybe we're not being fair to Dad. Here, read this," Susan said. "There's nothing here that's so terrible." She handed me a couple of fortune cookie pamphlets: "And When I Die?" "Glimpsing the Eternal?"

I waved them away. "Not for me."

"Who said it has to be for you? Or me? Or us? If it's okay for him—then it's okay." She might have sounded all visceral to herself, but as far as I was concerned, her willingness to go only so deep was the problem as well as the answer. I was not willing to take this Dad at face value.

.   .   .

I TOOK THE phone out to the balcony. Allan was still awake, watching a 007 TV marathon. First, *From Russia with Love,* with Sean Connery, and now he was in the middle of *Tomorrow Never Dies,* with Pierce Brosnan, In his mind, Sean Connery was the one and only real James Bond, and he only tolerated the others. Poseurs, he said. So this phone call he was more talkative and listening better. I couldn't figure out why Susan's "I'm OK, you're OK" got under my skin. All I knew was that it sounded better than it was, especially if it led her to spout off shamelessly about our own generation gap between my firsthand knowledge of our parents' family life and her ignorance. Allan didn't have more to say than what I knew already.

"That's not even the issue right now. You'll have plenty of chances to put her in her place when you get back. At least she didn't get religion too. And don't forget that Susan's 'inspiration'—if that's what you call it—will pass as quickly as it came." I didn't know if it felt better or worse when he reminded me that for a year she was Buddhist, until the retreats were too long a drive away; another year she studied Baha'i but found it hard to explain the theology to anyone; and she was a vegetarian for five years, until she became a lacto-ovo, then dropped the whole thing when she married Steve and the seafood restaurant. Then, Allan thought he was distracting me with down-home news: "There's been an article in the Metro section of the paper about your case with Brookline Hebrew Day." He chuckled. "They called the school Brookline Hebe and referred to the case as Jew vs. Jew."

"Where did that come from? Who's the reporter?"

"It says '*Globe* Staff.' But they're not so wrong. They listed the names of complainants, including you: Black, Stark, Goldberg, Hochberg, Glassman, Susan, her decorator, Carnie Goldstein . . ."

"That's racial—typecasting."

"More like reality—in Brookline at least." He switched to small talk. "The boys and I might not go to Gillette Stadium after all, and it's a snap to get rid of my Patriots tickets." Besides a nor'easter heading in, Ronnie was sleepy, sluggish, he would need a bulldozer to get him out of bed.

I wished Allan would stop with Ronnie's travail already. Couldn't he get it? My mission was spinning wheels. I needed his advice. I didn't want to believe what Susan said was true, that Dad's happiness, not the religion, bothered me, that what it came to was that Dad had broken our pact of mourning. "My arguments aren't convincing, and your Big Talk idea was a flop. Ended before I began."

"Well . . ." Allan paused, a significant overpause. An ominous windup usually to something smart. "This might come out of left field. But, you know, every time I've spoken to you, you tell me something about the place he's living in or how he lives—"

"And talks about it. Life—and death."

"And rain dance—okay. Stop interjecting and hear me out," Allan said. "You may not like this because it's an old Jewish proverb my grandmother used to say. 'Change the place, change the luck.' 'Change the place, change the results.' Something like that. How can you clarify what's the man and what's the place? Maybe you and Susan should shake him loose a little. Get him out of that apartment. Out of Jerusalem. See what he has left."

For the sake of efficiency, for the sake of six thousand miles between us, I didn't challenge him about the part he thought I would mind. Maybe he minded that it came from his grandmother and that it was a Jewish proverb. I wasn't indicting everything Jewish, historically, socially, or demographically, or bagels and lox, smoked fish, corned beef. Just the rules and regulations parts. And the fact that my father operated under a Jewish spell. But a practical suggestion was like breathing air into my lungs or getting chiropractic on my skeletal system. Before he hung up, Allan reminded me that getting Dad out of his cult milieu was—cult or not—anyhow, straight from the deprogramming book.

DAD AND EVELYN barreled in, palm-size umbrellas in hand, and I was about to tell them full frontal that we should leave, just leave, but it was they who caught me off guard first—when they saw me standing there—by shorting out a conversation in midsentence and pointed to their umbrellas. "See! We put our money where our mouth is."

"No, in the closet." Evelyn pointed, with elevated fluster, either real and true or part of the attempt to disarm the awkwardness.

"No. We will need it. Anytime now," Dad said, pitch-perfect. Too pitch-perfect. I was supposed to interpret his jittery laugh as self-deprecation, the kind when the faithful lapse into unfaithful moments or exposure. Ah! They had an agenda also.

In fact, Dad pulled out two dining room chairs and motioned Susan and me to sit. "We thought of something."

Evelyn threw him a sharp, cautious look, which didn't square with the pleasantry she offered. "You would be doing us a favor," she said.

"Let's get out of here," he said to us.

Evelyn's face dipped back into her neck. "He didn't mean escape. We meant we could travel north. See the country a little." She softened.

"Yeah, right. We haven't been north since our first week in the country altogether. It's so pretty," Dad said. Out of his mouth, the word *pretty* sounded hollow, the way a tap might sound when you search for a beam behind a wall.

The crazy part was that, in spite of being spared from the same suggestion coming from me, in spite of stepping up my aggression with an agenda to finally, finally break him, I reacted like a daughter. I didn't want to hear that he wanted us to leave his home: Was he suggesting that we'd interrupted routine and that we should be sorry?

"You *will* be doing us a favor," Evelyn urged.

Right to the point as always, I thought. But I didn't want to do them a favor. I wanted to do myself a favor.

ON THE OTHER hand, a vacation—even within a vacation—was a gift Dad would give himself regularly. Dad wasn't thematically a self-sacrificing man, and that might be an odd inconsistency about someone who lost his first wife after years of close and detailed caretaking. To his credit he used to literally bundle up Mom and carry her out the door and take her on spontaneous overnights, once in a while to Old Orchard Beach, but usually to Newport, Rhode Island, where he swore he didn't mind cutting back on the Cliff Walk, if that's what it came to. They would climb into the car with Mom narrating her limits of walking about, no downhill, no cobblestones, sneakers only, please, and Dad insisting the change would be good for her, and when they came back he would admit it had been at least as good for him too. So even as we kickboxed all his changes, I hated to admit that pulling a driver and Mercedes sedan out of a hat (in a single hour) was as much good-old-Dad as we'd seen the entire trip.

In the car Evelyn was all chittery. "I've brought Bumble Bee tuna with Hellmann's mayonnaise on bagels, onion crackers, whole wheat crackers, carrot sticks, pears, croissants that your dad got at the bakery." Then she emended the list with personal user options. The sandwiches and fruit were in a plastic shopping bag, *which ripped so hold it tightly underneath*, and bottles of springwater and cheap plastic cups *that cracked like glass if they were held too tightly.* And so on. Pretending this was a normal visit. In the meantime, I would rise to the battle. I was awake, refreshed, buoyed by my husband's confidence, working off my sister's benign uselessness and Evelyn's stream of consciousness. Because I'd wanted to, I'd forgotten Dad's obsessive focus.

"Safed," Dad announced. "We're going to Safed." He smacked his lips and faced forward.

"What is Safed?" I asked.

Before he opened his mouth, Evelyn piped up with a sidebar comment. "The little northern mountain city of Safed, about three hours away. Very spiritual. Lots of artists too. No wonder," she said, tucking the bags of food around her feet.

"Nn-nn," the driver said only to Dad, dropping his vowel sounds and shaking his head vigorously. "Two—two and a half hours away, if you go on Road Six. Road Six?"

"Road Six? Red Sox?" I whispered to Susan. I was giddily confident; the change of place just might do the trick.

Dad and Evelyn bent their heads together and whispered until Dad thundered their hands-down agreement. "Please. Go ahead. Save us time on Road Six."

Their whispering rubbed me the wrong way, and even though it wasn't fair, it was more convenient to focus on Evelyn than on Dad: Evelyn, default wife, I thought. Default mother figure. Default nurturer. I was meanly satisfied that her sandwiches and fruit stayed in the bag. I was going to get in my two cents and more, but the entire two and a half hours we (including the driver) ate minicroissants from the Angel bakery, one box after another, greasy plain and greasy chocolate. It was the first time the whole trip that my physiology trumped my agenda and I was punished for my nasty thoughts: By the last couple of miles, a wide zigzag ride into the mountains, the croissants had sunk my stomach and my ears wheezed at the elevation. Evelyn offered us fruit gum, and at least my ears snapped back to normal. An A plus to Evelyn for good nurturing.

"Eleven kilometers to Safed," Dad said, reading the signs. All along he'd pronounced the word in one nipped, foreign syllable, "*Svat*," and I was surprised to see the spelling on the sign.

In front of us, the road began to narrow as it rose up on the mountainside. The angles and drops below reminded me of the steep hazards on the children's board game Chutes and Ladders. A few minutes later, no longer air bound, we found ourselves on a city street, looping between twin-size billboards, one for cigarettes and the other for a black-hatted rabbi peddling something . After a city block of high stone walls, the Mercedes engine paddled hard and loud, then stopped short in front of a wooden door set into a flagging blue mosaic façade.

"The Eucalyptus. It's an old family house turned into an inn," Evelyn whispered as we entered the small lobby with a glass wall overlooking a small mountain range. "The original family grew and the house sprouted wings."

With a uselessness that was becoming consistent, Susan purred over the accurate poetry of Evelyn's description. "And the oil paintings too," she added, pointing toward the primitive landscapes, two deep, wobbling everywhere there wasn't a window. All purples and teals. I looked up—and down quickly. No time for art appreciation. I still had our work to do.

THE GUEST ROOMS were in the general direction of up and numbered sequentially, 104 and 106, but the two rooms were arranged with a courtyard space between them. Our room opened to a mountain view off a set of grille doors on a thick window ledge. After our suitcases arrived, we set off to see Dad and Evelyn, whose room, it turned out, opened to a private garden patio. Dad sat inside on the bed, looking pale, puffy, tired, in one of the spare moments, maybe the first moment the whole trip that I caught a function of his not-old old age. Maybe it was travel deflation: like when you arrive some-where after a twelve-hour flight, all the hours you've missed suddenly forfeited from the body at one moment.

When he looked like that, I could shut him down in a minute. Did I dare? I've thought about that one moment over and over, whether it was weakness or strength that restrained me. I mean, after everything I'd been through and in spite of myself, I choked up from the love I felt for him, to the care I felt for Evelyn. Dad took this trip only because of us, and I was going to break him sooner or later, shake him loose, and maybe he wasn't sick, but maybe he was too old—no, not that—maybe he couldn't take it.

"Sorry," I said. "Sorry you're tired."

But Evelyn and Dad rejected my "Sorry" with matched, choreo-graphed waves of the hand. "Wait and see what we have in mind," Dad said.

Twenty minutes later we met in the hotel dining room and ate what Susan called a tired chef's meal: warmed-over fried chicken cutlets and tomato-cucumber salad hand-cut to button-size pieces. With a full belly, Dad's fatigue converted to a recharge, and he got talkative about all the sites to see, like the olive trees from the time of the Patriarchs. Or at least from the time of the Prophets. Or maybe not the time of the Prophets, but he would have to look that up. Evelyn quieted him by pressing his shoulder a first time, then his arm, until Dad and Evelyn made a loud decision to take a walk and after dinner they disappeared through an alleyway behind the inn.

Meanwhile, Susan and I barely climbed the stairs to our room. Before she turned out the light, Susan called Steve at work, and when she hung up the phone she was shaking her head merrily about what it sounded like from six thousand miles away, all that healthy, pitchy restaurant noise in the background, the way she liked to hear it.

I sat up in bed, a single flimsy pillow behind my back, trying to tick off on one hand any inroads I'd made in our agenda. Not even one finger. I envied how quickly Susan fell into a gauzy, high-altitude, thin-air sleep.

nine

D AD HAS FINISHED IMPROVING THE INSIDE OF MY HOUSE. This morning he walked the perimeter of my yard with a notepad in hand, and now he's come inside. I'd fallen asleep sitting up at the kitchen table. The turn of his key in the lock jolts me awake, and he recognizes my sleep-not-sleep. He's good at blocking those first waking thoughts, and he leans over me with his hands behind his back. "Trim out the forsythia, you have a half dozen dead maple saplings, and the larger maple tree has dead branches. But the good news is that the buds are fattening up on the rhododendrons and I thought your dogwood tree was dead but it's not, and the first crocus is out." I wipe dry things off my mouth. "A peace offering," he says, laying a purple crocus on the table.

"A peace offering? For nothing," I answer, and then—don't I know it!—just the way that a bad thing happens out of the blue, like the time last spring when a policeman rear-ended my car when I was on the way to a Zoning Board meeting, a good thing can happen just as suddenly. Dad and I are talking and he apologizes for some of his attitude last December, when we visited him in Jerusalem.

He settles himself across from me, pushing the crocus into my hands in case I haven't noticed it. "I tried to bring this up the other day," he says. "Just stop and just listen: My rabbi at the Torah Lights had been warning us to take it slow. There's a fear factor with people like Evelyn and me who jump in, who go from zero to sixty in a major lifestyle turnaround. They don't always last. It's like infatuation. After you left I had lots of things to talk to him about, and your visit was a gift to me in many ways. Because he sent me to speak to a Rabbi Horowitz, who's used to dealing with older returnees who want to take everything in and influence everyone."

"Yes, in your own quiet way you were quite the heavy hitter," I say. "The relentless heavy hitter." I stop short of real criticism. Because Dad's influence in the holy spheres might come in handy just about now; I can't help think about the scale that has measured my fate since this story began, something like the way you picture fate as a child: a metal jurists' scale with two trays hanging for balance. Dad is on one side, pushing down with his forearms, and the Brookline Hebrew Day School and all its complications is heaped like coal on the bad side. Dad's face is tired, pointy, drawn. Not that it makes him more endearing and more human and less the object of battle. It's just that my experience battling for truth and justice hasn't usually involved what it takes out of my loved ones.

BACK IN SAFED on our little mission last December, I saw that same crimped look on his face. Except that morning I still clung to the fantasy that I would change his world, enact magic, or enact an instant reversion to his good sense, easy as a scene change in a fantasy movie. Except the distractions began that first morning, as soon as I went downstairs to the dining room.

First of all, on a real vacation, Allan and I would have been cracking up at the hotel breakfast. Conspicuous consumption. Miles and miles of food. But Israeli hotel breakfasts were legend, Susan told me. It wasn't just the Eucalyptus Inn. Later, when I heard her speak the list of hot entrées to Steve, even she couldn't do it justice: quiche baked with soft, unsalty cheese, cinnamon rolls, potato and cheese soufflé. Then the cold salads: mushroom, cabbage, tomato, tomato-cucumber, tomato-cucumber-dill, tomato-cucumber-dill-feta. Olive oil. On and on. Finally, after our second cup of coffee, Dad announced he'd arranged a private tour for us, which meant we would spend the day in our little group sitting in rows, at best talking to the back or side of a head. And with a stranger as our "leader." Not what I'd planned.

Somehow I was the last into the lobby and came upon a meet-and-greet scene already in progress. Mr. Alfasi was our tour guide driver and, as it would turn out, our wannabe life coach. He was shaking hands, laughing, talking, and exhaling a cigarette, which poufed a cloud of smoke around his head—a comfortable Aladdin image.

"Ready? We've been waiting for you," Susan said, as if we were there for fun and bonding and my lateness was the obstacle. Not a wink or a nod to the fact that we had an agenda and that time was short and getting shorter.

Dad introduced me. "This is Mr. Alfasi."

"Nice to meet you, Mr. Alfasi."

"No one call me mister I remember," he answered in English stripped of conjunctions and verb tenses. "Call me Na'tan."

Then Na'tan directed small talk to Dad, and I hopped frames of reference: The Aladdin image dissolved, and his dark, beaky face reminded me more of Gregor Samsa. He opened the right rear door of the car for Evelyn, the left rear door for Susan and me, and the front passenger door for Dad, all at the same time, a three-arm trick which might have confirmed he'd woken up as a bug.

Settled in the front seat, Dad announced the destination.

"Huh?" Na'tan gargled.

Without a blink, Dad wrung his statement into single-syllable words. "Where—we—go," Dad said. He pointed outward, then loop-de-looped his hand. "Wine. Old." A winery, an ancient winery was what he intended. "Goland winery."

"Goland? Golan?" Na'tan repeated the name with a question.

"Golan?" "Goland?" They traded the name into correct pronunciation. "Golan," Na'tan said finally. Dad absorbed the correction with a smile, and Na'tan celebrated truth and justice by double-revving the engine with a lead-heavy foot. He slammed the car off the road, tore out of the parking lot, eased to a just as sudden pause on the top of a mountain road. A high-up mountain road. But for the buildings and stone walls and pedestrians, we could have plummeted out of Safed on gravitational laws alone. Na'tan zoomed us out for another short block, then slowed to a sudden crawl at a traffic circle, "A new circle," he said, and, "mo-*dern* traffic."

I hadn't cared where we were going because my agenda wasn't physical, but I found myself gripping the seat back in front of me. In the hands of this driving maniac, my life goals had just gotten a little primitive. My adrenaline, primed for metaphysical battle, hummed in survival mode. Not that Na'tan's unsophistication didn't leverage his authority: The way he thought he was talking English to Dad, all that *heh-heh* and guttural laughing instead of words. Dad, in his former life so restrained and New England circumspect, responded with a spate of hand gestures, till even he—who had telegraphed nothing but cultural comfort and enthusiastic dissonance— was impatient. "All this hand jive," he said. "It's really not for me."

Which, I couldn't help notice, might have been the first moment of the trip we experienced something the same way: Dad directed the comment to all us women in one wide look as he turned from

Na'tan's front seat, a warm, sweet, inclusive gesture of us against the native country which was not ours. And sadly, because I was on a mission, because I'd woken up feeling desperate to keep my family together in the way I always knew it, I was obligated to slice the mood.

Susan told me later she saw all the warning signs of direct confrontation, the way I twisted off Mom's watch and twisted it back on again. (Susan thought I'd made up the nervous gesture, but it was Mom's, which came with the watch.)

You know, I always think that as a psychological defense denial works very well until it doesn't. What was working against us was that we reacted to the surface issues, like the yarmulke, or the light timers, and we didn't credit Dad with the depth of his changes. His aspirations. His desire to, as he put it, "work on himself." "I have to tell you what . . . we've been thinking about your mother, Evelyn and I," Dad said, snapping his shoulder belt forward and turning around.

"As if I don't?" I sounded angry. I *was* angry, even though I'd been telling Susan all along this had something to do with Mom. And not that I needed reinforcement of my sudden black, denuded mood, but the landscape changed abruptly. "Dad, we have to get a few things straight. You have created fresh wounds here. I don't care if you're wrong or right with this religion, but you have accountability. To us, to . . ."

After all that Dad couldn't hear me. Na'tan had rolled down his window; righteous and offended, he was busy chastising the driver of a ten-wheeler which had slowed us to neutral as the truck made a K-turn in the middle of the highway. I flopped back in my seat and saw what I might not have if we'd continued to speed along. The standing trees at the edge of the road were green and sprightly, but behind them the charred remains of a fire swept down the mountain;

what was supposed to be tall and imposing was instead chopped and uneven, like broken bones thrown in a fire pit when the barbecue is over.

Na'tan said something. Dad translated his pidgin English. "Bombs, air strikes. It takes fifty years to grow back those trees."

I didn't have time to sigh, to ask. To ponder the loss of wildlife; to imagine the bubble over Susan's head, bemoaning the maimed or starving Bambis and Thumpers. Dad barreled on. "Evelyn and I have been thinking about your mother. What she would want to see for all of us." His eyes were popping slightly.

But Na'tan interrupted. "This is not your mother?" He pointed to Evelyn. "Not your mother? Your mother she dead?"

I nodded.

"Orphans. You are orphans?" Na'tan asked, just as we drove into a scene with increasing personality: knobby hills, knobby mountaintops, and then ancient olive trees serious as sentries or grave markers.

Because sometimes I am made of steel and because I had my own agenda, I pretended I didn't hear the question. Below, on the other side of the road, were ditches, maybe bomb craters, what Dad called wadis: steep ledges, steep runoff paths for winter rain. Inside the wadis lay sickles and moons and bells of color, like the inside of a marble if you cracked it open. I hated when this happened to me. Call me an orphan, prick my skin like that, and you bet I'll have an association to Mom from any sound, smell, or sight: When I was a kid, the year before Mom died, one day coming home from the hospital from visiting Mom, I took Dad's hammer and cracked open all the marbles in my marble box. That's how I knew what the inside of a marble looked like.

There wasn't a guardrail in sight. Not having a mother was like driving without a guardrail. I could tell from the back of Na'tan's head that he was pulsing at the temple, about to work his mouth. Na'tan took the curves without braking, and Dad put his mouth to Na'tan's ear, as if the closer he got, the better Na'tan understood his English, an illusion I shared until Dad spaced his words a beat and a half, and said something needy and sympathetic about us.

"They are still daughters. They have me—and Evelyn."

"Orphans?" Na'tan wasn't having second thoughts.

"No," I finally piped up, "an orphan is bereft of both parents."

I'd used *bereft* aggressively, on purpose. A hundred-dollar word. But he wasn't intimidated.

Na'tan turned around and spoke directly to Susan and me, his beakiness flattening as his mouth moved. "You have no mother. You need someone to pray for you. Or you will have to do it yourself."

He turned forward and held my eye in the rearview mirror as we sped out of the curve. On the flat of the next hill he finally slowed down, discovered the brake pedal, and pulled over to the first narrow shoulder. The engine ticked as he turned off the car. Without the fan a breeze moved in, and the back of the car smelled faintly of cigarettes and broken leaves—like Oriental spices.

Na'tan got out, and he stood outside for a silent second, twitching his mouth, then motioned for us to get out too. "It's a special commandment to be nice to orphans."

"We are not orphans."

"Maybe it's cultural or something, but he means orphaned of just your mother," Evelyn whispered, trying to spread nice on the situation. Even Dad was stunned into silence. And the truth was, I don't think I ever felt like such an orphan as I did at that moment.

"Why did not you say me you are orphans? I have a special time to show you what's what," Na'tan said. He leaned against the hood of the car, pulled out a half cigarette from his pants pocket, and lit it with a clear plastic lighter. When he spoke again he spoke carefully, inhaling once, then exhaling the words as if they came from a deeper place than the smoke. "You need to pray. We go to the graves of the Holy Ones and pray there."

"Pray for what?" Now Susan was uncomfortable.

"We should go to the Golan winery as planned," Dad said. He waved his hand: to the general direction we'd been heading, *over there*, an empty gesture to empty space, where decision and aggression had no place to go.

Were they in cahoots? If they were, Na'tan didn't give up a conspiratorial wink. Instead, he bent to tie his sneaker, a neat trick with the cigarette stub between his knuckles. Like the stub and the shoelaces, we were in his hands. After a minute he shrugged and held the cigarette stub aloft to measure its worth, pinching the end and pocketing it. "It is a benefit to go to the graves of the Holy Ones and pray there." His denuded language was all colored in and didn't miss a beat as he threw his head toward the sunlight and directed our sight up the mountain. Once I adjusted my eyes, a pile of stones materialized, a mini-Stonehenge. We were at some kind of cemetery, and, in no more time than it took to look up and down, a handful of black-suited men appeared, wearing those black hats and climbing, climbing and descending, sidewise, spiral-like. Like angels up a ladder.

"Are they leaving or arriving?" Susan asked.

"She's the question," Na'tan answered.

I froze on the spot as if my feet were leaded down with anchor weights. And it reminded me of the way Richard looked when he was fourteen months old and we laced on his first pair of shoes, and he rooted himself to the floor like a punch-clown balloon. No budge, no way, no how.

I hate cemeteries. I mean, if I'd written the treatise on the history of grief, I would have skipped the chapter on catharsis and transcendence. The last time I visited Mom I had a negative experience; no, not a negative experience, but a full-bodied minus negative. I'd arrived at BaisYeshurun Field all hepped up, and then not two steps from my car I was lost, lost in a sea of brown grass and ice blots and indistinguishable granite slabs. Finally, finally, with help from the cemetery map I found it:

RACHEL BLACK

32 YEARS OLD, BELOVED WIFE AND MOTHER

It's not as if I didn't shoot for transcendence; I'd seen the movie *Ghost,* and I'd played with a Ouija board as a kid; if the moment had borne out my imagination, I would have seen a bird or butterfly hovering, fluttering, flying off to a distance where my eyes lost the dot to the blue sky, my breath turning white, my emotions vaporized, message taken. But with the slightest jiggle, the slightest sleight of mind, all I found myself doing was comparing the size of her headstone to the stones right and left, as well as the color and quality of the marble; I didn't find anything, there was no emptying, and definitely no motion—not animal, not mineral, not vegetable— and no woo-woo ghost story; lingering and going were equal acts.

Na'tan had locked in our agenda instead. On the mountain the black-hat men pulled small prayer books out of the pockets of their big coats—not overcoats but long suit jackets cut at the knees. They stood and prayed, swaying from the ankles. I told myself I could resist, like a schoolgirl pinned to her desk; they would have my body but not my mind. Then, the way your life is supposed to play back to you in the seconds before you die, snapshots of Allan at home popped up rapidly, man against the world: Allan out the front door Sunday morning, showing off for me by kicking the advertising dailies off the porch like a hockey puck; crunching the snow in a manly way as he spread ice melt and sand on the front steps; Allan's righteous ire, insisting he was going to return our Honda to the dealer if he got that electric shock from the driver's door one more time.

Na'tan motioned us to follow him down the road. "You enter the cemetery here," he said. And we followed. Past the army radar installation where two, maybe three big dishes looked as out of place as flying saucers. And so large that if it turned out all the deep-dish TVs in the world depended on the ingathering of beams just in this place, I wouldn't have been surprised. Beneath them was a cave where another half dozen worshipers flowed in and out, hardly looking earthbound. Every footstep crunched down thick stalks of purple thistle, as pretty as they were ugly.

"This is the grave of a Holy One" is what I thought Na'tan said. Maybe the radar broadcast the prayer. Now *that* was strange. We entered the cave and stopped at a mildewed trellis in front of a concrete hummock the size of a small delivery van. Fat melted candles lay on the floor, and, here and there, a still lit candle danced light on the black ceiling. "Here we pray," Na'tan announced.

"We pray to this person?" Susan asked, pointing to the hummock, probably, officially, a sarcophagus. She'd been so quiet, she'd been so out of my thoughts, I'd forgotten she was with us.

"Is praying to a person our religion?" I asked. "What does this have to do with orphans?" For the sake of efficiency, just for the moment, I'd given in to the term.

"No," Na'tan said, his impatience suddenly free of condescension, which had the effect of raising my impulse to be quiet and do what I was told. "Not to a person. See. This. Like telephone and wires here," he said, pointing to the hump.

"People have a little bit of soul, the soul lingering at their graves, and the soul carries up the prayers—like messengers they can go from here to on high," Dad explained. I wanted him to repeat that part, but I couldn't bring myself to ask.

So, in the shadows of the fat candles, and in this window to eternity, Na'tan's communication skills turned articulate and correct and conjugated. He rooted Susan and Dad in front, ordered Evelyn and me behind, and marked our position by pulling up a pitcher's mound of concrete rubble with the toe of his sneaker. There, a finger-size lizard dove on top of the mound and stitched through it, disappearing, reappearing. Allan wouldn't believe it. I mean, it wasn't the image of Mom that came up for me just that moment, but the image of Allan—really the image of the reasonable, rational, normal me in my normal life—which flattened the air out of the moment. Allan would never approve of this—this hocus-pocus, this irrational séancy thing, this reality you couldn't see.

I lifted my eyes, and then I couldn't help but notice that Dad and Evelyn had the right moves. Evelyn pulled two small brown prayer books out of her purse and handed one to Dad. In turn, he showed her which page to open. And how was I supposed to know what to do, much less to say, much less to think? The moisture and mildew, received and recycled, turned my breath gray and huffy. Was I supposed to be connecting with something? Someone? What did this have to do with being an orphan or a half orphan? For that matter, what did it have to do with bringing Dad home?

"Speak," Na'tan said. "Speak to the Almighty like you speak to your friend."

I looked over at Susan, whose face was as puzzled as mine.

"Speak. Ask. Thank. One. Do one. Or all three."

I was hard-pressed to thank abstractly. But ask, well, I could ask for things the way Ronnie came home from school once and said he prayed for hot dogs for dinner, and what were they having for dinner anyhow while I was gone? And then suddenly I thought of Allan

again, and an old argument we've had over and over: how many
times had he been so sure of something and then so wrong and how
many times had I relied on my instinct and even then got to use
something concrete and physical to say I told you so. It happened
once at an auction of a closing mental hospital in town when we
spotted a Louis XV armoire under a single high window outside the
administrator's office. Fruitwood with brass butterfly fittings, tout-
ing harmony. Allan got it into his head that when we moved it from
the wall it would be fake, empty, have no back, and I gritted my
teeth and insisted it was as solid as it turned out to be. And what
would Allan say if I told him that this cave, this grave was a portal,
from which you could deduce there was something on the other
side? And a soul was the link. Like the soul that Dad was feeding
and growing. And that's when thoughts of Mom locked into place.
Had Dad taken me here to experience the possibility that she could
live on in some form, really live on? Was that what I was seeing on
his face all the time?

Instead of being slippery and ungraspable, the insight pierced
me like a spear, struck me with lightning and thunder booms invisible and inaudible to the rest of them. So if there was a soul, and the
soul was eternal, then this life we have must take care of the eternal
soul, because that's what we take with us. It was everything that
Dad had been saying—and living.

The thought felt like an escaping balloon, which I lost the same
moment I grabbed it. And I thought of that old joke where a genie
gives you one wish and you outsmart him by wishing for a hundred
wishes. Well, I prayed to understand the prayer I was supposed to
be saying. (I think maybe since my prayer has come true.) I also
prayed for a clean resolution of the Brookline Hebrew Day School
case. Why not get support if it was there? Got that too, though not
the way I imagined.

I heard Susan open her mouth and ask for the restaurant renovations to go well. Just hearing her made the tears spring to the back of my eyes.

I must have sighed or groaned.

"Ended?" Na'tan asked.

Began, I said to myself. If I could call it that: Began, producing a navigating point from myself, picturing myself walking across a suspension bridge with something at the other end of it. But how in the world did you hold on to moments like that?

Then my nay-saying mind, my Allan mind, started up with me as soon as we filed out of the cave on the way to the car. I felt exposed, raw, as if my clothes suddenly dropped off. I'd had some kind of soul experience there. Or maybe I felt exposed-embarrassed: the way, in a movie, a bullied teenager feels when she discovers the laugh-out-loud Post-it stuck on the back of her T-shirt.

"Careful," Dad said.

It turned out he was talking about the slippery stone threshold on the way out of the cave. Na'tan held out his arm to sidle us rightward, against the mouth of the cave. Another couple of people were filing in.

"Careful or *otherwise*," Susan warbled. I wondered if my own face was as clear or transparent as hers, like Lucite or glass brick. I smacked a stubborn strand of spiderweb out of her hair.

I spent the rest of the day pawing my way through space, corded to my thoughts the way an astronaut hangs from the mother ship during a space walk. All I could think about was, would anything happen to me if I refused to believe in or accept the idea of a soul? Or would anything happen to my boys? What was I doing with my boys anyhow? Giving them animal life and nothing more?

But, as if nothing bigger than life had just happened, after the cave we continued to the Golan winery, where the English tour was given by an English-speaking French Israeli named Jacques or Jack or Jake or Yaakov, whatever we chose to call him. All the while I concentrated on how I would summarize the cave moment to Allan. *Strange* was too generic, and my boys' adjective du jour, *random,* was totally wrong. Very wrong.

Jacques the wine tour guide teased us with cartoon Frenchisms. "Amour," he said, pointing from the windowed balcony into the oak barrel rooms.

Back in the main building, he passed out glasses, uncorked a bottle of Chardonnay, and asked for questions.

"What did you mean by the wine journey through dinner?" asked one squat woman with an off-season straw sun hat.

"A question that's . . . *magnifique,*" he answered. "Aah—the wine journey from appetizer to main course to dessert." He had to be toying with her, with us. How could you live and work near those caves and think this was life?

Count on Susan to recognize the epicure's journey question. What came out of her mouth was a question for Jacques-Jack-Jake-Yaakov that was pure, a restaurateur's reflex: "Do you have a botrytis wine? The one that ends the meal?"

"Ooh-la-la, madame—yes. The botrytis," he explained to the group, "is dessert wine, naturally sweet. No sugars added. Merci, *madame!*" He lifted a house phone, mumbled into it, and a few moments later a young man with a green knit yarmulke handed him a small bottle.

"The botrytis spore is rot, controlled rot which turns to gold," Susan whispered to me. She'd established her superior knowledge, satisfied herself. No matter where we'd been, prayed, what we'd done, what we'd been exposed to, she was back to form. Then she crowned the day, buying table wine holders in the gift shop, a dozen for the restaurant, and one for Steve and her at home. Who'd ever seen anything like them?: shellacked avocado tree branches, about a foot long apiece, with an offside bagel hole and one flat sawed end. The wine bottles made them into something; when you set the flat end on the table and put the bottle through the hole, the branch held itself up, wine bottle aloft. When you took out the bottle and the support was gone, it collapsed like just another polished stick.

ten

THE NEXT AND OUR LAST MORNING IN ISRAEL I JOLTED awake to the rumble of thunder, not bowling-ball thunder, but dry, bongo-beating thunder, unconnected to any rain. I'd been in the middle of a dream about something I never found when we moved out of our house a year after Mom died, my Donkey Kong hand game (which had a monkey, not a donkey, fighting for his life through hoops, loops, and crashes). Mom used to play that Donkey Kong in the hospital, and one of the last weeks Mom was sitting up, she sat up for hours with the game, concentrating and pressing. One day, before I took the Donkey Kong home and lost it, when Mom's game was over and she handed it back to me because she was tired, she asked if I wanted to know what was the thing she liked best about Donkey Kong. That the monkey smiled, she said, always smiled, when you lost him. The dream ended back in my childhood bedroom, where I was rummaging, but rummaging confidently because I knew the things I'd lost would be there.

I knew the dream was inspired by the cave, and the prayers, and the literal soul-searching, and that you didn't have to be a mother or an orphan to blot up all that pathos. It would have been more of a stretch to connect the dream to the winery or the rest of the day after the winery, when we'd jumped into a waterfall, hiked into a wadi and hiked out again, worn our soggy sneakers to some forsaken antiquity museum where the woman said if we hadn't come when we did she would have already locked the doors for the day. Coins, pottery, shards, bronze jewelry; two fifteen-minute videos about Roman conquest. Even millennia ago, a village—a whole life—could be flattened like roadkill. Whoosh. If you didn't believe in the soul, gone—just like that. Then off to the shopping mall a half street away, where the new village filled in like a soundstage: voices, kids, dogs. We ate an early dinner of Greek salad and green olive pizza, Diet Coke and chocolate-filled pastry. I kept looking at Na'tan's face and Dad's and Evelyn's mouths: how could they jump from the sublime to the ridiculous? What kind of religion was this, with moods, questions, some answers, piety, unsustained piety, real hunger, desire to connect, afterlife?

I sat up in bed, clearing my head of the bongo thunder, with both Susan's and my flimsy pillows boxed up behind my back. Susan was awake too, sitting on the floor emptying and repacking her suitcase to make room for the avocado tree wine holders. For all of Susan's hand selection back in the gift shop, she'd only just then discovered the encryptions on their backs. "Look, this is weird," she said. She turned over a second one, then a third. "English words with Hebrew vowel notations underneath. This has got to mean something."

"Yeah. They don't know how to spell," I said, smart-alecking for comfort. Who wouldn't have wished such a top-heavy day would have dissipated naturally like fog or dew? But it had only sunk me, and I couldn't believe how we'd prayed and then toured, a kind of enactment of ideas. I wasn't quite articulating it, but the entire trip I'd seen Dad in balance, and that's what stuck with me. Of course I'd called Allan when I got in, but had gotten his voice mail. Just as well; I couldn't assimilate all this anyhow, and Allan would have

ended the conversation as soon as it began. Anyway, I don't know
what made me think I could process this with Susan. "How did we
ever go from that cave to touring?"

"One feels good, the other feels good," Susan said.

"That's not what it's about."

"How do you know?"

"You don't find your connecting soul points, pray, and then forget about it. You're supposed to carry it with you. Or something.
Did you *feel* anything, there, in that cave?" I asked.

Susan's hands suddenly became very busy, rolling her wine holders into a stack of logs, and she began to pack them tightly and verti-
cally back into a large plastic shopping bag. "You mean when we were
praying?"

"Yes—*pray*ing." I elongated the first syllable, the way I would
back up air quotes. If Susan interpreted it as irony, well, that was all
the self-protection I needed.

Susan heaved her bag of wine holders to the corner of the room.
"I was trying to be polite," she said. "It's not as if I suddenly believe
in eternal anything. I'm not a kosher hot-dog commercial. It was
like—like—experiencing fresh air or a magnificent view—"

"You don't get it, do you? This is religion fundamentals, entry-
level Soul, Bible class 101. What Dad's been working on the whole
time. I mean, if you follow his logic—is what occurred to me:
maybe—for Dad—Mom lives on in some form."

"You can't know that."

"This is going to be hard to explain. I mean, just think of the
way we feel inside, when we're alone, in bed, in the tub, singing
in the shower, speeding down the Mass Pike, listening to our iPods,
the thing we feel. We might have a name for it, but I think that's the
thing Dad is calling a soul. *Soul business.*" I sounded like I was introducing James Brown.

"Honestly, Honey. Take it easy. I was just being polite. Experiencing. Like Dad said."

Oh, Susan's analysis, if you could call it that, was a bunt if I ever heard one. Just a glance into the fog of how Susan's mind worked this experience forced an insight into how anyone's mind worked about this thing. And what exactly would "being polite" mean when you were dealing with the corridor, with the portals to the other world?

"Okay. I wasn't being polite—just polite. I was . . . meditating. People really believe this—meditation—can work," Susan said. "It felt good."

"Felt good?" I said. "It wasn't about feeling good. Or about mental massaging. We were supposed to be connecting with something from someplace inside us."

"I connected with myself."

"You can do that anywhere. But that's not what we were supposed to be doing. It was about our soul and another soul. Another soul in the sky. Eternity." There, I was saying it. "Here and someplace beyond. The cave was like a connecting place. And if that's the case, it means the essence of Mom is really out there somewhere."

Susan's face twisted. Would she dare challenge the possibility of Eternal Mom?

"Look. Don't feel bad," she said, responding to something. "Here's what I think: It's about heavy thinking but more . . . contemplative. And it's okay that Dad and Evelyn and all of them who are used to it are getting more out of it. They already tell themselves that's what works for them."

"This isn't some relativistic thing." My frustration rose, and an ache struck up in my temples, as if my mind was trying to put together two things that resisted, like opposing poles of magnets held face-to-face. "If there's anything I can conclude from seeing Dad, it's how reality driven he is. I know it sounds stupid—in spite of all the soul business, in spite of the fact that you can't see a soul—"

"And you can't touch it—" Susan said.

"But you can feel it. The point is, if it's true for them, it's true for everyone. I'm not asking for "I'm OK, you're OK" stuff."

Because if Dad thought this way and lived his life this way, the implications, the obligations would rest on us also. If you believed in a soul, you were obligated to take care of it. Everything he'd been saying. Like a spiritual inheritance. And it was bigger than I thought. Bigger than an apartment building, bigger than a dozen Starbucks or Barnes & Noble stores, bigger than anything I had ever come up against. Well, it was still easier to argue with Susan than discuss it with Dad or hack it to bits with Allan. Because I was trap-mouthed by a flowchart: what I was thinking but didn't want to say; what I said instead but didn't want to mean. And it was certainly easier to project annoyance onto Susan when I found myself wondering if self-deception could be fatal.

BY BREAKFAST, EVERY word out of Susan's mouth, every nod to the waitress pouring coffee, every bite into a crisp croissant which flaked on her sweater got under my skin. The way she smiled up at the cocoa-skinned waitress with the pidgin English and overmouthed the Hebrew word for mushrooms she'd learned a day earlier: *pi-tri-ot*. She wanted a special-order mushroom omelette, and her attempt at a guttural *r* honked in my ears like a plastic party horn; plus, the way she'd given Evelyn rein to take her emotional pulse as if Evelyn were her mother, when she ran over the minutes of her day so far: the pumping adrenaline when the phone rang in the hotel room that morning, though it was only our wake-up call; feeling unanchored and afloat without her husband; feeling ready to get back to

work, not to degrade this trip, which wasn't after all any old vacation. Like an emotional beggar, Evelyn was overly grateful, responding to intimacies and complaints, reciprocating where she
could. She invited Susan to join her in sneaking out croissant and
egg sandwiches in paper napkins and a half dozen of those flat-
topped yogurts, which turned out both mornings to be vanilla pud-
ding. The policy of this particular hotel, Evelyn explained, was to
look the other way. They even provided plastic bags.

And I, battered or not by some basic new ideas, I was still telling
myself I was going to finish what I'd come for, put one foot ahead
of the other, soldier on. I scurried out of the dining room to catch
up with Dad where he was studying the brochure rack between the
dining room door and the stairs to the lobby. Left to right, then top
to bottom, he picked, looked, and grew a stack of flyers in his jacket
pocket. Over his shoulder, a picture window, taller and wider than
both of us, reflected Dad's figure against the terraced green hills
and the cemeteries and houses, that old, dead, live, civilizing stone.
Dad settled on a glossy four-by-six card with happy, genderless,
helmeted clients of Ro'ni's ATV and Mountain Jeeping. He held
the card out to me.

"Dad, you don't have to keep filling up our dance card. We're
fine. We will be fine. We can just hang out," I said. "We don't need
another activity. We still have to come to some parity here."

"The brochures are just a nervous gesture. You and I have some
straightening out to do. So I think you and Susan should go your
separate ways for the morning."

"You noticed?" And for a minute I flashed on a primitive hope, the
kind I'd come with, that because we loved and cared for each other
and noticed all the little things, we could fix whatever divided us.
I could even tell him about the school case and he wouldn't react
much. If only Dad hadn't kept talking.

"I always notice how you and Susan are doing. I have better language for conflict these days. Some souls come into this world after much recycling, some come in on a first round. The jobs, the challenges, the lessons are more primitive. Even before religion, I always thought that the two of you had different capacities for depth. All this if you care to hear about it."

"You're luring me into a trap." I was about to be right, though not the way I thought.

Dad pulled me into a hug, and I fit my head into his shoulder. I flashed on that closeness again. This time he didn't disappoint me. "Look," he said, "I'll be a father today and send you two on different activities. Evelyn has this friend who owns a cheese factory. We were going to take you on a tour. Let Evelyn take Susan alone. You and I will walk around. Let's head up this way." Out the front door, he led me up a path between buildings.

We forged uphill, following signs to a candle store, and Dad, now silent, concentrated hard on our nimbleness of foot. The lanes were slippery, and from the top, wherever that was—a street above, a half mile above—some invisible street cleaner hosed water down the cobblestones. The water spliced the previous day's dirt down the edge of the cobbled walk, and we goose-stepped around the dirty, steady stream. "Honey," Dad said, squinting into the sun. "I've got to tell you something."

"Tell me at home, Dad, when you come home—"

"The point is we have to deal with it here. I want to tell you I am moving forward, and I can't change the past but I can change the future."

"That's not a proper send-off. That's the same thing you've been saying all week."

"Not exactly. Hear me out: Evelyn and I are so excited. About something: You and Susan will be the first to know, before a public announcement. We've endowed a women's Jewish study program. For women with no traditional Jewish background who want to catch up and learn everything we've come to appreciate here. The program is called Bnos Rochel, Daughters of Rachel. For your mother, in her memory and in her honor. Just so you'll know, the acronym D-O-R, *dor*, is the Hebrew word for generation."

"Generation? Mom?" I sputtered. "Mom? You're naming a religious studies school in honor of Mom? But *we're* her generations, her honor. Susan and I are the daughters."

"There's the literal and the figurative. It's a symbolic gesture, sure, like the path that wasn't." Somehow we'd landed in front of one small store as it rolled up its shutters.

"But Mom wasn't traditional. Or orthodox. And we daughters aren't."

"It's not as if I don't know that. But you'll come to see. You'll come to appreciate it."

My first thought was reactive and spiteful. I would tell him about the case and see what he thought: Take that, Dad. But the invoking of Mom slowed me to a halt. I conjured her, oddly, in present-tense verbs: Is she going to be happy? Is she smiling there in her other reality—the one we can't see but are supposed to know is there?

I looked at Dad, who was smiling, yes, beatifically at me. Oh, this Daughters of Rachel thing was going to be like the bungee jumping of personal challenge. I felt as if my brain had been turned inside out. And was leaking. And then, I popped my hand over the lid. "You can't do that," I said. "Your DOR—if Susan and I aren't religious, then it makes us the un-DOR, the—disinherited." When the word came out of my mouth, my stomach sucked in by itself.

"It's not like that," Dad said. "You could become . . ."

Now, this was the trap I'd expected, but never in this context.

I don't know how or why or when we stepped inside the store, where, on the back wall, little landscape oils hung in purples and teals, exactly like the ones in lobby at the inn. On the next wall, above a paint-splashed enamel sink, rose a dozen black and white sketches: men who looked like the worshipers we'd seen on the mountain, outside the cave. The third wall was covered in photographs, photographs of grave sites and burial caves and, judging from the gradations of light and shadow, arranged in a sequence from right to left, night to day to night. I found a picture of our cave; the radar installation and the thistle were giveaways.

Dad pulled my arm. "You've got to understand. We've put a lot of thought into this endowment. You girls will come to appreciate it."

"You've got to be kidding. Take it back." Even I heard the whine, the little-girl whine in my voice.

"I can't. We already gave the money." I might have asked him about how much money. He might have told me or said it was none of my business, but I turned away to the picture of the caves and the radar installation. The little woman proprietor with a blue paisley scarf wrapped around her head like a bandage unhooked the grave-radar-thistle photo from the wall, and I found myself nodding yes, she could ship it to me. The woman took my address and ran my credit card through an old-fashioned handle press.

SO BY THE end of our trip, which I couldn't in all honesty still call our mission, the only part of my original agenda that I'd achieved was not telling Dad about the Brookline Hebrew Day School case. Because, not only did I not change Dad's mind, and not only was I estranged from my father, but now I was disinherited of my mother. Before I dragged my hand luggage to the lobby of the Eucalyptus Inn, I called home once more with a croaky voice and a thump in my chest. Richard answered with a long version of a domestic tale that Allan might have sweetened if he'd answered the phone first. In short, Ronnie was still sluggish, achy, probably the flu, but the guys were excited about a big snow forecast, as big as March the year before, when three storms in a row had choked up the city for a week. Did I remember the thrill? Plus, the school battle had moved from the local paper to the front page of the *Globe* with that same catchy headline: JEW VS. JEW. With my name in the first paragraph. Did I remember last year's blizzard?

Did I ever—the sounds of plows and sand trucks like clarion calls and how the boys and Allan went out to be the best shovelers in the neighborhood. Richard picked an old straw broom from the basement to whack the car tops, and Ronnie found a hoe and chopped ice off the neighbor's step, ice which had spilled over and frozen from a punctured downspout. They played, pushed, rolled, brushed the snow off the tops of the cars as high they could reach. When our neighbor came to the door to say thank you, she'd liked my joke about shovelers, the next generation. I hadn't been joking.

Dad and Evelyn waited with us in the Eucalyptus lobby. Our airport driver was late, which unfortunately stretched out the time we had for wrap-up and leave-taking. Our first round of good-bye hugs were open-to-interpretation brief. Either there couldn't be more emotion or enough was already said or not enough was said, which had my vote. The best I figured, Dad had also told Susan about the endowment. Yet she was still smiling. As we sat on a pair of leather benches against the window with the mountain view, I could see the sugarplums dancing over her head: cheese fondue or rotted wine. Avocado somethings. And there I was mining philosophy of death, which turned into random parenting thoughts, which another time might have calmed or at least neutralized me: how you learn to be a parent from a parent, how you love because you give to them. How you give children what you want them to give of themselves. Or be.

The driver finally came, and I hugged Dad and Evelyn, briefer hugs than before. Susan and I climbed into the car, and I braced myself for the ear-popping curl out of town on the narrow mountain roads. The new driver looked beaky enough, like Na'tan, dark skinned too. By then I recognized him as a racial type of Jew, his style a genre: He spoke a spare English, which I didn't trust on the surface, aware of other realities that created their own need for language. If I began with pleasantries, he might, like Na'tan, turn too articulate or metaphysical on us. Susan's head bobbed back on the car seat, her eyes closed. I was desperate to calm—not detonate— the experience we were traveling away from. I didn't engage Susan about the endowment or say a word to the driver until the thank-you at the airport. In return, he didn't help us out with our luggage. At least the luggage carts were plentiful, free for the taking and strewn across the curbside.

Outside the terminal, thunder and clouds rumbled above in a grand, showy way, and a downpour began that had personnel and passengers scrambling like mice. I couldn't shake the picture of Dad, even as I walked through security, the ticket counter, and passport control. I could track that rain like a radar screen across the flat coastal land and wide-open sky and craggy mountains back to Dad at a hotel lunch in Safed spreading *za'atar* spice across a fresh baguette. Being good the way he should, a good Jew, feeding his soul, feeding his body in that order. Building his eternal soul. Bringing the two worlds together.

We were settled in an open waiting area when Susan cast her eye on a bakery and coffee café a good hundred feet across. She went and returned with a pair of baguettes and two cappuccinos. We pulled our hand luggage to a little metal table and ate silently. The baguettes were dry and chewy, and with one expert *aha!* Susan flipped her baguette over and peeled off baking paper stuck on the bottom. She launched into an explanation about silicone-coated baking paper (good) and quilon-coated baking paper (bad, toxic). "No explanation possible for the lousy coffee," she said, throwing her full cup in the trash can, a gesture which rose to as far as her perceptions could take her. Even if she'd peaked on a little inspiration, it was already fading like a firework show. She was done with this trip, finished. Lucky her.

BOOK II

eleven

TEN MINUTES AFTER I TUCKED MY HAND LUGGAGE INTO the overhead and belted myself into the seat, the pilot's voice broke through the trickle of loudspeaker music. Gliding from one language to another, he apologized: We would have a half-hour departure delay. The sudden rain, the torrential rain, especially on the tail end of a dry spell, had stirred fuel oils out on the runway, causing slick conditions unsafe for takeoff. Through our milky, double-paned porthole, we watched airline personnel unroll hydrant hoses out on the runway and flush the oily top water into huge curb drains.

The delay took more like an hour and a half. Which was all the time I needed to work into as opposed to work out of what I was feeling. Because if there was such a thing as a twelve-step anger process, one that has you build up—not let go—when I thought about the whole trip and how it ended with Daughters of Rachel, I was heading to number twelve, and by the time the seat belt sign flashed off, the very words *Daughters of Rachel* had hot-wired my brain.

I had nowhere to walk it off but the forward cabin, half a dozen rows ahead, where the kitchen galley was floor-to-ceiling stainless drawers and hatch handles. A steward and stewardess—Israelis? Euro-somethings?—leaned on the counter. Whatever their origin, their moussed yellow curls and epauletted shoulders made them look as if they'd come in a matched set; and if they weren't specifically *on*, they didn't appear to be especially service oriented either, bent over a Beach Bum guidebook. Reading the Bs out loud, comparing average beach temperatures in Bar Harbor, Bermuda, Boston, Brisbane. I uh-hummed into their conversation, my mind jumping about in a cognitive hangover. A little Allan, a little me, my sarcastic best. "I'll pray for your good weather in Bermuda if you get me a cup of coffee."

They looked up at me with matched round, alerted eyes. "Pray for good weather?" the man said.

They'd heard my words; didn't they get the sarcasm? In their defense, back in Boston, before this trip, incredulous would have been my first response too: people who prayed for weather were—for lack of a better phrase—held in suspicion. Weird. Strange. Alien. Out of it. Pariahs. Backwards. Oppressed. Lepers. Uneducated. My list could go on and on. The woman blinked first and opened a drawer, as it turned out, full of ice and water bottles. The man snapped down a long handle and opened a cabinet full of coffee filter packs. He set one into the cabinet wall as he flipped down a countertop and snugged a small pot into the niche. The gush of coffee was near instant. Then, with a quick canned smile, the stewardess said something in lightning Eurobabble to the steward before she pushed off with a tray of cups and a tall bottle of springwater. He poured coffee from the pot into a foam cup, in an artful overhigh pour—the kind of thing you practice. Politely, he mumbled something about prayers, and then, not so politely, he added that we'd left Israel now.

"Don't I know it," I said.

He looked at me again. Had I not picked up on the snub? On how he looked at me the same way I'd looked at the Fabio prophet guy on the steps in the Old City of Jerusalem. Okay, so maybe the scoffing was my own form of Jerusalem syndrome, but the strength of it coursed through my body like a transfusion of blood, of my real life. I sat down with my coffee, mumbling to myself: *Thanks to Dad and his rain dance*, we were going to land in Zurich an hour later than schedule. And later, *thanks to Dad*, we landed in Zurich off schedule so that we were forced to run mazes and ride miles and miles of tunnel trains in order to board our Boston connector at Gate E3.

And later, on the overseas leg from Zurich to Boston: *Thanks to Dad*, the same storm that brought rain to Israel and crackled across the whole of the Middle East and North Africa, lay over Europe too, said the pilot. The crosswind was therefore stronger than usual. At least the word *crosswind* was a fine picture to doze to, a name for the feeling I had when I closed my eyes, bobbling away on a sailboat or a pontoon. Floating, unanchored. No shoreline, no trees in sight.

I slept fitfully and woke desperate for distraction, but the movies were adventure and boxing; the music channels Euro dance, hip-hop. Temptations and Otis Redding on the American midcentury station version called, I couldn't help but notice, Heart and Soul. Next to me, Susan slept, woke and read, then dozed. I filched her books out of the seat sleeve: The first one an introduction to olive trees. The second, a slick periodical on arches and teal, decor of the Middle East.

Susan opened an eye and brought her seat up. "I picked these up when I went out with Evelyn—this morning?" She looked at her watch. "Tomorrow morning? Yesterday? Whenever—in Safed." She sank back in her seat.

The dynamic stormed in, about to be as immature as it was

sisterly, but after everything we'd been through, its power didn't
surprise me: I couldn't believe after all we'd seen and done in a week,
Susan ended up at her starting point. Externalities. Decoration. Renovation. I tried to hold my tongue. I did. For at least thirty seconds,
while, at my right elbow, a stewardess appeared and bent to the man
across the aisle, a paterfamilias if there ever was one, there with his
woman of valor and, besides a toddler on his lap, three children in a
row who looked like the baby ducklings in my college psych text-
book under the heading "Imprinting," or heavy black lines in a family tree. The stewardess balanced a tray piled with squares of tinfoil.
"Kosher?" she asked the man.

"Here—and here," the man answered, pointing to himself and
his wife. "And, here, and here, and here."

I turned back to Susan and pointed to her books. "Arches—and
teal. They're the sum total of your trip to Israel?"

"What, look at you. Is there a perfect formula? Dad took too
much from Israel, I take too little. Are you the one who's just
right?"

"Yeah, me, Goldilocks. Far from it . . ."

"I'm looking at the olive tree book for the color," Susan said.
"The teal that the other book is talking about comes from the olive
trees. Teal. Silver. Turquoise. Remember those old olive trees, those
gnarled old trees we saw when we were out driving with our good
friend Na'tan? Did you notice the color of the leaves?" She spread
the book open on her tray. "And the paintings at the Eucalyptus
Inn were an exaggeration in intensity, but the color was accurate.
See?"

I saw what she meant, I saw it was pretty, and my frustration
tangled my brain. Meanwhile, a steward hovered with our food and
Susan held the book in the air as he slid a steaming block of not-
kosher chicken paella onto her tray. Not before Susan pulled out a

centerfold picture of a teal olive tree panorama on a hill. And suddenly I thought about the society women on the *Titanic* who were trying to figure out which pair of shoes to put on when they were heading to the deck for the lifeboats, or maybe the musicians arguing about which to play, a waltz or a symphony overture. You always think these people are heroic, but on second look maybe they're obtuse or shallow. "I can't believe you got these books," I said.

"What is wrong with you?" Susan asked.

I didn't know. I did know. I didn't know. The steward laid down my not-kosher paella, and I tried to compensate for my crabbiness with little traveling companion gestures to Susan, like steadying her tray as she slipped the book into the seat sleeve. But, because I'd nagged at her, Susan shut down, and we ate in silence.

Afterward, I dozed with my neck at twenty degrees to my shoulder, my seat arm the parameter of my world, as if Susan were a stranger and we held to a no-touch zone. In between my dozes, I watched with envy as my kosher neighbors pulled out a set of red pleather skeins from their seat sleeves. With a huff and a puff they inflated their neck pillows into fat half doughnuts. Not without adjustment. The man popped the plug and hissed out some air, then closed his eyes. Many restless hours later, the lights went on and outside it was daylight. We were thirty miles out of Boston, but our landing ended up taking closer to two hours.

Maybe Dad prayed too hard, because the storm pursued us and we couldn't touch down at Logan from the south or east. We circled up to New Hampshire, where the storm hadn't yet hit, and landed from the northwest, dropping onto the runway inside a snow squall, frosty and white as if we were real people inside a snow globe of Boston. Queasy, a little off balance, we collected our luggage, got through customs, not as quickly as I make it sound. Oh, I'd worked myself up to make it back home and back to Allan.

Sweet, sweet arrival, the relief of the streamlined goal, getting from one place to another, the way an adrenaline rush blanks out what you've left behind in favor of the getting there. When I spotted Allan on the other side of customs, I felt as if I were landing all over again.

YESTERDAY, DAD AND Evelyn and I were shopping at Target in the Watertown Mall, which was a twenty-minute drive from my house but which felt like a big excursion to me. They were stockpiling, getting ready for their move—not just a *trip* anymore—back to Jerusalem. They'd filled a shopping cart with snap-lid plastic storage containers in five sizes, about half a suitcase worth, and they were busy explaining that if they bought six months' worth for half the price they would have to pay in Jerusalem, it would be the same as a quarter of a ticket back to the States. We rolled on to small appliances, the kind that can work with a 110/230 converter. Evelyn wanted to buy a Crock-Pot for her cholent. Setting that gas flame up or down to the right twenty-four-hour simmer was excruciating—as I'd seen that Friday afternoon in their apartment—and every Friday afternoon the guesswork started all over again. But as she stood in the double row of Crock-Pot choices, the decision began to get away with her.

"Digital timers. Four-level heat. Holding: Warm. Hot. Very hot. I just want a simple Crock-Pot, off-low-high," Evelyn said. "Simple, simple. And none of this timer stuff. Coming from Israel, you'd think this was appliance heaven, but it feels like Crock-Pot hell." She caught the attention of two stock boys, according to their red shirts, Sean and Sean.

I didn't need the little outburst to point arrows to me; there is no natural world, Boston or elsewhere, where I wouldn't feel self-conscious standing there in the small appliance aisle, what with Dad wearing a yarmulke and Evelyn wearing one of her strange little snood caps. Jew. One Jewess. Or, by association, two. Do people anyhow say the word *Jewess* except in old movies? Dad's born-again does not let us blend and turns on its head a couple hundred years of Jewish-American experience. Dad says that *is* the point, an observation that flips the challenge back to me. Anyhow, after expressing herself so eloquently, Evelyn tromped off to the front of the store to get cell phone reception and call one of her religious friends for Crock-Pot advice, and, speaking of hell, Dad just had to get in his licks, a definition that he'd heard in a lecture back in Jerusalem: the feeling that, when you're traveling, traveling, about to get to your destination, about to get there, just a moment from arrival, a half a moment, a split second, almost there—and then, instead of arriving, instead of landing, you get slung back out on your journey.

Oh, I've gotten better at hearing what Dad has to say, hoping it doesn't gouge too deeply, and grabbing the wisdom for my own purposes. For example, if *not* getting there is hell, then all that feeling when I landed in Boston and saw Allan at the airport was something like heaven.

For Allan too, apparently. On the other side of customs, when I pushed out my luggage cart, he whooped, grabbed me by the shoulders, hugged me tightly, each one of those gestures out of character. "Steve and I came in his truck" (*truck* was what he called Steve's Jeep Commander, a car that looked more fit for a presidential entourage than the likes of us). "I'm so glad—I'm so glad—" He kept interrupting himself and not finishing the sentence. All that chirp and chatter got me nervous.

I understood when I saw the *Globe* the next morning and read all about our flight: Swiss Flight LX 52 circling over New Hampshire. When, hours earlier, an American Airlines jet had had a very near slide off the landing runway because of inadequate deicing. As if I needed reinforcement of the idea, but Dad clearly hadn't considered the consequences of his special effects.

twelve

ACK HOME IN BROOKLINE, THE MORNING AFTER I LANDED,
I made Richard and Allan a glorious breakfast. It turned
out that Ronnie wasn't simply tired. Richard and Allan
hadn't wanted to worry me, but Ronnie was in bed with the flu the
whole week I was gone and that was why they never made it to Gillette Stadium. That morning his fever was still inching up, not
down, and after breakfast I ran out and got him a couple of sickbed
DVDs, guy stuff he'd warbled in a list, Season 6 of *24* and maybe
some *Prison Break* too, which when he was little had him running
around the house imitating the danger talk: "Go-go-go!" And "Patch
me through to the president." After which I ran downstairs to my
office, sealing my commitment to reason, purpose, and meaning
the way I knew it—even if it meant a cup of coffee per hour. Outside, the snowstorm hovered over Boston spinelessly, laid a few final
inches of fresh powder. Snow here, Dad's rain *there*: In spite of my
resolve, the connection snagged me: Dad back in Jerusalem, *Om-
ming* his rain evocations, praying at the Wall for our spiritual elucidation. Dad, his soul and Truth, the endowment. Pushing those
thoughts aside was my unsung heroic act of the morning.

I was grateful to behold my desk piled higher than I'd left it.

Mail. Publications. Several tubes of architects' plans, the *Globe*, the *Tab* (the local rag), good for a down-dirty read on Brookline news like the Hebrew Day School case. I stacked them on the floor, flipped on my computer calendar, listened to my messages, scratched out a to-do list, which, short and sweet, rang like music to my ears. I worked my way down the list until I got to Brookline Hebrew Day business and returned a call to the Planning Board. Joan, the town clerk, had been waiting to hear back from me: Turned out I was just in time to say yes to a neighborhood forum with the association and Brookline Hebrew Day School. I hung up politely, saving my scowl for the moment the receiver hit the cradle because the request undermined the legal position. Of all fragile mornings I didn't have to be reminded about Jew vs. Jew, that the case was less about the law and more social, more attitudinal, that, like big boys and girls, we should figure out how to share the sandbox.

Then I had a 10:00 A.M. appointment. Made confidently for the morning after I got back, assuming I would be clearheaded and ready for my usual charge. But instead it felt especially provocative because the client was none other than the lead name on town stationery, the town administrator, Michael Marder. At least he was coming for business of his own. A land-use probate workout, inheritance business, which, as he pointed out at our intake meeting, was like being born, that is, no fault of his own. Got that one right. At least his parents didn't abandon him or give his inheritance away to someone else. Or ask him to be someone else so he could get it back. Or dangle eternity and redemption in front of him like a carrot on a stick. They did the normal thing and passed everything straightforwardly. Just as I refilled my coffee cup, Michael Marder rang, not my basement office door but my front door, where he stood in a shearling coat more stylish than the bright ski parkas of my usual earthy plaintiffs.

"How was your trip?" he asked, breathing frost, stomping his feet. If this were a murder mystery, there would be no mystery: He headed down the basement steps blazing a trail of gray ice.

"The trip was informative—" I bit my tongue on a defensive snap. I owed no explanations. All he'd known was that I had gone to Israel, that my father was vaguely vacationing there. But his face had lit up to the come-on sound of the word *informative,* and now I was stuck for some explanation. "My father—he—well, he's got some lifestyle changes which have gotten the better of him."

"Lifestyle changes?" Michael Marder grabbed the comment with a silky dip in his voice. "What's *that* all about?"

What did he think I meant, a polygamy cult? Or a back-to-nature retirement beach community with, ahem, *implications?* My eyes bounced from Michael Marder folding his shearling onto the back of his chair to my vertical files to the yet-to-be-read *Mass Lawyers Weekly*s stacked directly behind his head. Back to his frozen and silly R-rated expression, which I was honor bound to emend.

"Didn't I tell you why I flew out on such sudden notice? My father and his wife, Evelyn, have become orthodox. Religious." There: Outed. Dad. Me. Now. And then the rest of the town would know. I forced a hearty drumroll on the word *religious.*

I HAD MY due diligence. What I told myself was one thing. What I was going to tell Allan might be another, because, endowment aside, how could I summarize Dad, his religious experience (and mine), for public consumption, no less? Oh, it wasn't going to be the last time my interior rebound screamed *Liar.* After all, those rules and regulations and prayers, those robotics (from the outside looking in) hadn't changed Dad a bit. Actually, Dad was exactly the same. No, make that *more* of the same, as if he'd grown into his shoes, his habits, his orderliness. I mean, the food, the art, the trip north. Even his pleasure seeking had undertow, meaning.

"YOUR FATHER? DAN? Build-a-Scaffold Dan?" Michael Marder said.

"Yes."

"Your father who does the breast cancer 12K walkathon and finishes top one hundred? Your father who has the biggest scaffold business in New England?"

"That's the same one."

Michael Marder didn't answer. He fussed his shearling to make a point of what he wasn't going to say, then screwed his face into a dried fruit. Religion was certainly a mood detonator, and, on that note, that time, we got down to business.

Forty years earlier, his parents, Frank and Helen Marder, bought a three-story brick-façade office building near Brookline's little downtown crossing, Coolidge Corner, and now, after their passing, Michael Marder and his brother were developing the property into office condos. But the development had ground to a halt under order from the Environmental Protection Agency. Before Frank and Helen's day, the property had been a gas station and the underground tanks were emptied, but an inspection by the EPA had strangled the condo development with an upscale demand that he go back into what they were calling a petroleum brownfield, that he must pull out the empty underground tanks and start building all over again. His brother wanted to sell his share, but not to Michael. He didn't want his parents' legacy to have to do anything with a brownfield. On the other hand, Michael Marder had inherited a problem and wasn't disinherited by it.

I caught myself reacting to that thought as he refolded that shearling. He and it wouldn't get comfortable till it was on and they were out the door.

"Do you understand that we have to get a trust and estates litigator?" I said. "There's someone good in my husband's firm. You might have seen his name in the paper. Did you hear about the Big Day whistle-blower who died and his estate was in probate because the reward money came into his estate after he died? That's the guy—"

"Okay. So we have a game plan. Thank heaven," Michael Marder said.

"Thank heaven," I repeated. The first crack of relief. A little religious vernacular here, a little religious vernacular there. I could be normal again. "Got religion?" I asked. Joked, like in the "Got milk?" ads.

Which he didn't get. "Not really," he said, glancing at his watch and stiffening his back. What I got was his message. Not funny. Plus, if I was the one who'd sparked a joke, it was on my time, not his.

"We'll get to the bottom of this," I said. "I'll call ahead and give you some idea of when he's available."

At that, Michael Marder stood up, readying his shearling for service, and finally noticed his puddling boots and the trail of ice turning into gray puddles the size of half dollars. "Sorry," he said, pointing to the floor.

I waved the "sorry" away, making the usual polite noise about puddles which came and went all the time. In other words, exculpating responsibility, vindicating him by waving away cause and effect, mostly cause. And then it hit me like a sudden slap: This was a really stupid line of reasoning. Ex nihilo and all that: Because if puddles came like that, the world did. I did. Dad did. Mom did. And the more ex nihilo my interior monologue got, the sillier it sounded, bound and gagged as I was by Dad's universe of truth and meaning.

And just for spite, Michael Marder didn't look as ready to leave as he'd looked a minute earlier. I tried to end the meeting by saying I was tired in all large and small ways, because, besides the longer travel time, jet lag across the north-south meridians from east to west was double the jet lag of the west-east direction. To my dismay, Michael Marder sat back down, petting his shearling coat across his lap, ready to pontificate or opine. I've come to see how religion does that to people, as if everyone owns a part of the discussion, entitled just by being in the human race, and every discussion, whether informed or uninformed, has the same value because there's a delusion that it's all opinion anyhow, or feeling and not fact or intellect or logic.

"Religion? You know"—he sighed—"our parents died within six months of each other. My brother and I aren't religious, but we had the same fight with our father, then with each other about our mother. I didn't see why we couldn't cremate. Even religious people—don't they say: dust to dust, ashes to ashes?"

"Your parents left no particular instructions?"

"I'm not sure they thought about . . . options. They were a little traditional."

A week earlier it wouldn't have occurred to me to ask what religion that was. I held my tongue. What difference did it make? But I or my confession about Dad had stimulated something. "Religion is a hot button," he said. "Necessary to discuss, debate. Though it's always easier to watch someone else haggle over it than to do it yourself. Your case with the school. Now that's a battle a long time coming."

That was uncalled for. Unfair, even. He of all people knew the intelligence behind the neighborhood complaint. He knew we were within rightful bounds to grandstand any and every assault on community development.

"Putting religion as the center of Jewish identity. Any identity. These days we see how dangerous it is," he said.

"You make it sound like the Crusades," I said. "The school case is all about land usage, and I'm defending constitutional rights for appropriate land usage with appropriate borders." What I'd been telling myself. I wished he would shut up and leave.

"It's in the newspapers," he said. "I guess when you were away. Your husband probably spared you, but there was an interview. Not even with Rae but with other people on the association who don't want fundamentalism in our face." I thought I saw him wink: This conversation with Michael Marder, the town administrator, was off record, of course.

"It's not fundamentalism. The case isn't about fundamentalism. It's about law and land usage."

"You can tell yourself that, but you know and I know. And now . . ." That racy, juicy look returned to his face. Could he have been referring to Dad? I wouldn't know because suddenly he was too "polite" to finish the sentence the way he first intended. "You know you have to prepare yourself because you'll be the enemy for a certain group of people. The *group*—"

"You mean the religious neighbors? I'm not against religion. If it makes them feel good, they should just be well," I said. Now all of a sudden I was the warbly defender, sounding like Susan back in the hotel room: "I'm OK, you're OK," the polite equivocations.

"They have their Truth. You represent another truth," he said.

My left sinus throbbed like a traffic blinker; the last thing I wanted to talk about was truth or Truth or the desire for truth and what happens when people think they've found Truth, or people who run away from Truth, and if I did, I'd want to have the conversation with Allan, especially about the cave we visited near Safed. But, just as quickly—apparently a better cue reader than I'd given him

credit for—Michael Marder acquitted himself of the religion discussion with two wagging hands in the air. Acquitted himself of
ideas, obligations, and consequences. His hands were fine and hair-
less, his fingers manicured, his nails glossy and clear; he answered
to no higher authority than his own reaction.

And I'd never show it. I've gotten far professionally with my glib
tongue and my emotions checked at the door. But his wagging fingers sank me with dislike. For that matter, his EPA problem didn't
compel me either, for all the wrong and personal reasons, mostly for
the entitlement, for him taking everything for granted. By what
merit did some people see their parents to adulthood, old age, and
then inherit . . . normal properties with normal problems? By what
curse did children like Susan and I get clobbered with little daily
things scarred with loss or overendowed with depth of meaning?
Or get disinherited.

Then, in case I hadn't heard, he was ready to end the conversation at the door a second time. Maybe it was the public figure in
him that drove him to summarize with, in his eyes, a bow and a
ribbon. "Face it. We're here. Now. And then we're not. That's why I
live . . . well. You know what I mean?" I knew he meant to make
nice, but to me he sounded like a nihilist, or the close-up actor in a
beer commercial. We dropped the conversation as nimbly as it had
started.

I shut the door behind Michael Marder, against a low, sharp
wind, which had iced the foyer threshold with snow, a fitting final
annoyance with his material struggles and my decision not to let
Dad affect me. I could have used another day to debrief and put
myself back together again, and it was inappropriate to focus on a
client when I was trying to coordinate my reentry and bleach the
exterior look of internal turmoil.

I climbed the steps in rhythm, compartmentalizing, forcing my thoughts to turn to Ronnie. Maybe I was supposed to get baseball caps made? I thought. Sweatshirts? I'VE BEEN TO ISRAEL TO VISIT MY RELIGIOUS FAMILY AND . . . And what?

I tapped on Ronnie's bedroom door and walked into his silent room. The DVDs were stacked the way I'd left them. His bulletin board, which he'd begun this past school year, was slathered with mementos, mostly kid puns and pictures of school field trips. Ronnie with his friends: free on the Freedom Trail, bunking on Bunker Hill. The last picture was taken at the Paul Revere House, and Ronnie and friends had rounded their eyes, bobbling them out of their sockets. But they'd confused instructions. "Not till you see the whites of their eyes" belonged to William Prescott back at Bunker Hill. What they meant was "One if by land and two if by sea." Some illusions of childhood were good enough unless you carried them to adulthood and had to hack them to bits.

"My head hurts so much I can't concentrate," he said. He was sitting up in bed looking like Casper the Ghost, a white soccer ball of a head, round, misunderstood eyes, feet tapered into the bottom of his blanket. This was the same boy who whumped in my shower and sang songs about letting the dogs out or showing off his grillz. He doesn't have a dog or grillz, but try telling him that. At least when he's sick he doesn't resist my affection. "Are you there?" I asked, cupping my hand on his chin.

"Barely," he croaked. "Aunt Susan called. She wants you to see something she did or she wants to do—something at Beacon Seafood. And my throat hurts."

I tried to jolly him out of self-pity with a frog imitation.

He shook his head stop, and I sat on the edge of his bed and slid my hand over his forehead. "You are very cool." I meant to make him laugh with the corny double entendre, but I found myself turning my head away so he wouldn't see me wipe my eyes on my sleeve. Something primitive was rattling my chest. I stroked Ronnie's cheek; as I expected, he pushed me off again, and it was easy enough to tell myself how I was mushy because of him.

thirteen

DAD HAS COME UPSTAIRS FOR A COFFEE BREAK. HE'S BEEN installing a shelf system in my basement to hold all the boxes he's dragged out of his place. The boxes include what he calls Mom's Passover dishes; maybe he would use them, but in any case they're too bulky to schlep back to Jerusalem in their suitcases. Mom's Passover dishes in my house: He's trying to get us to say that we'll use them, that when he goes we will have a sort of Passover without him. I know why he's so bent on being religious future oriented, if that's a concept. He wants me to know that he, the religion, and I will be around—for all seasons.

Instead of answering back, I can't help but think how it is these days that one look at him looking like a Jew puts my clacking neurons on guard against exaggeration and false avowals. Or self-expiation. Or excuses.

After Dad's unloaded the Passover dishes and steadied the shelves, we take an outing, in our Brookline radius but not my normal route. We eat pizza at the kosher pizza shop on Harvard Street and then we head into the Jewish bookstore back on Beacon Street. I get the feeling he's staging me, cramming in all his agendas before he leaves. The lightest, the neutral, the one we should agree on is Susan, who's copied both of us on the flurry of e-mails with her decorator, Carnie Goldstein, her partner in the new Middle East–seafood theme. We both had a laugh, for different reasons. When Susan came back from Israel, she'd halted the renovations in progress and researched a Middle East look. In her e-mail today, she's included the sketches for the restaurant bar: a double-dome ceiling with six arches, recessed lighting, rough stone walls, teal leather stools. I have to think before I align myself with Dad's outburst. I don't want to agree, but neither am I in any position to argue that just because she's obsessed with the physical in this world she is seriously flawed.

We enter the bookstore through a hanging display of khaki and denim caps with Patriots and Red Sox insignias in Hebrew writing.

"I can get these in Jerusalem. In the tourist shops in town. They're cheaper there too," Dad says. "Next time I'll bring some back with me."

"When you come back to stay?"

"Whenever that is . . . ," Dad says. He trails off because he wants to finish the conversation we started in the pizza shop. "If only Susan would turn some of that energy for renovation back onto herself." Dad sighs. "You—at least—got messed up and confused."

"It's not like I've become . . . anything."

"Circumstances have conspired—you're poised to get smarter. Poised to act. You just don't know it yet." Dad heads down a narrow aisle and makes a right toward the back wall, floor-to-ceiling English Judaica.

"I haven't had a choice. But I hate when you say things like that; they're so judgmental." That one's been on the tip of my tongue.

"Judgmental? That's an old saw. Being called judgmental is the occupational hazard of the religious. Susan's inability to grow, to work on herself rather than things doesn't have to have anything to do with religion, even though it does. All I'm lamenting is that if

Susan took half that outward drive, a tenth of the outward drive, and turned it inward—"

"What if shallow people become religious? Or are religious? Or if a religious couple has a shallow kid? What happens then?"

"There's nothing the system can't bear. Like people gravitate to light, so do animals . . . even plants—"

"One way, your way. All the way." I'm hoping I sound convincing.

He looks at me over the title of a book he's grabbed and holds to his chest. The cover's yellow and black stripes remind me of police tape at a crime scene. "Here: *Passover for Dummies.*"

"I don't need your fine sense of humor. It's just that when you look down on Susan, you make me feel like you're looking down on me."

"How can I convince you that you're the one supplying most of that feeling? It's not coming from me. Have you noticed that I never say anything about Susan's absolutely nonkosher seafood restaurant? Not just any restaurant, the very antithesis of kosher. I'm not sure she feels like I'm looking down at her."

"I don't think she cares."

"Maybe that's the point. But you wouldn't feel like I was looking down on you unless you recognized there are certain issues of right and wrong, better, best, truth—"

"Listen to yourself. This is exactly why religious people make nonreligious people feel uncomfortable. It's like I prick your skin and get the lecture I suspected was waiting for me all along."

"Why can't it be the fact that I'm your father? And I want what's best for you. Since when was I afraid to lecture you?"

In the background, over invisible speakers, I hear choral music, men, and I think I hear the word *Jerusalem*. "So don't take it back then. It's just that . . . you know how when you're little you think of heaven or some Deity as a big wagging finger in the sky? That's what religious people make you feel like. Make *me* feel like. What *you* make me feel like." Primitive, basic, this is our iron curtain.

He doesn't answer, he's thinking. Which gives me an opening to go back to automatic pilot. I'm not just defending Susan, I'm defending choices, a way of life. "Dad, you're not eating in Beacon Seafood these days anyhow. What's it to you?"

"Okay," he says after a minute. "Let's call a truce between us. Even about what you know and I know is wrong with Susan's constant renovation. But I have to say she's been renovating that restaurant or her house since she married Steve. I mean, can't she ever stop working on things and start working on herself?"

"Susan's perfectly normal—in this culture—in case you've forgotten. In her eyes, she's already formed and complete. It's just that the world around her isn't."

And then, because even if Dad doesn't realize he's judgmental, I'm feeling it, and my little punishing, get-even impulses rise up: I want to remind him how much decorative art he'd gotten in the short months between the time he arrived in Jerusalem and the time we'd gotten there, but it sounds tit for tat, and I know they're not the same thing.

And then, apparently because I've shut down one artery, he feels obligated to open another and enact the next subject: religion and suffering. We're standing inside a square of floor-to-ceiling book displays. On my right is the shelf called "Prayer and Meaning," to my left a shelf called "Women and Jewish Femininity." In front of us, "Religion and Suffering." He pulls out a volume he recognizes, called *Growing Through Suffering*.

I get it now. "Is this why we've come into this store?" It's getting harder and harder to ho-hum him.

It's Mom's kind of suffering, not mine—he's quick to say. A distinction I'm not in the mood for. I don't want to hear about how he's reframing her illness and her death into spiritual growth, spiritual tests. For Mom, him, us. How hard he's worked on reframing her passing into a system of meaning.

"You can't imagine how grateful I am, what a stroke of divine intervention it was that I let Mom's family intercede for a proper Jewish burial."

"The same divine intervention that didn't let her lead a proper life, a proper—Jewish—life?"

That quiets him down.

BACK IN MY office, Dad keeps his four new books in their bag, and he's lightened up, changing the subject to social historical Jewish stuff, including what he really knows firsthand, how a returnee (a *ba'al teshuvah*), which he is, is not the same as a Jewish evangelical. There's no such thing as Jewish evangelicals. Once and for all there is no such thing as a Jewish born-again. "There are all kinds of religious types." Chassidish, for example, which he is not. Or Yeshivish, where rational argument is the trump card.

"I have a new friend," he says. "Closer to your age. A rabbi who works in my yeshiva, and his becoming religious became famous when his sister wrote it up for her Harvard alumni magazine. He'd written her a long letter. He told her he'd had his 'nihilism annihilated'—that's what he said."

"Not so funny," I say. But it is funny; smart too. I would think about it, except from the beginning of the conversation back in the pizza shop I'd intended to boycott all his engendering talk by accusing Dad of fronting, of aligning himself with some pious image he's projecting outward. But it doesn't take much to be reminded of how naturally good Dad is. How if his religion is the enactment of that drive to good, he was a religious man waiting to happen: All I need to do is take a look at the dense double row of rhododendrons on the other side of the bay window behind my desk. Today, even all these weeks after the groundhog saw his shadow and winter's eased off, their frozen, brittle branches stretch and clench like spastic human arms. As a matter of fact, they look like the black and white stills of World War I soldiers mowed down and frozen in the trenches of the Pyrenees. Usually, the leaves are unfurled and fecund, a testimony to the ability of people to get along.

The month after we'd built my home office, the next-door neighbors brought in road pavers and expanded their blacktop driveway to three feet from my new window and, as it turned out, slightly over our property line. I was furious, out of my mind. But, precisely because I spend my day so litigiously, Dad insisted that the most important thing was to get along with neighbors and let sleeping dogs lie.

Dad follows my line of vision to the rhodies. "I remember how angry you were," he says. "And then how you didn't say a word."

"Proud of me, huh? How I turned the other cheek?"

"Honey, that's an aphorism from another religion. We treat others the way we want to be treated. Empathy. Not denial. That's our core activity."

"Let me guess—and it's all for the best, at the same time?"

"Now *you're* the one being judgmental and unfair," he says. "I don't sit here telling you to work on yourself, to change the universe by working on yourself, to take on one mitzvah. Lighting Shabbos candles, for example. How hard can that be? One little act that can illuminate your home, affect your family."

I wanted judgmental, he is going to give it to me. Is that it? This time I change the subject. Evelyn has taken my car. "When will Evelyn be back?"

"Well, she's gone shopping . . . *again*," Dad says. He labors the word *again* to bring up my smile. It's not misogyny but a kind of insider affection when Dad categorizes women in activities like shopping. And lest I think Evelyn has fallen off the all-spiritual-all-the-time wagon, Dad reminds me she's self-declared the shopping to be recreational, the way you might eat for a couple of days in rebalance after you've been starved for one. Israel has terrible shopping, unless you're fluent in Hebrew and can manage the native souk markets. She's discounting, enjoying the hunt and kill, good stuff cheap, not cheap stuff cheap. She's going to Marshalls, T. J. Maxx, Filene's Basement. You can't get discount in Israel, Dad reminds me, though someone had the bright idea to open up an Ace hardware chain.

"Just up Evelyn's alley," I say.

Dad's quiet. I am too. I can't imagine what will come next; truncated banter is dangerous, and I'm waiting for a piece of conversation to pop. It's like watching the blob on a Lava lamp congeal, form, and break away. Which it does. With a direct hit.

"You know. Allan is still just giving me the time of day," Dad says. "Cordial. A handshake. Decent enough so that I wouldn't have a real complaint, but I'm guessing he's still angry at me about the endowment."

"Not because of what, if anything, it takes from us financially." What I'm obligated to say, very quickly, like all gracious adult kids. Though it's not the entire truth. "But I'll be honest, he worries about me, the hard time I've had with it."

"Or the hard time *he's* had with it. Just as long as it's something like that. In time . . . It's one of those things that time will have you forget even your first reaction. Or your resistance to change."

His last words prick me, because he always thinks he knows me best. I hope he's right, because as far as Allan's natural skepticism hardening up like a defensive shield, I was actively and passively to blame.

THE FIRST WEEK after I got back from Israel, Allan showered and dressed down the hall in the guest room, gave me seven mornings of grace on behalf of my physical reentry, my sleepy late mornings, early bedtimes, and uneven energy. All of which helped me lay a numbing net over the business with Dad, endowment and all.

Though, as much as I wanted avoidance, when Allan signed off his morning courtesy and moved back to the master bath, I was the one who wanted to talk. That morning I had competition: On the other side of the door I heard the very loud sports radio. Red Sox. Red Sox. Red Sox. Even those winter months before spring training. The sportscaster barked and moaned over the contract negotiations with Theo Epstein; at least it was the single sports complaint I could understand or relate to, since the motivation to keep a fine-looking front man onboard was so public and obvious.

Then the sportscaster spoke about being in love. They called this man's radio? About the pull you feel toward something when it's right and true and meant for you. And the fear of change. They couldn't let their manager go. The main sportscaster burst into laughter. His buddy said he was kidding, and then they were ranting again about money buying loyalty, symbolizing loyalty; then they sidetracked to the prodigal Beacon Hill mansion once owned by the manager of a Florida ball team. The same couple—he Boston Brahmin and she, the former nanny, had bid for the Red Sox and switched allegiances just like that when they moved south. Like a lie, they said. As if their whole life before had been a lie. I jumped into the bathroom and ran the hot water in the sink to wash my face. In this old house, that was enough to affect Allan's shower.

"Hey," he said, over the shower wall. "That's hot. Very hot." A minute later he stepped out onto the rug, toweling himself in the steam, turning down the radio.

"I have to talk to you about something," I said. Try as I might to build some kind of callus around it, it kept coming down to the DOR endowment. As a single symbol, it had taken over my brain, lurked around every emotional corner. What it took from me. What it asked of me. My own desire for truth and then fear. Fear of change, and the need for self-preservation. Being unseated as a daughter also meant I could be unseated as a mother. Being unseated as my mother's daughter meant I would have to change.

Talking about it altogether was one thing, but I did have a choice about the way I presented it to Allan: as a question-raising act or as an assault. Through a conscious choice to affirm Dad's ideas as crazy or mistaken by ganging up on the bad part of the idea. I'm not making excuses now. It's just the facts. I didn't have to begin the conversation by talking about the uncomfortable outcome of the trip. If I wanted to talk about it, I could have begun with the connection, the sense, the sensible.

"Susan and I were disinherited."

"What?" Allan snapped off the radio, gulping words above the steam.

"Not entirely. Not of Dad. Of our mother." My tongue stumbled it out, and once it came, it came in a torrent of bad intentions.

"What was your father thinking?" Allan said. He grabbed his robe and threw his towel onto the hook.

At that first shot of sympathy, I began to weep. I explained everything I knew, which wasn't much.

"What does he think, you're going to get born-again too and be a proper heir? Your father was always too easy—always susceptible to extremes."

Though I'd played for the sympathy, even then I didn't like the way it came back to me. What did Allan mean by that? Dad was a builder, a doer. To this day, when I close my eyes, I see Dad clambering up side ladders, sure-footed as a cleft-hoofed animal.

"Let me rewind just a little." I tried to tell him about the cave, the smell, how I thought of Allan, how this transcendence of the spirit is a serious matter. How maybe, just maybe, Mom could be out there somewhere. But I'd picked a scab on Allan and made it bleed.

"It might be transcendence of spirit for some people," he said, "and they lose the transcendence of *brain*." He stomped into the bedroom with a towel around his waist. On the way past the closet, he grabbed two orange striped neckties. He turned on the overhead light, bent into the bureau mirror as he laid them against folded shirts on the bureau, and picked the tie with an orangier orange and the wider swathes. "Don't get distracted, and don't forgive your father by getting all eternal soul on me." He spoke to me from his reflection.

I'M SITTING AT my desk trying to work, which has devolved into pretending that I'm trying to work, and Dad has come down to tell me he's on his way out to the travel agent to pick up their tickets. Before he goes he shows me his new watch, which Evelyn found at the fine jewelry counter at Filene's Basement in Newton. Two watch faces, so he can live in two time zones, Israel and here. He's carrying a large book with a picture of a matzo on the cover, a picture that's so real looking I'm almost wiping the crumbs. "What is that?"

"After I pick up our tickets, it's time to meet my learning partner. Passover's coming, and we're learning the Passover Haggadah. You know, the Passover book," he says.

"Just because I don't know much doesn't mean I know nothing," I say.

"I didn't mean to patronize. I'd meant to explain why I was going out the door." He looks at his watches. "If I were in Jerusalem, I would be going out the door now too."

"You're serious about this studying stuff," I say. I'd seen the insides of his oversize red Talmud books, Aramaic jigsawed across one page, English on the other.

"You want to know why I'm *learning* with my partner? Not *studying* with my partner?"

He doesn't give me a chance to say no.

"*Learning* the holy books is the common usage. It's more passive, how we receive what's already there. Because there's so much to absorb, to take in." He smiles up at me; then I'm not sure what he sees on my face because he switches gears quickly. "On the other hand—" he shrugs, too casually—"the program's called Study with a Buddy."

"Maybe it should be called Learning with a Yearning."

His face relaxes. He thinks, when I make a joke, I "get" it.

He means closeness, and I feel distance in the pit of my stomach. But when he leaves my office, I feel oddly vacated. I'll be happy for all reasons when he goes back, but in spite of my resistance every time he opens his mouth, I miss him already. Outside, the rhododendrons shimmy and shake by themselves, roots to leafy tips. Not according to the neighbors' "goodwill" plan, the rhodies trap the basketballs from the two-basket court that was the other half of their project. I should be happy for the neighbors, really, that their teenage son is the most popular boy this side of the Charles River and how the bass which comes up on their exterior Bose speakers obscures the yelling and the salt-of-the-earth *f*-words on the basketball court; but today, the bass combined with the noise inside my head makes me think I'm listening to a motor operate with my head underwater, the way a drowning person might hear the boat that's come to save her but with all the floundering and fluttering can't see where it is.

fourteen

Two weeks after we got back from Jerusalem, the neighborhood association and Brookline Hebrew Day School squared off at the town-mandated neighborhood meeting. In the good, scripted version, all the big children would say why they had a hard time sharing the playground and the town would shake a stern stick. It was a clear winter night, streets and sidewalks clean of snow, and my mind should have been free of Dad and his outpourings, but my mind was clearly elsewhere, and my usual Brookline politically correct perceptions were off-kilter. When I walked into the Runkle School cafeteria, when I looked at the two ponytailed, earringed, wide-bottomed men from Brookline Cable TV affixing their video tripods into the north and northeast corners, I asked out loud who those *women* were. I kicked myself right away, but I knew the source of the fungal, something's-off feeling: Allan, who now had stake in all my matters.

By complaining so bitterly to Allan, I'd provoked the scoffer into a steady, midgrade dissident. Anything having to do with religion had become a sand-in-the-oyster irritant, except for Allan there was no pearl. Just that morning, when Allan was leaving for work, he needed some Ricola drops, which he swore he'd dropped into

the top of the secretaire in our foyer. Usually, the secretaire over-
flowed like a lavatory with a mind of its own, or I'd called it a time
capsule stuffed with clipped Sunday comics, bank statements, coffee
coupons, foil flasks of in-the-mail shampoo, and the Ricola drops.
Allan lifted the desktop, and I remembered when the Safed photo
came the day before I'd shoved it in there and never shown it to him.

Without a word, Allan brought the photo up to the sunlight and
squinted into it. He looked back and forth between me and the picture several times with the neutered, blank eyes he saved for manly
tasks like scraping roadkill out of our driveway, and he shoved the
photo back in the drawer and shut the drawer hard over the sticky
dowel; he asked me if Ronnie's doctor's appointment was that day
or the next, and on the way out the door he stomped to reiterate,
practically in poetic meter: A picture, of a grave, will never, go up,
on our walls. The floorboards trembled through the foyer all the way
into the dining room, where the wineglasses began to ring in the
cabinet. Even Ronnie, back in bed after a day in school, asked what
that ringing was. I found it hard to believe, but the ringing in my
ears lasted all day. I should have been grateful; wasn't Allan protecting me, defending me by keeping the barriers up?

Meanwhile, the high cafeteria windows, most recently deco-
rated in green and red, were now a pink-a-thon of paper shutters
and large mobiles of cutout hearts. In spite of the gingerbread, as
the room filled with neighbors, it sifted out so that it reminded
me of a college lecture hall. The first seats to fill were the rear, then the
wings on either side; front and center seats were punishment for being late—except for the central, earnest characters in the front
row, including Rae Stark, leader of the pack. I was surprised—and
relieved—to see that Rae made it to her own party. She'd called me
earlier in the day to say her father, our old friend Moe, was in the

hospital with congestive heart failure, and I wouldn't have been surprised if she didn't leave his side, but here she was. Next to Susan was the unmistakable stylish helmet of spiky blond hair with dark roots belonging to Carnie Goldstein, not only Susan's decorator but, increasingly since we'd gotten back, her constant companion. Rae yoo-hooed my attention as soon as I entered the room. Of course I'd be sitting in the front row with them.

In his official town capacity, Michael Marder looked less compromised than he should have for a man who waved away the afterlife so confidently. He tapped on the microphone to bring the meeting to order, introducing himself with grave self-awareness and a heavy dose of the pomp he showed one to one. But he was brief, and he turned the mike over immediately to the chair of the Planning Board, Grace Heller.

"She comes into Beacon Seafood all the time," Susan whispered to Carnie, loud enough for me to hear. I didn't need to be reminded. I'd seen Grace Heller in action, the kind of person who liked to stump the waitstaff, ordering scallops and squid by asking for bivalves and cephalopods. Shoring things up into their most complicated parts with their biggest names was a petty tease, exclusionary, not a little unlike what was happening there that night—that was, turning the raising and educating of children into a cultural filibuster.

Grace Heller settled herself to the left of a lavish easel decked with an enlarged aerial picture of the proposed building. In her right hand, she rolled a red laser pointer, a town-provided prop, ready to go. At Michael Marder's long, slow nod, she trained the laser beam onto the map and traced the line of the projected wider road, and then apparently she couldn't help herself and grimaced miserably. Her breach of objectivity was small, maybe unnoticeable to most, but unethical, retro-unconscionable. Coca-Cola did subliminal messaging like this in the fifties, in movie theaters.

My back lit with tension, I looked around, but no one else seemed to have noticed, especially since, in spite of the little grimace gaffe, Grace Heller articulated a neutral introduction with a good-vibrations overstatement. "We are talking about a serious community restructure, and what we as an entire community can tolerate for our own mutual benefit." Behind me someone emitted a low breath utterance, a soft "blah, blah, blah." Grace returned the laser line to the row of x's, the residential houses abutting the proposed building. "Tonight we'll try to get a sense of that community and meet each other, hear our plans and our concerns." Then, with a very serious face, Grace introduced the principal of the school. "Here is Rabbi Abraham Mandelbaum."

Mandelbaum? I froze.

I looked at my notes; I looked at Susan, who didn't register anything.

I would have to scour the fine print on my paperwork. Rabbi Rothstein—wasn't he the executive director? Oh. I looked again. The papers I'd gotten that week: On the petition response, Mandelbaum—this Mandelbaum—was the principal. I looked up at him: This Rabbi Mandelbaum had a red beard. Mom's Mandelbaum signature auburn red. Oh, my interior lights blinked like a pinball machine on tilt. Could this be one of Mom's Mandelbaum family?

My stomach clenched as Rabbi Mandelbaum lifted the mike stiffly and raised his eyes to the crowd. "Good evening to our deah friends and neighbahs. Our good neighbahs," he said. No r's, only ahs, a Boston native. Which made him even more possibly a relative of Mom's. Oh, a flame of anxiety dropped through my chest, sizzling with the complications.

To his credit, Rabbi Mandelbaum was, appropriate for the circumstances, *sort of smooth*, not a polished litigant—in the way of
someone who's generally skilled but naïve to a process. Unfortunately, his directness was another recognizable Mandelbaum trait.
Without any drumroll, he headed straight to the bottom line:

"The Dover Amendment will be my savior, my messiah," he
said. Which sounded, in his Boston accent, like "save-yah" and
"mis-i-yah."

The crowd murmured. Maybe his accent was a play to the crowd.
Maybe not. He continued: "The Dover Amendment is a state law
that exempts religious and educational institutions from many
zoning restrictions. A safety hazard is the only argument against
development of these institutions and their sites. And I'm here to
show you there is no safety hazahd whatsoever," he said. "No hazahd. Unless you consider hard feelings a safety hazahd." To his
credit, he didn't direct the comment to Rae Stark or me, or anyone
in particular; his eyes rested on the notes in his hand.

After that first exegesis, Rabbi Mandelbaum didn't exactly drone
on; I'd heard worse, more numbing technical defense of a building
project, and to his credit he was orderly, moving along from the
daily use of the site to the occasional use. The school would commit
to paying privately for crossing guards at drop-off and dismissal
time. They were not a community with school buses, no worry about
buses swallowing up the road. Friday afternoons were clear, few if
any evening activities except parent-teacher conferences several times
a year. No gymnasium and night games—couldn't afford such lux-
uries. He made solid points, but did he convince the crowd? If
Brookline statistics bore out, the crowd was more than half Jewish
and entirely liberal, left, green, blue—in the bluest of the blue
states, which by definition meant you should do what you want to do.
Feel good, do good. Multicultural. Be mindful of others—there's

the rub: as long as you weren't rubbed the wrong way. So why was *this* multicultural different from all other multiculturals?

And then the other half of the crowd, the school supporters, believed that afterlife was the real deal—so why were they struggling so hard to make their points in this one? I mean, if you listened to Dad, how much did it matter anyhow? I pursed my lips, hard, lest some inanity pop out.

When Rabbi Mandelbaum sat down, Grace Heller popped up to the mike and called Rae Stark to speak on behalf of the neighborhood association. Rae swept to the front of the room. Her tilt, her build, her gotta-do-it attitude predisposed her walk to an eagerness which looked sweet at first intake but a little too determined the next, when she grabbed the mike out of the stand like a professional singer or stand-up comic and began to pace. "My sleep. My work at home. My road. When I think of my neighbors, well—I already have very good neigh*bahs*. Neigh*bahs*," she repeated, not to be outdone as an indigenous dweller.

With that, I was already kicking myself for being too tired and too preoccupied with my before- and Dad's afterlife to give Rae a walk-through on her presentation. No matter where my personal thoughts took me, if I was Rae's lawyer, I should have reminded her that she couldn't construct a decent argument with her bellowing personality as the epicenter.

But I hadn't given Rae enough credit. Considering her initial animation and confidence, she constructed the argument carefully, in language she'd mustered specially for the occasion. Lest she be taken for a Philistine, she evoked the traditions of her fathers and mothers. "By way of introduction, I am the Boston North coordinator for the breast cancer walkathon and the manager of Coffee-Cocosh, a family business, a New England family business which was the first in town to ban trans fats; give paternity leave; offer dental plans, on-site day care, and domestic partner health benefits, and I donate ten percent of my profit to the City of Boston mothers and literacy program, which earned us a governor's citation for community service."

So, there was no risk to her charm as she raised the moral stakes, carefully: Instead of religious coercion, she spoke about the "boundaries of personal identity." Instead of a war cry for civil liberties, she'd revved up her key phrase: "infringing on individual personal choices." But she wasn't done. "When it comes to religious institutions, the Dover Amendment," she said, "gives special rights to believers. We cannot get around the fact that the Dover Amendment bypasses all zoning mechanisms when it comes to reconciling different interest groups. The real problem is that the Commonwealth of Massachusetts violates our constitutional right to strict neutrality with respect to religion."

It's not as if I hadn't expected every word she said. And when she sat down, Michael Marder announced he would mediate a discussion, a thirty-minute discussion, no more. The crowd buzzed, timidly—who might have the guts to begin?

Carnie Goldstein, of course, reading from notes. "In addition to aiding religion, there's the issue of declining values of surrounding property." Her voice was Euro-something, as sanded and polished as her crow's-feet and forehead lines.

"Yes," said Michael Marder. "The zoning laws impact taxes, quality of life."

"The whole matrix of factors. The Dover Amendment discriminates against secularism, business, private individuals." Carnie apparently couldn't say it without her notes.

"Well, the orthodox typically have large families. Who's to say what this might grow to?" This break-in from a man with an Aztec ski hat. Wool ear braids hung to his shoulders.

"But one school breeds another. You always need a second school so you don't send to the first." Laughter. I couldn't see the source of the rejoinder. But the laughter was from both sides. A crossover joke, quite the accomplishment.

"What about a synagogue? I heard there will be a synagogue. The Dover Amendment allows for educational institutions—" Carnie Goldstein again, reading.

"Whatever that means." This from a woman who had been waving her hand wildly. She stood to call out, then made a great show of plumping her sweater and skirt before she sat back down, but then she popped up again. A gesture to casual afterthought, but she'd clearly done her research. "When it comes to the Dover Amendment, *educational* is a vague standard, which allowed a gun club to build because it gave riflery classes. And a methadone clinic had so-called life skills seminars." She air-quoted the phrase *life skills*.

"Yes. And what about the synagogue plans? Don't the plans include a synagogue?" Aztec man, once again.

Rabbi Mandelbaum stood to answer and directed himself to the whole crowd. "Just for the record, we don't shoot—out or up. And yes, we need a synagogue room—a room, not a building—because prayer is part of our curriculum. It's not intended for Saturday or holiday use." He articulated the last part loudly and aroused a buzz of voices as he sat down.

"Who would oversee this construction so the kids aren't peeping on my wife as she sunbathes?" Any of us in town had come to expect the wild-card, non sequitur comments, usually from the smartest of the bunch too. I recognized the speaker, Rae's neighbor on the other side of the school, a physician whose name was often in the paper for his overseas do-gooding, mostly in North African countries.

"What about substituting the Jewish school for a Hindu school or a Christian school? Would we have the same reaction?" That was Michael Marder, diversity trained, in his official capacity.

"That's a cheap shot at 'correctness,'" said a man with pincer glasses and an equally pinched face. He read from notes in his hand. "You know how Jewish Brookline is. I think it was Woodrow Wilson who said, and I quote: 'Intertribal disputes within the same nation are always more vicious precisely because the stakes are lower.'" I couldn't tell what side he was on until he sat down and shook hands with a yarmulked man.

"But these are high stakes." This from a white woman with a sand-colored Afro, practically a halo, transparent and chunky. "Why do orthodox families separate their kids and send them to their own schools anyhow? What's wrong with the public schools?"

"Why do they have so many kids anyhow?" Rae asked. She had to choose that moment to speak up.

"Look here." Carnie Goldstein stood up again. "There's no way these children will last this way. The problem of the school is a generation's worth. Then we can turn the building into a youth center or something." She coughed—or laughed, I couldn't tell.

Michael Marder bent in to the mike quickly. "Gentle people of the town. This is not a discussion about the Dover Amendment, religion, or religious values or family planning or intelligent design." Michael Marder would do that, interpolate the intelligent design comment. It—or something—finally provoked the crowd, whose group mumbling sounded like an airplane as it flew overhead. Then, a loud, derogatory catcall flew across the room like a missile shot.

"Say no to Yarmulke Street."

"Please, take your seats," Michael Marder boomed. "Pleeease, take your seats."

"Say nooooooooo to Yarmulke Street."

Behind me, the religious neighbors and Rabbi Mandelbaum

settled back, several men on one side and a half dozen women on the other side. The woman next to Rabbi Mandelbaum, wearing a purple turtleneck, stood up. No notes or prompts, she knew what she was saying about the Dover Amendment and First Amendment rights. "The school building is within the boundaries of the law. A change in law is another discussion, not for here, not for now. Not regarding Brookline Hebrew Day. It's a job for Beacon Hill. The lawmakers' discussion."

She couldn't have been more right. I recognized this woman and her calm balance from the board of the Women's Bar Association, though I never knew she was part of this religious crowd. I could only imagine her thoughts: weighing the world to come against her earthly endeavors like this. Or maybe I was projecting: If this woman looked at me, what would she see inside my thoughts? Anything?

fifteen

THE NEXT DAY I FOUND OUT THAT CARNIE GOLDSTEIN and the man in the Aztec ski hat were founding members of STREPP, Stop Religious Property Provocation, and the agitators were friends they'd planted around the meeting. It could have been worse. My one consolation was that Dad still knew nothing about the case; witness, his e-mails were still chock-full of epiphanies about the weather and his soul classes.

The complications were squashed inside me, waiting to spring: not only did Dad's desire for meaning and Truth cut us loose from our mother unless we aligned with his ideals, but he was aligned with a group whose land monolith I was fighting against. I had to admit it was tricky: two battlefronts against the same body of people; and it was all pushing Dad further and further away, which was not what we orphans wanted.

I shouldn't say I was relieved, but a couple of days after the town meeting, all talk of stopping the Jews ground to a halt: Rae Stark's father, our old friend Moe Stark, died of his congestive heart failure.

At Kampinsky Brothers Funeral Home, the ushers in the black yarmulkes scooped Susan and me (among the last cluster of guests) to the seats everyone else had avoided for decency's sake, the voyeur seats directly behind Rae and her brother, where they were busy draping and heaving themselves across the shoulders and lap of Moses's second wife, Joan. The same Joan who, with proper lack of respect for the second wife, Susan and I used to call Joan Jetson because of her harsh middle hair part and turned-up collars. Since we were kids, her blue-black hair had thinned, pinked, and puffed, but today her stand-up collar was in place. Black, of course.

Never mind the petty petty things. The larger petty things were more telling: Rae and her brother peeled off Joan's shoulders as the rabbi came up to the microphone. The rabbi incanted a prayer and then let out the *o* word: *orphan*.

Rae wailed. The back of her neck and ears reddened. Even my own stomach clenched. I hated that word.

Rae redraped herself onto Joan. The last time I'd been even near the front row at a funeral was Mom's, of course, and who knew what we looked like from behind or if we draped or clung. *You need each other now*, were the over and over words of comfort, and I'd been so young that I thought the *now* meant then, that the need was fixed in time and then it would be over. What a vapid, mean thought to thrust on children. To thrust on anyone.

"This world is a corridor to the next world," the rabbi said, pinching his eyeglasses at the corner, a gesture he repeated a dozen times during his short eulogy. "And Moe Stark has passed through the corridor."

Corridor? Did he use the word *corridor*? I smacked Susan with my elbow. "The corridor," I mouthed to her.

"The huh?" she whispered. "Shhh . . ." She put her finger to her lips.

Did rabbis always talk about corridors? Did funerals always involve rabbis who talked about corridors? Was I the only one who heard the word *corridor*? The only one who processed it? I looked around. Around me, the funeral guests blinked and nodded, closed their eyes, laid their heads back or forward, examined their hands, pulled their chins.

By the time they rolled the casket out to the hearse, an image had shoved itself into my mind: Moe Stark dressed in one of his natty suits, walking down a long hallway, toward a double-height door that opened into something large, like a conference center or a wedding hall. Moe turned a beaming smile on the rest of us as he entered the door. And then he waved from inside that room and disappeared.

AFTER THE CEMETERY, Susan went back to work and I made my way back with the crowd to Rae's house. As luck would have it, we pulled into Rae's street just as the cars belonging to Brookline Hebrew Day School lined up on either side, narrowing the roadway to one lane. I checked my watch: two o'clock. Clearly we'd driven into preschool dismissal time. Three-foot-high kids in colored coats with hanging clipped mittens shot out in straight Madeline lines, met their car-pool moms. Rabbi Mandelbaum stood at the door of the school, then walked out to direct traffic; but yes, the road was clogged up for the other owners and for us, who had sympathy business there. Nothing I would mention to Rae, but information I would store.

Inside, Rae's house looked as if it hadn't expected company, even though Moe had been sick and lingering, and his death was not sudden. Not that I'd have expected Rae to uproot her past-is-past collections. A wall of built-in wooden cubes in her living room held nineteenth-century baking tools and antique nutcrackers. In the dining room, ornate crown molding set off Rae's mountable knick-knacks: door knockers, wall pockets, hand mirrors—all flat backed and already used and useless. Someone had moved her collection of silver bread baskets off the cherrywood table and replaced them with the platters Susan sent from Beacon Seafood, fish and seafood salads, egg salad, and garlic knots. Chocolate cake. Jalapeño corn muffins. The food chittered up the atmosphere, and we sat in chairs pulled back from the table and ate with our plates on our laps.

A half dozen of us watched with great interest as Rae's husband heaved around boxes of breast cancer walk T-shirts, from the buffet to a spare chair and finally to a corner of the floor. Abruptly, Rae set down her plate, grabbed a T-shirt off the top of the box, and stood to shake out the folds. "I designed these myself," she said, pointing to the Boston skyline with the Zakim Bridge, black on pink, with a space on the bridge ramp to write the name of your loved one.

"Great—you did a great job," I said. Now the silence was broken, I expected her to circle on to Moe, but when she sat back down and picked up her plate from the floor, put the fork of egg salad to her mouth, she reconsidered and spoke about her mother.

"My mother's cancer was the kind you get with the BRCA one and two genes."

This was an old discussion for us.

"I get examined every three months," Rae said. She took a sip of her Diet Coke. "I fight back. What about you and Susan?" She knew we did not have the genes. She was talking about the check-ups. "Which doesn't limit your susceptibility. I'm happy I can fight."

"We fight too. Just with less frequent examinations. Or the volume of worry." I found myself clarifying for the crowd. A little too intimate.

And then, just as quickly as she jousted with her future, Rae's attention strayed to the bustle at the front door. Carnie Goldstein, walking in with Michael Marder and his wife. They shook hands with Rae, sat, smiled, talked. Later, when we were done with our egg salad and Rae's husband was circulating with a white lemon-scented trash bag open in his hand, Rae had the first soft moment I'd seen all day. "Losing my father is like losing my mother all over again," she confided.

Of all people, I was in no position to comfort her on that one, but I told her I was sure I knew what she meant.

BY THE TIME I left Rae's, it was after 3:00 P.M. I'd lost my concentration for work and found myself bottom-lining, enumerating: listing the things I still had, the things I should be grateful for. Dad—alive, at least. Susan. Allan. The boys. My work when it's not so complicated. Even Beacon Seafood. Because sometimes when Susan and I try to coordinate a meal, it isn't for real hunger but for the satisfaction of riling each other up and then toasting it off with a glass of wine or, in the daytime, a cup of cappuccino. When I called Susan, she wasn't too busy between late lunch and early dinner, and ten minutes later, I found myself climbing the half dozen brick stairs next to the loading dock. The back door of the restaurant was so short even a child would have to bend over to press the buzzer.

From the basement office, Steve hawked an annoyed and drawn-out "Yes."

"It's Honey," I said. Without buzzing me in yet, he held the intercom open and I heard him talking with someone, a phrase that sounded like *cornflake crumbs* and then a pitched voice yelling "Plums," which was the word I might have heard to begin with.

It was a damp, gray afternoon, the kind where texture and color and air collide, different from the still, white cemetery air. A small, low wind huffed a fish smell in from the harbor. I pushed the buzzer again, tapping my foot in a puddle of melting ice, fish shipment ice most likely. A thin stream of water ran across the top step and dropped into a groove along the far edge. The water ran after itself, like anger or fear, searching for the conduits it had already made. Finally, Steve buzzed me in.

I headed straight to the back office and sat on the far side of the desk Susan shared with Steve and the night captain.

"Let's eat back here. I'm not in the mood to go out there on the floor," Susan said.

"Since when is your restaurant 'out there'?"

But she'd already ordered us shrimp-orzo salad and onion rings, not exactly comfort food but good food. "What's made you so moody?" I asked.

"What's made *you* so moody?"

Instead of a direct answer, the thought occurred to me: "Did you notice the rabbi's language?" I asked. "Passed through the corridor. Dad's corridor, and all that. I know I'm speculating, but wouldn't it be wonderful if Rae realized she is looking for comfort in a system aligned with the people she's fighting and she should logically drop the school case?"

"Or be respectfully out of commission for a while since it's her turn to gather comfort there? Keep dreaming. The corridor is just funeral language, the comfort package, like the tissues and candles. I wouldn't put much stock in the way the rabbi said Moe passed. People always say: "pass on," "pass away." The TV psychics say "pass over." They're euphemisms."

"But for Dad—funeral talk is Dad's vernacular."

"Now that you put it that way." I couldn't tell if Susan was going to laugh. She stifled it and quieted for a minute. "You didn't realize that? I'd told Steve the day we got back that Dad sounded like a eulogy."

"I was hopeful that Rae could face the core eternity issue and calm down a little."

"You *would*."

What did that mean? Her features banked as she shrugged her shoulders and tossed her gaze around the room, to nothing. "You've become obsessed with Dad, with our trip. Did you realize how much you talk about our trip? And about the endowment for Mom. Sometimes I think you attach more importance . . ." She adjusted Mom's picture that she kept in the four-inch spot between the computer monitor and her in-box. "Somehow—for you—everything always comes down to Mom. Mom and loss. I've been thinking about that."

"Finally . . ."

"No, not finally. More like actually. Since we got back from Israel, it's like you have Dad, Mom, life, and death as a brain filter. The endowment is just the symbol of it all."

"It's just a mutation of the regular, normal—"

"And circumstances bring the feelings out. Yeah, yeah, yeah."

"Just because you never obsess this way . . ."

"I can't help it that it wasn't me, that you and Dad always had the first-tier sufferer thing, the front-row seat in common. He's pulled out, given himself a way to make closure—finally, finally, and no wonder you feel afloat. Here, read this."

I don't know why I expected something better or more, but she'd handed me an article she'd cut from *The Boston Globe*. The Monday Health/Science section: CADMIUM IN SEAFOOD CRUSTACEANS A LINK TO BREAST CANCER.

"What does this have to do with anything?" I said.

"Kind of sobering. Considering what I eat for lunch every day."

"A reason to be kosher?" I couldn't believe I said that.

She couldn't either. "More like a reason to be proactive. You know, you talk about religion all the time. All the time, like it's your new knee-jerk reaction to everything."

"I do not."

"Yes, you do. You and I were having a conversation about breast cancer and then you started talking about kosher food."

"What?" I huffed. "What are you talking about?" My defensive hackles rose.

She led me into the dining room to scale out her new ideas for her Middle East bar. At the bank of espresso machines, the wait-staff lined up like soldiers, filling dolphin-shaped water pitchers at the bus stations, smacking the bottoms of the saltshakers, pouring peppercorns into the tableside pepper mills, setting wine in the avocado wood holders she'd bought on our trip north.

"I put them out last week for Valentine's Day and never took them off."

"And . . . ?" I waited for her to zoom back into focus.

But when the words came out, her harshness sounded like Allan and her hissy whisper sounded like a talk radio shrink enunciating into the mike. "You know what your problem is? Dad has severed the purity of your loss," she said. "What's he supposed to do? Mourn forever? Never change?"

"You're only seeing the external effects—on him, on me. It has to affect inside us too. He's the one who made the point. The closure he's found has to be our closure too." Truer words I hadn't spoken, and in her silence the coffee machine espressoed with a life of its own. The beans smelled black, not mineral black, like tar or coal, but woodsy, ebony black.

Back in her office, sipping my espresso, I couldn't help think about how dangerous it was sometimes to articulate an idea. I mean, once it's taken form into words, who knows? It could spread like a germ. That's when I noticed for the first time how without windows Susan's office looked like a cave, how that and walls the color of peat moss which curved down into the back of the room made me think that if I was a prisoner there, I knew exactly where I would start tunneling out.

sixteen

IS IT ALWAYS THIS WAY? HOW SOME IDEAS LOOK FOR CRACKS IN the wall and seep through no matter how tight you've made it? Something happened between the first neighborhood meeting and the town Planning Board meeting: the born-agains began to pop up everywhere in Brookline. In proportion or not; or maybe I was like a medical student freshly immersed in anatomy and physiology watching the person standing in front of her in Dunkin' Donuts pay for coffee with a radius bone instead of an arm. It turned out there was a born-again son in my book group, a grandson in my Women's Bar Association Public Forum, and my secretary's niece was born-again in Israel, circuitously through Morocco, then finding out there's no place like home.

I'd begun to fantasize that Rae would make my life easier and recant, even a little. But she was one of those people whom confrontations with mortality made harder, not softer. What I noticed at her shivah visiting week (work friendly, evenings only): She sat on a folding chair wearing frog green Crocs and a torn ribbon at her collar, surrounded by sign-up sheets for breast cancer walk sponsors. Among her friends and townspeople who filed in and out of her front door, no one missed a comment on the pictures of both her parents on her living room mantel. Each picture had a Jewish story, a be-all-you-can-be-type Jewish story; for example, Moe's matriculation at Tufts in 1947. Beating the odds of the Jewish quotas because he was a four-letter athlete. And Rae's mom—I never knew—she'd been a bathing suit model at Filene's downtown until her religious father made her stop. To hear her, Rae's parents were tigers, voracious Jews out to stake turf in the world outside the enclaves, the world where no Jews had gone before.

Here's where my prod for truth makes me twitch in my chair: I drove home from Rae's feeling peculiarly empowered. After all, until Dad changed his mind and tried to change ours, Rae's was the type of Jewish charge I was used to: onward, upward—outward. The best of all Jewish expression was being the finest and strongest physical specimen you could be in this world, here and now. So when I walked in my front door and found Ronnie on the sofa clicking, clicking, clicking away on the remote control and complaining he was bored, the last thing I wanted to see was a fey Jew. Dad might call it soulful. In defense, I would call it passive. Ronnie was feeling better. He'd been back to school for a day; his fever was gone. So I pushed him outside to play basketball with the next-door neighbor, and a half hour later, Ronnie fell over the boy's sneakered foot. I heard Ronnie's crash and saw his slump through my office window. He didn't bump his head, get a concussion, break his front teeth. Ronnie lacerated his liver.

Well, the doctor explained, she'd seen worse damage from events just as simple: a kid falling off a bike, a kid walking to school on an icy sidewalk lacerating a pancreas, which doesn't regenerate the way a liver does. I mouthed proper gratitude, but it wasn't more than skin deep.

Waiting Room B on the third floor of Children's Hospital was blandly tan and symmetrical, with banks of square chairs in back-to-back rows, which created the impression that there was no front or center to the room. If it had been a classroom, I wouldn't have known where to look at the teacher, the blackboard, the answers, the questions. Susan arrived; she brought Ronnie a get-well card, poster size, something she made herself, really more of a cheerleading card: get well, be well, stay well. We tiptoed to his room, and she tacked it up on his half of the bulletin board, next to Dad's e-mail about a whole army of supplicants at the Western Wall on his behalf. But Ronnie was sleeping, and Susan said his body looked like a snowman's, a very little kid's snowman: a ball of a face perched on a ball of a body, all that roundness making the limbs insignificant.

"I thought I was being a parent, driver's seat and all, but it's like skidding out of control on the highway," I said when Susan and I sat back in Waiting Room B.

"I know what you mean," Susan said. I wasn't sure she did. How could she know that a dose of Rae's type of Jew had me push Ronnie outside?

I slumped in my chair, clutching a Green Mountain coffee cup in the exact center of my lap; my coat was piled behind me, my purse rested on the floor between my feet, and I felt as if I were someone waiting in a crowded airport gate, afraid to spill over to the next seat or take more than her share of the microworld she finds herself in. The only other people—group? family group?—in the room, as fate would have it, included two men with yarmulkes and a handful of long-skirted, buttoned-up women.

What kind of cosmic joke was this? There I was in the hospital crashing because my dishonorable reaction to Rae's reaction to all those Jews had pushed me to push my son when he wasn't feeling well. Were the sins of the mothers really visited on the children? Oh, how the yarmulkes and the females with their long skirts and covered body parts provoked me to a wave of self-consciousness. I couldn't even fight the thought. By now I knew it was true: Spirituality had a physical prompt, and, sitting there with those people, I had to step up to the plate as if Dad and his ilk were the litmus test for the right and perfect thing to say. So, besides my general self-consciousness, I suddenly had to guard against being theologically provocative or circumstantially stainless. I mean, if your focus is the other world, are you allowed to say things like "Poor Ronnie, it's not fair"; or "Why does something like that have to happen to such a good boy?"

For a minute I actually wished Susan would offer me some "I'm OK, you're OK." Some equivocation. Any equivocation.

"You want to talk?" Susan asked. "You *need* to talk," she answered herself. "About anything?"

For a minute I brightened inside: Anything? The price for parking a car at the hospital for one hour? The male nurse on duty yesterday with the pec-rippling shirt. Dad. No, not Dad. The Brookline Hebrew Day School case? Instead, I nodded my head back to the chairs behind us, meaning the yarmulke gang. "They have an eighteen-year-old undergoing abdominal surgery as we speak, and I can't imagine they want to hear the ballad of Yarmulke Street."

"You mean they're people too?" I knew Susan meant the joke as a tension breaker.

I'd already surprised myself by the ability to break down the group into recognizable parts. The men wore black yarmulkes like Dad's, and one of the women wore a snood cap like Evelyn wore in the mornings. Another man wore a blue knit yarmulke, not a black velvet one, and the net look was about body covering, both the men and the women.

I noticed Susan pulling her skirt over her knees.

"What are you doing?" I asked.

"Ants in my pants," Susan said.

My sister was not a jokester, and the very sight of her getting self-conscious about her knees rattled me out of my stupor into a laugh.

"Don't laugh at me."

I covered for myself quickly. "I could make the dumb-things-people-say list. Even the doctors here," I said. "I can't keep hearing how it's not my fault or there is no fault or it is my fault. The effect is what I have to deal with. I can't keep beating myself up over the cause. That's what I keep telling myself."

"You flunk mommy school lately?"

"Yeah. But it *is* my fault, the fault of my consciously pushing, and I'm sure I'm being punished." For what list, I was formulating. Oh, I reined back my thoughts and began to hum. What sounded like the alphabet tune: A, B, C, D—

"Stop it already."

I stopped humming, acting as if that was what Susan meant, as if I hadn't recycled the crime and punishment loop for the past twelve hours.

"No," Susan said. "Not that. Stop the self-battering. It would be illegal if someone else did it to you." She was whispering. The religious presence could do that to you, though I'm not sure Susan and I felt self-conscious in different ways. And my head was spinning, my defenses broken down a little. Maybe it was my lack of sleep and maybe it came after a bad twenty-four hours trying to resurrect myself in my own eyes, but looking at that family of women, it occurred to me that their proudly unhip exteriors weren't as bad as I'd thought. Because they were *souls,* their clothes didn't call attention to their bodies.

They appeared to be a set of parents, two grandparents, and two teenage girls. The girls were reading from some prayer book and moving their lips rapidly. I would have been overcompensating for negative thoughts if I were to talk to them. I would have been over-compensating for that if I ignored them.

I closed my eyes. Now that I'd excreted my negativity onto Susan, I was tired; my head pulsed off my neck. If only the religious family didn't make my neck burn. If only I didn't have this childish impulse to . . . connect . . . to say I knew who (really what) they were, that Dad was one of them. That I wasn't such an *other*. Which of course reminded me of the way small children play next to each other in a wading pool. Looking, flirting really.

Susan went to the soda machine out in the hallway and came back with a Diet Coke. One of the grandmothers went to the machine and came back with a bag of ripple potato chips and a can of diet Sprite.

I bolted up in my chair. "How long was I asleep?"

"About a minute. Maybe less."

"I want coffee. Fresh coffee."

Susan recognized my tone, or maybe the feral look I'd squeezed on my face, and knew better than to give me any more instructions. She volunteered to find the cafeteria and returned with a pink cardboard tray, coffee for two, a heap of Splenda packets, a pile of mini creamer tubs. We each poured a half dozen creamers into a cup and all of the sweetener. One of the mothers in the other family watched and wagged her head and smiled as Susan and I recapped our coffees.

Susan couldn't help but explain. "We started drinking coffee when we were kids. We still drink coffee like little kids." What she didn't add was the why, how Dad made a big pot to get us all going in the morning and we had no out-of-bed mother to leaven the act. But the coffee had unfastened the kind of partition between us and the religious family.

"What are you here for?" Susan asked, even though I'd filled her in already.

"Our son is having GI surgery," the mother said. If it weren't the same conciseness as I'd used moments earlier, Susan would surely have read it as aloof and turned back around to face her own wall.

The father's cell phone rang, and he left the room to take the call. The mother twisted in her chair to talk. The only time you saw back-to-back rows like this in conversation was at a party game of musical chairs. But usually someone is crying because they're odd man out. Anyhow, one of us had to twist, and she'd taken it upon herself to be the twister. "We brought him back from Jerusalem, where he was studying. And he has some kind of colitis. An intestinal block. Not that they don't have hospitals and doctors there—but we're here. All our doctors are here. And we were scared by the distance."

Were we trading information, or could it be that we were trading anxiety and fear? From my narrow view of things, until that moment I assumed that religious people didn't get scared. So could we trade comfort? I wanted to ask. Were people of faith at least less scared, if they had so much purpose and so much belief in life after death anyhow? My assumptions tumbled into my questions and clogged my conversational grace.

Susan piped up. "We were in Jerusalem. A couple of weeks ago. For the first time."

"The only time," I said.

That's all it took for the mother and grandmother to come around to sit in the chairs facing us. "Do you mind?" the mother asked. She looked at us with a bobbing head, registering our faces, calculating something. "Sisters?"

"Mother, daughter?" Susan bobbed back. Silly question. Who couldn't tell a mother and a daughter?

Both women nodded. "Whereabouts were you in Jerusalem?"

I couldn't believe this woman was willing to have a normal conversation. Why were these women making small talk anyhow? Why weren't they making large talk with their higher powers? On the other hand, why should anything bother them anyhow if there's life after death and this world is just a corridor?

"We were in a neighborhood called Rechavia," Susan said. "Have you heard of it?"

"Of course—it's an old neighborhood, a fabulous neighborhood. Close to everything. Just visiting the country?"

"Visiting our father," Susan said.

"What's he doing there?"

"That's the problem," Susan said, a little artlessly, a little off guard.

"That's the *question*," I said, shooting Susan a look.

The mother and grandmother looked at each other to check responses. They laughed pleasantly but not a fun or funny laugh.

"Don't take it personally," Susan said. Which she shouldn't have said. Next thing I knew she'd be saying something like religious Jews were her best friends. Or something like that.

"Well, he doesn't really *live* there," I said. "He went for a visit, and he ended up staying, temporarily."

"Then we had to go see what was going on with him and his wife. He's studying. At Torah Lights." For someone for whom everything is okay, Susan stretched her syllables into words that would do better with air quotes.

"At Torah Lights?" To her credit, the woman ignored the tonal innuendo, that we'd implicated Dad in some off-balance scheme. Her face lit up fluorescently, with a smile that began at her chin and switched on some dance in her eyes. She called over to her husband, who had walked back into the room. "Listen to this," she said. "Their father is studying at Torah Lights in Jerusalem."

"Gotten in deep," Susan mumbled. "What? I'm joking," she whispered to me.

"My brother-in-law—my two brothers-in-law—teach there," the woman said. "One is actually the director. Their sister, my husband's sister, lives here in Boston. Her husband is a rabbi in town, a school principal actually."

I guessed what was coming next.

Not quite.

"They live near Beacon Street and Washington Street."

"That's right near my place," Susan said. She did not say her place was the best crab-shrimp-lobster-nonkosher restaurant in town.

"Where's that?"

"Food business," Susan said, suddenly curt, suddenly self-conscious.

"There's a supermarket. An ice cream parlor, the nail spa, yoga center . . ." The woman ticked off the list. She looked at Susan. "You're not the yoga center. You . . . you're the seafood restaurant? We pass it all the time. The place where everyone always walks out with leftovers from the meals."

"We make a point—my mother-in-law's Jewish joke: eat, eat. We serve big portions . . . no one should ever leave hungry."

The women looked puzzled, and I didn't blame them. The seafood restaurant was probably an anti-Jewish joke to her.

But she knew it: "Oh, you mean Mom." Everyone in town called Susan's mother-in-law Mom because of all the TV and radio ads. "The one who sings her jingles to *Fiddler on the Roof's* 'Tradition': 'Oysters,'" she imitated, singing, "unsafe to eat in a month that doesn't have the letter *r*; lobsters can be left handed or right handed; clams worth eating close their shells before cooking."

"That's me. *Us*," Susan said.

Now once this woman put out and sang the restaurant jingle, we had no choice but to take the lead on Jewish geography, the documented game of connection: not six degrees of separation, as in the general population, but three degrees of separation to get to how your cousin is married to her next-door neighbor. Or it took fewer degrees than that. Or no degrees, as it turned out. Because when the sister walked in, and she was introduced as Mrs. Mandelbuam, we knew right away she was the wife of Principal Rabbi Mandelbaum. And Susan and I already knew her.

We'd met her at a would-be turf war five years earlier during the first breast cancer walkathon, one of those Boston springs that had begun in fits and spurts, changed its mind, confused the tree blossoms and the rhododendron blossoms, and, overnight, the crocuses and Porta-Johns burst into color at curbside. The walk would come and go, and Susan would make sure that Beacon Seafood dominated the block. She set up an official lunch stop—all the perks: water, sports drinks, snacks, a nurses' station, and lunch: pasta and seafood salad. Except right next to them the religious women had set up a quick stop with orange slices, water, and Powerade. This woman had manned the table with a framed picture of three women, two old, one young.

Susan whispered her choice comments: old fashioned, out of time fashioned, like a storybook Mama Bear. She wore sturdy nun shoes on a pair of great legs. Great, long, athletic legs. "Missed communication," she'd said to Susan. "No need for both of us here manning tables for the locals." Without further ado, she'd handed Susan her orange slices and Powerade, and every year since, without knowing her name, we'd seen her cheering the walk, huzzahing from the sidelines on Beacon Street.

Oh, why did this have to happen and deepen my connections? The rabbi's wife, this Mrs. Mandelbaum, nodded to Susan, but she must have taken one look at my face and posture and figured who was the first-tier sufferer. Her sister-in-law whispered something to her as she leaned back against the window, crossed her lovely ankles, and turned to me. "What is your son's name?" she said.

"Ronnie."

"Does he have a Hebrew name? We'll add him to our prayer list." She paused. "Our get-well prayer list."

"Our father has a prayer group going," Susan said. She forced the lingua franca. I was impressed.

But I noticed the translating impulse of the rabbi's wife. Not exactly patronizing. Not exactly not patronizing either. "What's your son's Hebrew name?"

"Rachel. After our mother—the r," I said.

"Does he have a male name?"

"Ronnie. With the r."

"No Hebrew name?"

I shrugged.

Even if she didn't get the answer she expected, the rabbi's wife did not react. "What's your name, sweetie?"

I told her.

The rabbi's wife laughed. "Honey. Sweetie. So it's Ronnie, son of Honey. For illness we beg with the mother's name. Nothing like a mother to evoke mercy."

I held my tongue; the truth was, I wouldn't know.

seventeen

I'M IN MY KITCHEN, TYPING AWAY, POUNDING AT THE TRUTH to get it out and set the record straight. Dad pops up like the Where's Waldo? guy, trying to give me perspective on this, that, and everything. He's brought me another purple crocus. When there's more than one crocus, it's the first real sign that winter is receding. "April showers bring May flowers."

"It's only March, and a crocus is more tuber than flower. Like a potato plant," I say.

"I don't know where you get your information," he says, setting what I recognize as his glazing tools in the corner by the refrigerator. Yesterday, he finished my attic skylights, and now he's heading to Susan's house to reglaze the picture window in her foyer. I've asked him before, but I ask him again if he minds these small-scale projects, if he feels more or less useful because they are so little, and he mumbles an answer about doing, whatever, for us girls. I don't mind the way it sounds as if Susan and I have the same needs.

"Besides. You'll be happy to know that this chapter's almost over. We're going back to Jerusalem in two weeks."

"That's good. By then I'll be breaking things so you'll have something to do."

Next thing I know, Dad is poking through the freezer and finds some Häagen-Dazs vanilla and almond bars, which I didn't know till today are kosher. We sit at the kitchen table, and he unwraps mine for me. I bite off the top piece.

"Take it easy," he says. "Did you know that women are more prone to brain freeze?"

I didn't used to notice his trivia thrill. Since he's been born-again, unicorns might exist, there's a place inside the Western Wall where the wall cries tears, the traditional Jewish marriage contract is the first known example of female conjugal rights, and before a baby is born she knows everything from one end of the universe to the other and at birth an angel taps the upper lip and then she forgets—but only mostly: That's why sometimes aha moments aren't just discovery, they feel as if you're remembering. Whew, Dad, enough.

Outside, two kids roll a bicycle with a flat tire. A couple of after-school tennis players pass by in sweatpants and parkas, off to the town courts for preseason lessons. Dad pushes back in his chair, twirls his yarmulke, and settles it back on his head, as if it's blown off steam and has to land again. And I can see what's coming; the trivia is a casual prequel for one of his "talks," the talks which are palliative or which have the potential to transform me or give me perspective.

But stop eating the ice cream so quickly is all he says.

I'm relieved. That's what it has been like for weeks. Just when I expect a big thing, he's down-to-earth.

"If you eat so quickly, you stop tasting it." He gets me: That big-thing look returns to his face, he dips his head down and gets that darn-it expression. "We should strive—strive to master our desires for the good things, we should—"

"Dad, stop."

"I don't mean give up the good things." His face clears as he sits back. "That's not what I'm saying. It's just that we're a right-time-and-place kind of religion."

"This kind of roundelay has happened too many times," I say. "You want me to say 'huh?' and then you'll explain and then I'll get a lecture."

"You think you have it all figured out?" he says, getting up. "Do you mind?" he asks. In a minute he's unloaded the freezer of waffles, blocks of frozen vegetables, frozen steamed chicken dinners, frozen entrées. Lots of frozen foods for our family this season, and, of course, organizing is one of his natural and neutral talents.

"You know, for rookies, our religion is not 'all or nothing.'"

I ignore him. He shuts the freezer door, then opens it again, poking his finger along the gasket. "It's torn a little."

"How hard is that to fix?"

"I have to call GE." He pauses. "Maybe not. Maybe I can get something. Hey, do you need all this stuff?" Dad turns to the scraps and notes packed on the fridge door. They and all the magnets tell a life story.

"This?" He points: a menu from a Chinese takeout.

"You can throw it away."

"This?" He points to a coupon for Homer's hometown taxi: three dollars off on an airport ride. "Never mind. Evelyn and I can use it." He tacks it back up.

He lines the coupons up on the left, the pictures in the center, and get-well cards on the right. "This leaves a few odd men out," he says. "Oh this! I can throw this away."

He's pulling down the invitation. Obsolete as yesterday's sale coupons at Macy's, and not that he'll ever know the whole story, but the invitation was the beginning of the end of the Brookline Hebrew Day School case. After Ronnie's accident, before the Planning Board meeting and the final showdown at the Zoning Board of

Appeals, the invitation slipped through the mail slot like radioactive fallout, except all white linen and raised letters: We were cordially invited to the Boston dinner honoring Dad and Evelyn for their generous contribution and endowment of Daughters of Rachel to the Torah Lights institution. Dad and Evelyn were coming to town. No warning. No heads-up. Addressed to the whole family, and the price to attend was $250 a person, $150 tax deductible. When I called Dad, he said the invitation was the real thing, but the price, a mistake. We were invited as his guests at the family table. In the middle of the Brookline Hebrew Day School case, Dad and Evelyn were coming to town.

It had been a very busy week, the same week we brought Ronnie home from the hospital. The same week Susan's in-laws flew in from West Palm Beach for tandem cardiology checkups. Who wouldn't notice the new theme in my life? Both the dinner and the visit raised the same mortality issues, what a parent was giving over, in whatever the allotted lifetime. I couldn't change the facts of the dinner, but Susan begged me to be the buffer between her and her in-laws at Beacon Seafood. I felt the crackly static as soon as I crossed the threshold into the restaurant, the way an overheated room might hit you or if you could actually bump into microwaves or TV transmissions or cathode particles.

"Hey, Mom." We air-kissed across the table. In a public place, an airport line, for example, she might smile at her constituents. But privately, Mom's signature snippiness is intimidating, forever signed and sealed for me the first time I met her, when Susan took me back to the restaurant kitchen and Mom was standing there in a suit and strappy three-inch heels, so petite that she came up to the shoulder of the chef as she balanced a twenty-pound tuna horizontally by the head and tail, demanding that the chef heed the sag in the midsection.

Susan chattered nonstop, buffing the blade of her butter knife with her forefinger, placing it down exactly at the top edge of the butter plate. She'd begun the last three sentences with the words *in spite of,* this last one finishing with . . . *may as well have.* Mom was taking her through the paces: Were they handling their inheritance well? Were the guests as pleased as in her day? Did the customers smile after their entrées? After their desserts? Did they manipulate the pasta servings so that customers carried out the plastic-lid tins and told their friends and neighbors about the portions?

Susan introduced the concept of the Middle East bar.

"With . . . flavors?" Mom asked.

Susan nodded. "New sauces. Saffron. Red—it's just called red sauce."

I swore I heard Steve begin to hum an old Donovan song: I'm just mad about Saffron, Saffron's mad about me.

I tried not to get distracted by imbalanced subtexts: Susan wasn't exactly asking permission, and Mom assumed her involvement was an entitlement, instead of a courtesy. And I always hated the way Steve made Susan the front woman for the legacy. Steve sat and occasionally sipped his water, his smiles and frowns equally bland, and where tears might track if he ever showed emotion were what you could call movie star lines, which theoretically should make him look handsomer.

Then, as if the real conversations weren't subterranean enough, Nava, the best day waitress, was plumbing the depths of obsequiousness. When she came over to take our orders, her hands were trembling. Of course Mom ordered without looking at a menu. Shrimp with both of the proposed new sauces. We ordered two onion flowers to share and a large plate of coated fries served on edible rice-paper newsprint, Mom's favorite enactment from thirty years earlier. Nava made tableside theater with Caesar salad and served it out. I watched Mom carve up the salad with a knife and a fork and eat the salad in parts: croutons first, then anchovies, then the romaine, as if a person had the power to make the parts into a whole. Mom's shrimp arrived retroussé on a plate that was extralarge and extraprimped with parsley and red-radish shavings. Then Mom smiled—good? She dipped, took one more bite, then laid her fork down. "So far, the saffron sauce is wonderful. What's that . . . cayenne? But where are the shrimp coming from?"

A rhetorical question she answered herself. "Either you've been buying seawater shrimp or you've been buying cheap. It smacks of preservative. Iodine." She dipped a shrimp in the red sauce. "I don't mind . . . I don't mind the paprika. The tumeric . . . is that tumeric? But the cilantro. Too heavy on the cilantro. You know there are two types of people in the world, those who love cilantro and those who hate cilantro."

This was why Susan had asked me to come along. The moment Mom pushed the shrimp and sauce away, I changed the subject. "Mom, did you hear about our trip to Israel?"

"Sure I heard. About your father too. How does your Dad look?" Mom said, with the swirl of a pointed finger at her head, lightly enough so that I wouldn't know for sure if she meant nutsy, or if she meant was he wearing a yarmulke? Either way a plain old question in her default mode, that good old hauteur, that little mood blast, as if someone had opened the door to the walk-in freezer.

"He *looks* . . . like he's having fun," I said.

But Mom, a straighter than straight talker, of course meant the question literally. "I meant is he wearing different clothes, his look? A beard and side locks? You know that dinner scene from *Annie Hall*?"

She meant the scene where midwestern Granny Hall eats dinner with the New York Woody Allen character, and all she can see is the black-hatted, side-locked ghetto dweller. "We had the same first reaction. But, yes. No. Same old clothes. A yarmulke," I said, not wanting to satisfy Mom by telling her Dad was clean shaven. "He just looks a little more Jewish."

"Perfect." Mom clapped, but it was a complicating gesture: approving, condescending, both, neither.

Just in case she appreciated the joke but found Dad's Jewishness the thing to patronize, I said the most positive thing I could manage. "Dad seems to rise to the top, wherever he is. The dinner is a good example." Later, when I asked Susan's forgiveness for egging Mom on, I reminded her that taking the truth and reducing it to its best points is what lawyers do all the time.

"I got the invitation to that dinner," Mom said. "We won't go, I'm sure. But I'm sure we'll send some kind of a donation. After all, he's our *mechutan*."

What did she say? *Mechutan?* It sounded . . . Yiddish. I didn't know Mom knew any type of *mama loschen* that didn't involve non-kosher crustaceans.

"You thought I was such a Brahmin? My parents spoke Yiddish in the house to my grandparents, and I happen to know there's no English word that translates to *mechutan*, that is, your child's father-in-law. Or *machetanister*: Your child's mother-in-law." Then, from across the table, Mom embraced me, kind of: a no-man's-land of touch, part kiss, part hug, part air. Which ended in a strong-arm surprise when she slid her hand down my shoulder and pulled the back of my hand. "Don't run off. I want to hear more about my *mechutan*. What *is* he doing there?"

"Your . . ." I couldn't pronounce the word, but I knew she meant Dad. "He's being Jewish," I said, wiggling free of Mom's grasp. The thoughtful, truthful answer. Now that she'd asked, Mom grabbed my hand again, the pitying grab. For what now? I'd felt this from every hospital visitor since Ronnie's diagnosis. Except this pitying grab had more to do with Dad.

"He can't do the same thing here?"

The problem was, it was hard to differentiate between Mom's signature straight talk and a provocation.

"What, just the way we are? Nonkosher seafood and all?" I swept my eyes in a way to show I might not mean to implicate the restaurant but couldn't help if it was the truth.

"Nothing personal, Honey. I always admired your dad."

Sure she did. Mom took up her water glass and chipped at something only visible to her expert good eye. "And how is Ronnie doing?" An observer would have thought that Mom only meant to be catching up instead of sawing me into logs.

"Better. Better than the first couple of days. He was lucky that his liver regenerated altogether." I hoped the medical jargon might be a conversation closer.

But Mom was still in control, nodding her head to signal Nava from the door of the kitchen, which Nava understood correctly, rumbling a dessert cart over to the table. The dessert cart was a sore subject for Susan. Historically, it wasn't one of Mom's favorite Susan-generated restaurant changes because Mom prioritized the need for refrigerated desserts over the need to display. (Susan had slowly done away with the creams, the brûlées and they no longer pushed ice creams or cheesecake.)

Nava placed a dessert wine on the table and poured out small glasses.

Mom acted as if the wine made her contemplative, even before tasting. "Funny," she said. "My grandparents, your dad's grandparents, they all came to this country. American dreams. Your father, he can't be serious about staying. Why can't he come back to Boston? He can be the same Jew here."

As if I hadn't had the same thoughts. Hadn't I just spent a week in the hospital watching the rabbi family, imagining Dad picking out some kosher potato chips for himself at the vending machine? What if Dad had been there for me? Isn't being a good Jew being a family player?

But when Mom asked the same question, the phrase *family player* pricked like a bee sting and aroused the little rebel in me. Not the rebel who knocked back Barnes & Noble stores, Lenscrafters, too many BabyGaps, and all symptoms of body snatcher industrialization.

No, the rebel that wanted to declare: Dad's okay. Really okay, and I might as well have admitted it. No, it wasn't the rebel in me. It was the Pursuer of Truth. I agreed with Dad. I viscerally, intuitively, intellectually, emotionally agreed with Dad, approved of Dad. Would be like Dad, if only.

If only, what? Oh, for Susan's sake, for all our sakes, I had to tiptoe around that one and forget direct communication, just play to Mom's empathy. I grabbed an actress's gesture of discomfort, looking at my hands in my lap as if they'd suddenly turned into cast extras, mumbling a cheap canard about Ronnie and having left him home alone for too long. I walked out with another air kiss as Susan pushed an aluminum tin of leftover shrimp and saffron sauce plus shrimp and red sauce into my hands.

eighteen

THE MORNING OF THE SHOWDOWN AT THE OK CORRAL, there I was pumping gas at EconoGas up on Commonwealth Avenue and I spotted a yarmulke man at the parallel pump. The week before I was seeing the born-agains everywhere, and now it was the yarmulkes. The same phenomenon, how medical students stand behind a woman in the Super Stop & Shop and she's not a person but a skeleton with a liver or a gallbladder with tendons, whatever part of the body they're dissecting that week. Thanks to Mom and to my mom, the story of my before and after life had taken a terribly self-conscious turn. Like the born-agains, the yarmulkes were souls in the corridor; no, make that souls in the corridor minding their eternity, and what was I doing for mine?

I just didn't know how to act with souls anymore. Normally I would ignore the man, or figure he'd go away, or just not see him, or, if I saw him, make grand assumptions about a man with a yarmulke, that he was less than a real person, not a type of *more*. Or, when he slid his credit card into the slot and couldn't get the pump working, when he asked me if there was some trick here, I would use large hand gestures and shrugs because I assumed that his otherness meant we didn't speak the same language. Literally and figuratively.

There I was, cold but dry under the corrugated overhang, and I bucked the shelter in order to bring him to the cashier you got to from the side street, where just a couple of minutes earlier I'd knocked on the window at the glass tube and handed over my credit card in a space big enough for a child's hand and too small to turn up a gun barrel at the cashier (though I guess that was the point). Back at my car, I reclutched the gas pump and held steady. The yarmulke man returned to his car and, finishing before me, thanked me with a wave; I found myself relieved to see that he wasn't one of the locals, that his car had Connecticut plates and bound stacks of newspapers in the backseat and that he was speaking, Hebrew I guessed, into a snappy, up-to-the-minute cell phone.

As I got back into the car, small bits of swirling snow pressed against the windshield and melted to high and rising sunshine. There went my imaginative out. If only a nor'easter would knock out the rest of the day. If only the nor 'easter would take town electricity with it. The Planning Board meeting was bound to be a high-wire act. If the Planning Board didn't come up with equitable, reasonable terms acceptable to both sides, we would push ahead to the Zoning Board of Appeals. The ZBA was always the show of shows. What if the ZBA meeting was the same time Dad came to town for his Torah Lights dinner?

I felt as if I were crawling to my own execution. I was only fulfilling my fiduciary duties, but how had I become the ringleader of the deniers of eternity?

AT LEAST THE Planning Board sessions enacted town law and procedure, which meant they were open for the public to come see but only the principals participated. Which distinction would be lost, I suspected, as I walked into the extralarge space at the main function

room at the main library. Extralarge space for an extralarge expected turnout. Extra-animated, extra excitement—extra innings,
probably.

Even a half hour before showtime the room was filled up to capacity. The ceilings were cathedral high, and the room held stacks
and shelves of local talent, books by Brookline authors. I'd read many
of them: the geisha book; a book on the Dunkin' Donuts founder; a
book about how doctors think; a biography of Marie Curie; short
stories on requited love but in all the wrong places; a book of short
stories with the word *effigy* in the title. That one had me pause a
minute. Oh, Brookline was a lovely, educated, liberal, literate, enlightened place, but maybe not so when it came to other people's
enlightenment. Where was the logic in that? Be what you want to
be except if someone else doesn't like it.

I scanned the crowd for telltale headgear, religious or weather
driven: three black beaver hats, Dr. Zhivago style; innumerable
women's berets, wool or knit, primary winter colors; two red and
blue Patriots hats; one fleece ski cap; one black knit cap with an Israeli army logo; a dozen black fedoras; one women's Burberry cap,
wide brim. Not to forget the purity-of-face people, the bonnet faces.
The woman at the Wall in Jerusalem had a couple of sister-clones. If
I read the hats right, the room was filling up evenly, school advo-
cates to school opposers.

"Honey Black." A yarmulke man, tall, broad shouldered, and
slim, with a trim beard, approached me. He did not shake my hand.
"I just wanted to put the face together with the name. I'm Hank
Firestein. The lawyer in Allan's office. We've been speaking about
your client's brownfield probate problem. We have a meeting set up
for next week, but I knew I would see you here."

Now, someone upstairs had a sense of humor. The attorney in
Allan's firm who was consulting on Michael Marder's case wore a

yarmulke. I didn't want to lose focus. "Nice to meet you—and we'll see you next week," I said.

Just then the Planning Board walked in, one by one and gravely, taking their seats behind a raised desk in front of the room. In the corners, the ponytailed fellows adjusted their cameras, and I noticed—which brought me to a sweat—Kerry Caritan, the Channel 4 newscaster. A woman puffed powder on his face, getting him camera ready. All of which enhanced the predatory feel of the meeting. I took a seat in the front row and waited.

We were the second of two items on the agenda. The first petitioners were a couple, both speaking with accented English—Spanish, Portuguese maybe—and the wife wept softly behind a yellow cloth handkerchief. They stood at the left corner of the dais, able to see and be seen. They lived in the home her father had bought after he'd come to America and labored twenty years as a housepainter. All they wanted was to build a second parking space, and they had the room to pave a new spot, right across their front lawn.

But no one was allowed to park on the front lawn in Brookline. Even if it was her family home and even if it was paved. Worse to have it paved: The board was emphatic. The woman's weeping turned into a loud moan. They needed two parking spots, and now they would have to sell their home instead.

If she'd been my client, I'd have stayed the tears after the intake moment. Recognizing land-use principles is the very heart and soul of municipal responsibility, and anyone knew that Grace Heller needed quick categories and too much crying made her dismissive. Grace and the board decided a unanimous no.

When it was our turn, I got up to speak first. I said, simply enough, the cul-de-sac was fit for residential use only. Anything else endangered the residents. Nothing new. Nothing that hadn't been heard already. My eyes rested on the crowd; Hank Firestein listened carefully. Then I realized he was sitting next to a rabbi. One of the rabbis. Did that mean he was the lawyer on their team? A lawyer? Did that mean I was getting distracted?

Who said that because I was rational I was right? I meant, for example, why was murder bad? Not because it wasn't rational or logical. The Japanese kamikazes weren't crazy. They were brilliant pilots who sacrificed themselves for their military national goals. Or the suicide bombers. What about suicide bombers? You read their diaries, see their videos. What's the relationship between logic and reason and doing the right thing? Why did I think I was right because I sounded so reasonable? With that I lost steam, quickly. On the other hand, I was bound by my fiduciary duty to continue; I cut and pasted mentally, but I retained my last shot, which was, all said, really my best shot: the traffic. The noise in a residential neighborhood. Finally, there were not enough parking spaces planned to support the use of the building. When I sat down, I was hot around the forehead and face, the rims of my ears. Even my chest burned.

To my surprise, the people of faith also had an unhealthy dose of bad nerves. And I'd second-guessed the sweet passivity of Rabbi Mandelbaum, who would have the town hang its head in shame at the core issue. He walked to the front of the room slowly and described a case in New Jersey, one that I was familiar with, one that I'd hoped he wouldn't bring to the town's attention with its fuzzy application of the law. A synagogue was denied a building permit because it did not have enough parking spaces for the allotted seats and size of gatherings. So they drew parking spaces into their plans, spaces which would remain empty and unused since this was a crowd that would only walk to services on Shabbos. Then the permit was finally denied because all those parking spaces bespoke a wildly aggravated traffic condition.

"Would he just come out and accuse us of anti-Semitism?" Rae leaned over to me but didn't bother to whisper.

Grace Heller asked the first question: "Are you saying the plans will be emended to include parking or to exclude parking?"

He barely opened his mouth when a voice flew across like a put shot.

"Not in America." The heckler wore one of the Dr. Zhivago hats.

"Go home." A shout from the middle of the room.

"Go to your home in Israel."

"Go to your home in Africa." The voices volleyed.

"What if," shouted a black fedora hat, stepping out from the crowd pressed against the side wall. Uh-oh. He was one of the real religious ones. The cable TV cameras spun to catch him. "What if we were to substitute another type of school there, another denomination? What would the response be?"

"The same response, the same," Rae stood up and shouted. When she sat back down, she wiped her brow with a tissue, an oddly Victorian gesture.

A Patriots hat—or was it a beret? I don't remember—stood up. Before he got to speak, the rabbi's wife sitting a row ahead leaned over to the woman sitting next to her, who stood up and waved her hands about like a TV weatherman in front of a camera. "Not so. It's not the same response. This is particularly, specifically, totally against a religious institution. It's like Germany here. Germany, 1939."

"Sit down. Calm down," Grace Heller screamed. "This meeting is in session. We have a meeting to conduct."

The cross fire zinged around the room, too loud and too quick to be controlled by Grace Heller. This was ball game volume with no goodwill, and I'll never know if the hecklers were plants from STREPP.

And for a minute, I didn't know where to align myself. Civil liberties should apply to everyone, even when the cause doesn't appear "liberal."

"Say no to Yarmulke Street." A young man in black on black with a black vest moved forward from the side wall.

"Say no to Place de la Faithful." This was a local psychologist whose heart tore for displaced, disadvantaged humanity.

And then, of course, depending on who you ask, a scuffle began when Ms. Germany 1939 waved her fists. Or did it begin when Dr. Place de la Faithful threw down his backpack and charged to the dais? The first camera stopped when Dr. Faithful ran to the corner and knocked down the video tripod. And Mr. Germany ran to the far corner and pulled the plug on the second video and sound system. By then, the crowd stood up, and I only saw what was going on because I was in the front row.

In minutes, the Brookline police stomped in, several soldiering pairs of them, flashing handcuffs. Their nightsticks smacked at their hips as they picked out the rabble-rousers, one per side. In the history of the Planning Board, this had never happened before. Not here. Not in our town. What had I wrought?

LATER THAT NIGHT, the snow I would have prayed for early in the day if I'd known how to pray fell steadily. I sat in my kitchen watching through the window as the road disappeared into the horizon line, a perfect metaphor for the way I felt snapped off from the rest of the world—my world. All of my worlds. A tow truck chugged up the street, hitting the curb with pit-pats of sand. My chest hurt, muscular and large, a phantom response, as if I'd been sobbing for hours.

In the morning I had an icky, caddish feeling as I opened the front door to check on the morning paper. Coddled in a tube of green plastic, in spite of the snow, the paper was there, delivered on time. I flipped to Metro section: There it was again, the new favorite catchphrase: "Jew vs. Jew." "Trouble in the town," the article began. I folded the paper back, set the thing on the kitchen counter, but couldn't bring myself to read it.

I would have liked to think that, on the domestic side of the law, life went on smoothly, but I also had to break their own bad news to Richard and Ronnie. They'd gone to bed hoping for a snow day, but the morning was one of those conciliatory after-storm mornings, like since you suffered *that*, now I'll give you *this*: The temperature would spike and the sun would brighten and the snow would be gone by noon. I called up to the boys a couple of times until Richard's uneven footsteps tapped out on the stairs.

"Anyhow, snow always makes me think like a kid," he said when he finally came into the kitchen. He walked up to the pantry and stood there. "You got any instant oatmeal? Cocoa Puffs? Trix? Hot chocolate mix?"

"Sorry," I said. "I have leftover shrimp from the other day."

The joke was a mood killer. Richard sighed into his morning routine, popping a bagel out of the bread box and slipping it into the bagel toaster. He ate his bagels naked, medium toast, on a napkin, and he regularly snubbed my shelf of condiments and spreads: all-fruit strawberry preserves, apricot jelly, chive cream cheese, lox tip cream cheese, garlic-boursin cheese, butter, and it's-not-butter spread. I didn't even bother to lay them on the table anymore, or make a suggestion. I could only imagine the look or the face or the smart-aleck answer if I ever suggested kosher.

He crunched away, dropping crumbs on his chin and the chest of his sweatshirt, and his oblivion made him look more child than adolescent or like an obviously senile person.

"Ever wonder what I'd look like with normal hair?" he asked.

"Where did that come from?"

"Where it always comes from. Why can't our family be normal. Brown, black, blond. Not red." The whole list was singsong until the word *red*, which he spit out.

"Do me a favor. This is not the morning for that conversation." I couldn't take being a double family loser, on the giving and the getting ends.

Richard leaned over the *Globe* at the page I'd turned back but couldn't bring myself to read. "Is that you?" He pointed and asked and, before I could answer, "Last bagel?"

Easy enough for him to equivocate. Maybe I should have been happy that in our house, love, food, attention, bagels flowed on tap or like mother's milk. Or happy for Richard that there was a mother altogether. I could tell him that life wasn't all about what you receive or what you pass forward. But listening to myself was half the problem already. And getting harder. Ever since we'd been in Jerusalem, it was like the thing that I didn't know was my soul had grown a mouth of its own, and it was getting a little bit too Jiminy Cricket sometimes, the way it wanted to moralize or wag a finger and say things like right, wrong, insignificant, hmm, no, yes, don't do it.

nineteen

W ITHIN A WEEK OF THE PLANNING BOARD MEETING, Dr. Faithful, a man of color, filed a lawsuit against the police department for discrimination. Ms. Germany, a man of strong principles, filed a lawsuit against the police department for use of excessive force. The town lawyers had their hands full. Though neither suit affected the forward movement of the school case, bad will abounded. Allan came home from Dean Park, where he'd thrown some balls with the boys, and repeated a story, apocryphal maybe but telling. It seemed that a yarmulked dog owner and a not-yarmulked dog owner fought over a slobbery tennis ball thrown across the dedicated dog field. Once one dog dropped it, the other man didn't want his dog to retrieve it.

"Why are you repeating such a stupid story?" I asked.

"It proves a point. Religious people—"

"Or not religious. How are you so sure about assigning blame?"

"How are you?" Because I'd heard about harassment: The Brookline police were ticketing cars for over-two-hour parking absolutely everywhere within three blocks of Rae's street and the school. And at dismissal, at recess time, the children walked in sidewalk lines so perfectly to the letter of the law that the *Globe* quoted Rae when she said the school community was being aggressively passive.

Would the town burst before the next step? Before the Zoning Board of Appeals session? And I heard a louder drumroll than that: The ZBA meeting was scheduled for the day after the Torah Lights dinner. Which meant that Dad would be in town for the ZBA showdown. I still hadn't told him about the school case. It was bad enough that I was a traitor at heart, at soul. A bit of a sympathizer for the other side. With Dad in town, I would have to fess up, one way or the other. My colliding lives were not working out, not working out at all.

Four weeks, three weeks, two weeks. Dad's dinner was one week and three days away, and the ZBA meeting was one week and four days away. Dad and Evelyn were on their way to Boston, and I'd begun to feel as if my body were divided, but not down the middle, not down any lines I could recognize. And then, Susan and I realized we had to feed Dad and Evelyn and house them. In the last e-mail they told us that next bit of news, that they'd rented out their Brookline condo and would stay with Susan or me.

Ever true to the life of externalities, Susan was convinced that once we wrestled down Dad's upcoming visit to the plain mechanics of making a kosher kitchen within a kitchen, everything else would flow. It was her idea to shop at Tablelocity at the Atrium Mall. I'd agreed; we'd shop, get coffee, sit and talk. But there I was, off-balance with my body because I was suddenly an eternal soul. Like I was a tuning fork that measured world frequencies against something deep inside me, as if—all along—my outrages and actions had stemmed from that small place.

I couldn't help myself: The floating, untethered sensation only got worse as we stepped from the underground parking onto the massive, endless escalator; past each rising floor, each passing sideshow of lights, all those rings of commerce for personalized calendars, the best and latest cell phone, fashion watches with this year's colored bands. I held on to the rails and stumbled off where the escalator ended, precisely under the atrium dome, precisely across from the entrance to Tablelocity at less of a door and more of an aggressively displayed landing that featured an eye-catching table of the new AeroGarden 2, which was—if the sign was to be believed—a cubic foot larger than AeroGarden 1 and, to the best of my knowledge from a quick glance, a dome-topped, self-contained world for perfect at-home kitchen herb growth. A perfect metaphor, I remember thinking: I used to live and grow my family and my job in a contained and covered world like that. Then someone took the lid off.

Susan grabbed a cart and piled up an expert cartful of four-, six-, and eight-quart pots, pot holders, ladles, and red and blue utility knives—times two, for dairy and meat. I wandered between oddities, lunch boxes sewn up from wet suit fabric, stackable cups for poolside drinking. We settled up quickly and parked the kitchenware bags behind the cash register; we would come back for them before we left the mall. Then, across from the escalator, we scooted into a bagel-colored banquette at the Coffee Cantino, where the atrium was exposed and the heights to all that great artificial top light pulled my eye outward.

I was about to say it reminded me of the scene in the movie *Ghost* where the undead Patrick Swayze character finishes his work in this world and moves to the light, to eternity, but I was a little gun-shy that Susan would accuse me of religious filter again. Susan got the napkins and sweetener, I set out both cappuccinos with skim, arranging a slice of carrot cake with two forks exactly between us. On the other hand, since when was I afraid to speak my mind? But it wasn't just my mind speaking. It was my soul speaking. Me sitting with Susan was like an apple trying to talk to an orange. As we popped the plastic lids off our coffee cups, I forced myself back into place and asked her why didn't she just get the cookware from one of her suppliers?

"It would take too long. Besides, I like to go out with the masses. Like a supermodel shopping at Target."

"Don't get carried away," I said. Her joke, my joke. I hadn't planned to see myself joking, but there I went again, seeing myself from the broad view, like a movie camera training in from the ceiling: down the walls of light, to our round wooden table for two. Why couldn't I fess up? I mean, by now, shouldn't it have been obvious that this kosher business wasn't all about technicalities but about meaning? Purpose?

"Seriously," Susan said. "You're not going to believe this—but I wanted colors. Nothing industrial, white, or stainless steel. I like to shop in those places. For me they're like toy stores. Or candy shops." She leaned in to her coffee and inhaled the steam. "Smells more like cardboard cup than coffee bean."

For a moment my heart flooded with appreciation, for the soft and sensitive side of Susan, the one who liked colors for a reason and smelled the roses and the coffee, the one who just might be able to hear what I'd been thinking about, the one who would give me the answer I wanted for the question I didn't want to ask. "What do you think Dad will make of the school case?"

"Don't know," Susan said, slashing the tip of a Splenda packet with her teeth, and her face brightened up. "You want to hear something funny? Did you ever hear of DAR, Daughters of the American Revolution? The American blue-blood, white Episcopalians? DAR, Daughters of Rachel, DOR—they're almost the same thing."

"Not quite. That's really stupid, really stupid. There's no comparison to what we're doing and to how we're supposed to be the Daughters of Rachel."

"I'm trying not to think about it."

"And I can't help it," I said. "Dad will be devastated by the school case. *I* will be devastated when he is."

"You don't know devastation," Susan said. She was outdevastating me. A sisterly thing. "My supplier for baby greens is so overworked from the baby green trend, even though we've been buying them for twenty years, that all he delivered was baby fennel and a half crate of baby bok choy." She grinned up at me. She was kidding. "No, but really, we *are* having a problem with the baby greens. And I think I'm having general food anxiety."

What made me imagine I could talk to her? "You think Dad's visit is all about accommodating the food? That once we *do* the food, everything else falls into place."

"Yes—basically," Susan said. "We can accommodate Dad without approving of him. And him—to us. That's family. We do it all the time."

"Or the opposite. This conversation is beginning to sound like a replay. If either of us had any guts, we'd have a different discussion altogether." This last comment was long in coming but felt good, once it was out.

"What's that supposed to mean?"

Should I have backed off? Why couldn't I bring myself to say that I wanted what Dad had to give me, that I wanted to be a Daughter of Rachel? What was I afraid of? Not Susan, of all people. Allan? If he ever got to see, got to really see, then he would at least soften his bark. But I backed off. I didn't want to provoke Susan. Or anyone. I told myself that it was strength that had me back off, and I dropped the conversation to low ground. "We don't know what we're doing. How did you know to get two of everything?" At least when you disappoint yourself, you're usually the only one who knows.

"I don't remember. Mom told me—or someone."

"Our mom was never so Jewish, so 'out.'" I looked into her face. She cast her eyes into her coffee cup; she didn't want to tell me. Then she couldn't hold it back.

"Okay. Carnie Goldstein." Her face crimped to the true confession. "Carnie has a religious brother. She's not exactly happy to say it out loud and to say it proud. He drives her crazy. His wife drives her crazier, but she said, 'You have to get two of everything.' Red and blue to tell them apart or at least pretend you're telling them apart."

I stirred back the milk foam with my little wooden stick and took a drink that was longer than necessary, wanting to give the impression the coffee and confidences were my full banquet. So, Carnie had an agenda too. Besides STREPP, all her whispering in Susan's ear was thirty-odd years of sibling baggage.

One last, long swill of my coffee left unconquerable and muddy foam swirling on the bottom of the cup. And why was it—was I imagining it? or did every song on the sound system have the same rhyming words, like *free, be, you, me*?

twenty

NOT THAT IT MATTERS TODAY, BUT SUSAN SAID IT WAS MY idea to go see our old-new friend Mrs. Mandelbaum and get a mini lesson on cooking kosher food for Dad and Evelyn. Now that we had the pots and pans, we needed expedience, the quick track, a kind of kosher in one lesson for dummies. I'd called Susan and pestered her for a day and a night until she agreed, and she was the one who pointed out that if we went during the schoolday, Rabbi Mandelbaum, the husband, would surely not be home and we would have no conflict.

What was with all the kosher angst? I told myself: Relating would be the soft touch, something I would do for the town, for my abstract goals of peaceful coexistence. Anyhow, I had to find out: Were they Mandelbaum relatives? Native New Englanders?

We were off to see . . . Mrs. Mandelbaum. No red shoes. No props, no little people. At least Susan owned skirts, a half dozen black skirts in graduated lengths and thicknesses for all restaurant seasons; I had to dig in the back of my closet. Not that anyone suggested we follow a dress code, but you had to be a social dolt to ignore this fundamental thing that religious women wore skirts and not pants.

When I came to Susan's door, she answered and sucked in her breath.

"What?" I said. I already had the feeling that my look in a skirt was the way I was feeling, bisected and short, a skewed piece of geometry.

"Skirts are good," Susan said. "When you wear a skirt you can be five pounds heavier than when you wear pants."

I wasn't sure why she had to say that. Meanwhile, I slipped into the bench in the kitchen bay as I watched Susan peel open a new bag of Morning Ecstasy coffee beans, funnel them into her home grinder, then her espresso machine, and touch the start pad. I leaned forward, then back, then forward again. It wasn't the first time I'd thought that her kitchen bench was built on two planes, like two dimensions, right for stick figures, not real bodies with meat on the bones and souls inside. But the discomfort wasn't physical—it was dread. Real dread. Now what was that all about? I found myself using the energy I might have used for pacing by twisting the hem of my skirt between two fingers. For all that, a skirt came in handy.

The espresso machine churned and chugged. "The beans smell black," Susan said.

"Rotten?"

Susan laughed. "No. Woodsy, ebony. Like that." She grabbed my hand, a gesture of warmth I wasn't in the mood to reciprocate. Susan stifled a laugh into a cough.

"What are you all affectionate about?" I asked.

"You have to *give* if you want to *get*," she said.

"You sound like a marriage book," I said.

"Hard to explain," Susan answered, sitting back again. "This stuff with Dad gets me all stirred up."

"Stuff. You mean the soul stuff? The afterlife stuff?" Maybe she was coming to. I sat up straight, as uncomfortable as the bench was. I wasn't hungry for food or thirsty for coffee. I was hungry for expression of my thoughts and confusion.

"What's on *your* brain? The food. *The kosher food.*"

The coffeemaker, a junior twin to the restaurant machine, continued to espresso. Not an inspiring noise, a reality noise, and I sank back into my dread. What if I would see this woman, open a door, and not be able to get back?

Detachment, that's what Susan was feeling. She pulled two small flowered cups out of a drawer beneath the machine, tapped the fill button, and a minute later pushed two steaming cups across the table. I felt responsible for neutralizing my dread and her dissociation. Before we left I got paper towels and spray from under the sink, wiped the tabletop, offered a summary we both could handle. "Just for the record, I'm doing this with two minds, a kind of scared but good for you combo. Like tough love or getting pulled over by a cop for speeding through a school zone."

But Susan one-upped me. "No reason for you to get soft on me now. We're doing it for the food. To accommodate the food."

"NO. NOT THAT there," I said, as we climbed up the wide front steps under a sign that said B'NAI DOVID. "We're supposed to go to the side door." We turned the corner.

Susan pointed to the word WOMEN embedded in a greened-over brass plaque next to a buzzer. "Are we in Brookline anymore?"

I shrugged; we climbed up the few narrow steps, with no help from a rusted and wobbly and thereby worthless iron railing. As per instructions, this door was unlocked.

"Sorry," I said.

"It's not *your* apology to make."

"I don't think separate but equal is the major theme. I was told the main synagogue entrance is already locked at this hour and the entrance to the women's side of the synagogue gets us directly to the offices upstairs."

Just inside the door, a small bulletin board hung with APT. FOR RENT signs. And a sign for a business: HATS 'N' HOSE. WINTER CLEARANCE, 25% OFF. Inside the main room, rows of folding chairs, lined up theater style, faced the front, Beacon Street side of the building. There were a couple of stairways and a small elevator. The elevator creaked up to the second floor. The door snarled open to steps directly in front of us.

Another half flight up. Just off the landing, the rabbi's wife sat in her own office with framed diplomas on the wall, a good resting place for nervous, disoriented eyes. She might have looked like Mama Bear, but Mama Bear didn't have advanced degrees: An M.S.W. from Boston University. An M.S.Ed. from Simmons College. Or citations: The next two parchments in frames were certificates, one from Governor William Weld, one from President Clinton regarding the Avon Walk for Breast Cancer. "My husband and I came from Minneapolis. He came from Europe when he was a kid." Okay, so they weren't New England Mandelbaums. But the thought didn't comfort me.

"My office used to be the kitchen. Or should I say, my kitchen used to be my office." Mrs. Mandelbaum looked less perplexed than anyone I'd ever seen, kind of Zen if you asked me, so her strain for precision confused me. Maybe we made her nervous, and not just the other way around.

"My office is the kitchen too," Susan said, finally, meaning it to be a joke, but the woman raised her eyebrows without moving the rest of her face, a look open to a dozen interpretations, not the least being that Susan had overestimated some free-floating need. Or connection. Or underestimated the solid ground that belonged to this woman. Because, even if Susan didn't know, I knew their kitchens would never be the same. I sat myself across from the desk on an upholstered shield-back chair; Susan sat on its double.

"You want to see mine?" Mrs. Mandelbaum said. She meant her kitchen, and she had a name. According to the diplomas and citations, her name was Mrs. Charna Mandelbaum.

Charna? What kind of name was Charna? She led us down a dark hall, not dark because of lack of light. In fact, a cord of fluorescent tubes pointed the way along the ceiling. The hall was dark from lack of real decor: The walls were the same thin wood veneer homeowners tack onto concrete basement walls to "finish" the look, and the rolled linoleum was raisin black. The house was built in an era that knew floors should be generically darker than walls and didn't mind the railroad hitch of one room beyond another.

After all that, the kitchen was a surprise. Not the finish work, which was much what I expected: Formica cabinets, the never-never land sheen of plastic wood grain. I saw Susan's eyebrows lift to the holy grail of utility. The kind you see at kitchen shows, what the pros call a home restaurant kitchen, or a restaurant home kitchen. Which led my eye down to the windows, two of them, each with a wide stainless sink beneath. Next to each sink was a dishwasher, extrawide. There were two wall ovens, an extralarge refrigerator and its extralarge freezer twin, and a bakery-size KitchenAid on a stainless cart. Capped by a 1960s mustard gold Formica scallop at the soffit line.

"Did you want a drink? A piece of cake?" she asked. Without waiting for our answer, she disappeared into a pantry and came out balancing paper plates and cups and a bottle of seltzer.

"Do you have some kind of restaurant here?" Susan asked. "My competition?"

Hardly, I wanted to say. I mean, there Susan was. It wasn't the first time she had a chance to get some meaning from the food. But there she was.

"I make meals for people."

"So do I." Susan wasn't getting it. "What do you mean, meals?"

"People come for Shabbos and holidays."

"You mean like . . . Yom Kippur?"

"Well, we don't exactly eat on Yom Kippur. But before and after, yes. Other times too. We have guests. Lots of guests. Hospitality is—how shall I say it?—a very Jewish thing. A mitzvah."

"You do all this cooking yourself?"

She laughed, out loud. An unrestrained laugh, and all the while, even when she threw her head back, the hat she wore didn't budge. And something was up with her hair, which didn't budge either. (Later, much later, I learned about the marriage wig that women wear, the partner to Evelyn's hats). "Though it was something I grew into." She lowered her voice. "When I was first married, of course, I knew how to cook. But not in this volume."

"What kinds of numbers?" Susan asked. "I mean, it's hard to imagine that what I do for a living, someone else is giving away."

"We might have twenty or thirty people for a Friday-night Shabbos meal. Students. There's lots of students. And every couple of months we have a huge group with speeches and lectures. Maybe a hundred people then. Three formal meals during a Shabbos. You do the numbers."

Which Susan had already—the equivalent of catering a small wedding on a regular Shabbos, a large wedding on the special ones. Susan's face closed up. I didn't usually think that she resembled Steve.

With Susan in retreat, my tongue tied. Our hostess pulled out three chairs in the middle of the kitchen, around the table. A clock just above the Formica scallops ticked loudly, a clock faced with—my best guess—Hebrew letters instead of numbers. A loud tick: I couldn't figure out if the clock was moving forward or backward. Counterclockwise, I thought.

The rabbi's wife, Charna Mandelbaum, followed my gaze. "It *is* going counterclockwise. It's a replica of a clock in the town center in Prague."

Susan poked some response through her social freeze. "Same era as the Golem of Prague?" Here we were, barely Jewish literate, but we knew a couple of things.

Then Mrs. Mandelbaum excused herself and returned with a small, full plate. Zucchini cake, she said, and though it was the color of the linoleum, it was happily moist and it had chocolate chips. Susan took a spiral pad out of her pocketbook, ready for facts and figures, but the rabbi's wife started with an overview. "You know how they say you are what you eat? That's the basic idea of kosher."

"And hygiene too," Susan said. "I mean, who hasn't heard of pork that used to have trichinosis."

"If that was the case, kosher wouldn't be relevant now, would it?" Mrs. Mandelbaum said. "It's more than hygiene. Kosher is like food for the soul as well as the body. Hashem's diet for spirituality." When she said things like that, Mrs. Mandelbaum looked like a pure soul in a pure body herself, as if all that kosher food had done its work. I mean, as if she wore her soul on the outside too, but she was oddly and enticingly still in this world. "The list of what we don't eat is long for a reason."

I held my breath. She wouldn't dare lecture us about shellfish, which was Susan's livelihood. "For example, we don't eat birds of prey. For their aggressiveness, their tension."

I let go my breath. The possibilities for insult and injury went right over Susan's head. That was the good part about her "I'm OK, you're OK" attitude. But it left me thinking that even though I still had my picket fence between me and "them," now I was propping it up on both sides.

twenty-one

NOW IF YOU'D ASKED SUSAN, THE OUTCOME OF THE CON-versation with the rabbi's wife was not affirmation of the soul business but nothing more and nothing less than the logical division of labor. I was game to keep all theology under the radar. So, Susan would cook kosher at her house and I would procure. Which is how, a couple of days later, I found myself climbing a snowbank turned ice mountain, using what gym masters call a core balance technique to open my purse in midair and dig quarters out of the bottom for a parking meter outside the kosher grocery. One step inside, a single glance took it in: The store was a bakery, deli counter, fast-food joint, kosher vitamin dealer, wine and cheese emporium, with a sign that said NEVER TO [sic] EARLY FOR YOUR PASSOVER ORDER, even though it was still winter on my calendar.

I couldn't find a shopping cart, but the brightly colored handbaskets were ergonomically designed, and I rose to the challenge. Was I any less a juggler than the woman in front of me who was steering a stroller with her free hand, or the woman grazing the wall of matzo meal products on Special Sale who was on double duty with both a stroller and a large baby forward-faced in a chest carrier, bobbing its head like a car ornament? I'd come armed with very few shopping specifics, but, according to Susan, and more important, the rabbi's wife, everything at this store was kosher enough to buy, and everything I needed except fresh produce was there.

What I hadn't counted on was the insider ambience, which could make an outsider feel like a leper. Shopper after shopper was on a first-name basis with the man behind the single cash register, who wore a trimmed beard and jeans and a baseball cap, and the etch lines around his eyes, chin, and cheeks turned upward, giving the impression of a smiley face, someone who's happy with his lot in life. He called to the first stroller woman, "Mimi, your beef ribs are cut and the salmon fillets are coming in this afternoon."

This Mimi nodded her thanks and turned to look at me. Stared at me, actually, then turned toward her fussing baby. The second woman, anchored between the packaged rugelach on an iron grille display and family-size sacks of rice strewn in a plastic bin, cast her eye on me and turned away. At the same time the man behind the counter leaned forward as I whizzed by on the way to the packaged croissants. "Aren't you . . . ?" Apparently he couldn't bring himself to say "the bad guy?"

Forget deer in the headlights. There's got to be a fresher and more apt description of sudden self-awareness, of impending doom bearing down on graceful creatures going about their daily business. Quickly and just as vaguely remembering what Dad ate, used to eat, or might eat, and remembering that Evelyn didn't like red meat at all, I stacked a couple of packages of boneless chicken breasts, a half dozen steaks, and a top-of-the-rib-cooks-like-brisket into my handbasket. The weight nearly sank me to the floor.

I spun back to the refrigerator and picked out what looked like a container of soft cheese because Dad ate soft cheese in Israel. Once again at the meat counter I picked up a chicken cut in eighths, only 2.8 pounds, but it finally demolished the balance in my handbasket; in fact, tilted it portside like the scales of justice on a bad day for the defendant. I barely had time to think between the moment I whipped out my credit card and the moment the smiling man behind the counter looked at my name and said, "Oh, I thought I recognized you."

"Yes. I'm—"

"I know, I know," he said. He didn't stop smiling, but he scanned my card without looking up and handed it back without looking up and looped my plastic bags off the bag rack without looking up.

I STAGGERED OUT to my car, fifteen pounds of kosher meat hanging off each wrist. I'd moved out as fast as I could. Because next to the cash register was a clipboard with a sign-up sheet, a petition against the people who were against the school. My name and Rae's were at the top of the list.

By the time I reached the car, climbed over the snowbank, and heaved the bags into the trunk, my wrists felt as if they'd been slashed and my biceps were straining. But I hadn't bought enough. I wasn't done, and, instead of holding my head high, I realized that my self-consciousness had limited me to animal proteins. I remembered what my intentions were, how I'd wanted to avoid a visit to a general supermarket, where only some things were kosher and I'd have to consult my special list of Orthodox Union labels and little kosher product insignia: stars, circles, backward *c*'s with *k*'s in the middle. So be it, so be it. Trying to accommodate religion at the same time I was grandstanding with the school case.

I drove over to the Stop & Shop on Harvard Street. After I parked my car in a real parking lot and got a cart with wheels this time, my adrenaline crashed into clarity: Susan was fooling herself with the possibility of parallel lives. Either religion is True or not, and Truth has obligations. All I had to do was look at myself: There I was in the Stop & Shop cracker aisle with a picture of kosher symbols in my hand: *o*'s with *u*'s in the middle, *o*'s with *k*'s in the middle. And at the same moment Dad and Evelyn were packing their bags in Jerusalem; Susan was holding teal and not quite teal leather samples up to the fluorescent light in her office; Allan sat behind his desk in his high-rise downtown, fine-tuning a brief against someone else's ideas. My life felt like the conference room in an old World War II movie where the generals stab colored pins onto a large map of the world, colored pins to indicate troop movement and, most important, colored pins to herald the hot spots and where the big battle might take place.

twenty-two

EXACTLY ONE WEEK LATER, SUSAN AND I MET DAD AND Evelyn at Terminal E at Logan Airport. It wasn't the first time I thought that if I ran the world, all family visits would be consistent with the force of first-moment greetings, when agendas are subsumed by the clean love and the complications are stored in the baggage. As yet unopened. We hugged, I cried. "You look so good, so good," I said, hanging on Dad's shoulders. Kissing Evelyn.

"I'm sure I look exhausted," Evelyn fussed. Susan demurred a no, no.

"Okay—you look good but tired," I said. In my intake love state, a kinder description of their pale and puffy faces, the way travel puts the fluid and ecosystems out of whack. Evelyn had taken a Dramamine, so her walk was loopy. I took her hand luggage, Susan linked her arm with hers; I linked with Dad, who said he had heartburn.

"From what?"

"I don't know. I wasn't thinking and I ate the kosher chicken meal they gave me for lunch and then before we landed I wanted to wake up so I had to have black coffee without milk. You know, no milk after meat. But I shouldn't be drinking black coffee."

The way a dream fizzles in a movie, the way the scene tinkles into pieces and drops out of sight, there went my greeting. It's not as if I'd thought for a minute that they'd leave the religion back in Jerusalem. Dad wore his big black yarmulke, and Evelyn wore a soft black beret of the same velvety material.

Evelyn and I slid into the backseat of Susan's truck. Before we got to the Ted Williams Tunnel, Evelyn was bobbing her head on her chest. Dad swung his head from side to side, comparing the size of Logan to Ben Gurion Airport. And the buildings: Coming in over Boston made Boston look more like Manhattan.

"Dad, there hasn't been a sudden outcrop of high-rises. You've just been gone six months," Susan said.

"I know; I sound like a hick. I feel like a hick. Where we live, seven stories is a high-rise."

"I love where we live . . . ," Evelyn said. She wasn't asleep after all.

"I love it too, but we have no visual scope from our windows, our trees. Just if we leave the neighborhood."

"Since when is a view so important to you?" Evelyn asked. Touchy, not especially a trait I remembered. She was wide awake now, leaning forward. "It's not like we have a view past Beacon Street in our condo."

I had a new one for Susan: Who was black and white and carried a whip? Apparently, Dad had to make amends for seeming to bad-mouth Jerusalem. "Some people live with a big view. Some people—like us—we are the view. Someone has to be the view," he said.

Evelyn sat back, satisfied.

WHEN WE GOT to Beacon Seafood, Steve was sitting in one of the back booths with the night captain scribbling something across a spreadsheet. The captain bowed from the waist and left. Hi's, hugs, handshakes. Did they want anything to eat? Being kosher sensitive, of course they offered: Salad? Coffee? Fruit? Anything?

Dad and Evelyn huddled together like refugees at Ellis Island, bent into each other and clutching their hand luggage. Satchels pulled up around their feet.

"Water," Evelyn said finally. "A glass of water is just fine."

They did not sit down. So this was going to be it, their stance on Beacon Seafood. After a couple of minutes, Steve finally slid out of the booth. "Hey," he said, hugging Dad. "I'll bring the mountain to Mohammed."

Nava was back with two glasses of water. "What else can I get you? The shrimp salad is fresh. Crab cakes right out of the fryer," she said.

"Fine, fine, Nava. Just fine," Steve said. "Don't bring anything."

"What can I get you, Mr. B? Mrs. B?"

"The water's fine, thanks," Evelyn said. "You know we haven't stepped into a nonkosher restaurant since—"

"Since Prague, probably," Dad said. "And that was too bad, too, for such a holy city."

Now their "holy" was expanding with them. I held my tongue as they stood and drank.

But count on Evelyn: She emptied her glass and turned to Dad. "Dan . . . we don't belong here." Her face registered real dismay. Real displeasure. Real distress. How could six months make such a difference in a psyche?

"She's right," Dad said. "Can you get us back to your place? Or just take me over to my garage and I'll get my car."

"What are you in such a rush to get your car for?" I asked.

"It's Thursday already," Evelyn said.

"Thursday," Dad repeated. "We just landed, but we have to go shopping, get ready for Shabbos."

"Oh, we have you covered for Shabbos," I said. "In the law if not in the spirit. Just you wait." I wished that Shabbos was all I was talking about.

THE NEXT DAY, Dad stepped into Susan's kitchen on the cat feet that come when someone is doing the other a favor, and all he said was that maybe he should buy stock in Reynolds Wrap.

I know Susan well enough: Even though she rode the wave of self-management, it was fragile. The best she could do was pretend her blowup was only fake. "Cheap humor. Cheap, cheap. You can laugh all you want, you can capitalize on my perceived weaknesses, you and Honey can pretend that my life is all external, all renovation and decoration. But if one more person walks into the kitchen and admires the luster, the sheen, the ambience, the inventiveness, or the sophistication of the tinfoil decor, I will scream." She slapped down a frying pan on the counter.

She wasn't done. "At your own risk to alienate the cook. Plus, if anyone bothered to look at the rabbi's wife's list taped to the refrigerator door, it says how—short of getting a new stove altogether—we had to cover the cooking surfaces with tinfoil, which was in the first half dozen double-underlined instructions. And now the soup is boiling over." A fleshy, sizzling smell rose in the air.

"It could be worse," Dad said. "At least you have the granite counters. If they were Formica, you'd have to cover them too."

The tinfoil talk flared up one of those mind-control accusations, but as I was sitting with Dad in Susan's kitchen, the accusation took off in a sad direction. We'd learned all about mind control the last year Mom was sick and Susan joined me at summer camp, the one in western Mass that prided itself on camping austerity: Our bathroom floors were plank boards; in our cabins the open windows had no screens and nightly bats swooped in one window and, if we were lucky, out the other. These were the days before VCRs, and the camp had one movie for rainy days: *Invasion of the Body Snatchers,* the pea pods that morphed people into zombie versions while they were sleeping. On rainy nights the campers gathered in the dining hall and saw that movie a dozen times a summer if they saw it once. Susan and I played the movie back at our house, on snow days when we didn't have to go to school. Other mothers would be baking with their kids or making thick soups with meat bones and hot dogs. Our mother stayed in bed and we played body snatchers.

I wanted to hug Dad, tell him it would be all right, but I wouldn't have been sure what I was talking about. Even then I had the sense that, after all was said and done, he was the one with the ability to reassure, not I. Objectively speaking, he still looked *normal,* more normal than normal, in spite of the yarmulke. Or maybe more formal, more off-putting than we'd seen him in Jerusalem. He seemed to have left off his jeans, he was wearing dress pants and a sports jacket with brass military buttons, and he was carrying one large and one small green velvet prayer bag, which he laid up on the counter at just the spot where tinfoil formed a seam with the granite.

"Poor Evelyn. She can't shake the fatigue. Sleeping off jet lag for twenty-four hours?" he said. He slid into the banquette, not before filching a paper cup from the stack and pouring himself orange juice from a carton with an *o* with a *k* in the middle at the ingredients line. "I think it's worse in this direction."

"How many times have you come in this direction?" Susan asked. I assumed she'd meant to bleach the sarcasm, though she hadn't quite. She bent into the celery she was chopping on a paper plate. All her confident kosher kitchen shopping had overlooked the luxury, nay the necessity, of a cutting board.

"It's what they say."

"They?" Susan looked up.

The very words shot up my back. I saw Susan shiver her lumbar up to a toss of her head. In the day since he landed, Dad also displayed a new penchant for referential talk, always seemed to have a *they* hovering in the background, like he'd come in a group and he was the spokesman for collective experience.

He slid back out of the banquette and pointed to an instant hot-water dispenser next to Susan's sink. He already knew his way around to the foam cups and plastic silver. Paper plates and bowls. There was more where that came from. After one phone call to her lobster bib supplier, Susan dragged home half a dozen hundred-count sleeves of paper plates in two sizes, cereal bowls, serving bowls. She was squeezing her eyes against onion gas and opened them to tears, looking out the window. The daylight had tamped down to another storm on the way, perhaps rain, or—on the sliding scale of misery—snow or ice. Or bad water pressure—oh, that had become a lost cause.

"Hey, I haven't seen instant hazelnut coffee for months," Dad said. He'd grabbed the plastic jar and held it up to the light. He put it down again and began to reach for the regular Maxwell House.

"What's the problem?" Susan asked.

"I don't see the kosher symbol. Sometimes it's easy to mistake the ℗ trademark sign for the U kosher sign."

"Maybe when you don't have your glasses on," Susan said. "Here." She pointed to a spot on the back of the jar.

"Well, I'll be darned. There it is," Dad said.

"What could be not kosher about coffee anyhow?" Susan asked.

"I don't know. Something about the flavorings. Some additive. The symbols give the go signal."

As if we didn't know that already. Hadn't he seen the kosher symbol list hanging on Susan's fridge, the twin of the list hanging on mine? What was the problem with additives, and what kinds of additives anyhow? But if I asked him, I'd be opening the spigot, so to speak. Susan chopped slowly and steadily against the paper plate.

He made a blessing out loud and drank his coffee. "Imagine," Dad said, "if my grandparents came down and saw this meal you're making, this home. They would recognize everything in it. They would sit down and eat here." Invoking inheritance issues—large, small, attitude, real property, or otherwise—was exactly the wrong thing to do. When he left the room to try to wake Evelyn, I found myself alone with Susan, who was still sniffing back onion tears. Whatever it was Susan could smell or taste, or even cry over, well, at least she had a name for it.

AFTER SHABBOS CANDLE lighting, Susan crawled on her hands and knees in her foyer closet, digging past the extra ice melt and wind-shield wiper fluid for the bag of old hats, gloves, and worn-out but not thrown-away boots. In their drive for internal perfection and shedding their past identities, Dad and Evelyn had also forgotten the climate they came from and weren't prepared for a wintery walk to Shabbos services. Susan handed Evelyn a pair of battered La Canadiennes. Evelyn sat on a dining room chair, grunting as she squeezed the boots over her ample calves. "Whatever kept you from throwing these boots away?" Susan rolled her eyes in my direction. I knew what she meant. Catching up on her sleep was good for Evelyn. She'd napped her way back to the usual loose connection between her mind and her mouth even as she found herself on the receiving end of Susan's beneficence.

RONNIE FELT THE lift of atmosphere, on perfect cue. "Are they gone?" he called from upstairs in the family room.

"The coast is clear," I called up. Then I heard the whiz and the click and the TV starting up, the dopplering swirl of the surround sound system as it turned on from speaker to speaker. They'd had to wait till Dad and Evelyn left because the TV was on the short Shabbos no-no list, like car, radio, and telephone. Part of the change-the-physical-world circuit of electricity that came from lighting fire that came . . . Oh, what did I know?

"You coming up?" Allan called down.

What was I supposed to do? I always watched TV on Friday night, but Shabbos was riding my back like a monkey: I felt the betrayal if I went upstairs to watch TV on Shabbos; on the other hand, Susan was organized, and there was nothing to do in the kitchen or dining room. I'd already read the *Globe* on her kitchen counter, twice. So I watched TV, but the rumbling feeling in my chest and stomach was almost something I could name. Hunger was part of it, but not the final analysis, as it turned out.

I made my way downstairs ten minutes before Dad and Evelyn returned from services an hour later. They blasted through the door so loudly that I figured Steve, Susan, Allan, Richard, and Ronnie would come downstairs on their own. I was almost right. Steve and Susan came down right away. Richard inched down slowly, as if he would take the banister with him. Feet, body, head, feeling self-conscious. I forgot to mention that a few days after the conversation we'd had in the kitchen about normal hair he'd dyed his red hair brown, and several shampoos later he still looked streaked and splotched, Halloween themed. He made it to the bottom of the stairs with a bit of a show, yelping from the cold at the open door, hopping from one bare foot to the other. I would talk to him later.

"Allan, Ronnie?" I went to the bottom of the stairwell and called up.

They didn't answer, and Dad and Evelyn did not shed their coats right away. They stood on the floor register and slipped off their coats to a blast of forced hot air.

"Dad, they're back. We're ready to eat," Richard yelled up, cupping his hands as we'd all learned to do at Susan's house, directing the sound with a megaphone effect.

We heard two electronic clicks and the back end of a weather report as it hopped off from speaker to speaker. I pictured it, Allan pushing against the swivel leather chair to pull himself up, and he answered—in deed, not words—what he'd agreed to by coming downstairs in loud treads on the rug runner. He made his point with actions, shock and then orientation on his face, like a time traveler who has to figure out what year he's landed in.

Under Evelyn's direction, Susan had left the soup on a low flame, which had to be covered for some reason, so she'd covered it with a disposable lasagna-size tin. The flame was too high, Evelyn said, and she could tell because of the sour smell of turnip and parsnip. I'd smelled it too, I said. And then I didn't say that I'd already had the thought of the roots they were, then of earth and something primordial without being primitive, something animate, definitely essential.

The candles we lit, also under Evelyn's direction, were white, unscented; the idea, Evelyn patiently explained, was that of bringing light, radiating the stuff a woman supplies to the home. Allan squeezed my arm as we walked into the dining room to remind me I'd asked a lot when I asked for his patience and patronage.

At least Steve and Susan knew that food has its rhythm. We sat around the table, set with a white paper cloth with plastic on the underside. And set elegantly with white paper goods and clear plastic cutlery. Dad with his big yarmulke, Evelyn with a maroon knit beret that glistened with the bits of snow turned to water. Dad began with his Kiddush on sweet wine, and after he drank

he poured cups for everyone. He made a blessing on the bread.
We ate.

"Susan, you're like the Little Red Hen," Dad said. Yes, she made
the challah loaves, shaped ground fish into patties for a first course,
ladled up chicken soup, which had cooked all morning and made
the house smell like a Shabbos meal since 10:00 A.M. She cooked,
she served, she cleared. The wine and the soup and the sitting spread
ambience, like—I hate to say it—a Tuscan restaurant or a private
cruise dining room. Steve ate a third helping of chicken soup, and
Allan ate two helpings. He wouldn't look up at me. He didn't say a
word, but if the boys were ambivalent, you couldn't tell from their appetites. They'd ignored the fish, but they pounded away at the sliced
brisket in gravy and the side dish: Susan had layered a white and
sweet potato soufflé into a new white serving dish she'd unpacked
from the restaurant office.

When the food slowed down, the conversation paced up and the
boys fidgeted. I'd told them earlier in the day and I reminded them
in the kitchen before dessert, no going back upstairs to the TV. I'd
taken all precautions about conversation; I had briefed Allan, Susan
had briefed Steve: No inflammatory talk. No talk about the endowment, the dinner, the school case, Town of Brookline anything. On
the permitted list: the food, sports, movies, summer vacation, the
boys' school. Ronnie's teacher, who turned out to play in a new-grass
bluegrass group on Thursday nights in Cambridge. After all, I felt
responsible, the motherless mother in me picking up the responsibility for everyone's satisfaction if not happiness. Susan did the food,
I created the ambience. Or so I wanted to think. Shabbos had its
good points.

I first noticed that look on Steve's face when he perched on the
edge of his chair. He'd gobbled dessert, a piece of pie with nondairy
ice cream, and I thought for a minute that he was going to ask for

seconds. I was wrong. His chiseled face tightened on its own lines as he sprang into the kitchen and brought back a water pitcher. Friday night is a big night at the Beacon, and we'd promised Steve we would take no more than an hour and a half, but there we were almost two hours later. I figured he wanted one more look at the clock without being obvious. It was his home, his table, and he'd promised time, unimpeded. Next to Steve's lined face, Allan's wide, unreadable face looked so amiable; it was almost over, this evening, this meeting of the worlds. And Allan, always mind driven, idea driven, had heard me when I said I wanted peace for one evening. That, yes, I had something to prove, if he wanted to look at it that way.

"The only time we sit like this with sweet wine is Passover," Steve observed.

I relaxed. Lifted my wine to my lips. Five minutes to go.

"So why is this night different from all other nights?" Allan asked—referring to the Passover Seder and its famous opening line. Then he laughed. All the adults laughed, but not the boys. My boys didn't get a Jewish joke. I would have lingered on the sad thought, but I saw Allan's face change very quickly. I saw it in the way his features stiffened, his eyes got smaller, more focused. He'd had enough, maybe. I had to clear the table and end the feel-good vibe.

Steve rose and announced, "Dear Dad, I have something special for you in honor of your . . . visit." He meant a special bottle of single-malt scotch. Did Steve and Dad have much in common ever? Besides single-malt scotch and high school football? Opinionated, not the opinions. A tendency to take his reality and act as if it's all reality. Dad broke away from this as he was seeking the truth.

"L'chaim," Steve said. "Or as they say in Scotland, sláinte."

"To Yarmulke Street," Allan said.

"To what?" Dad asked.

"He said 'Yarmulke Street,'" Richard said. "You know, like in the newspaper."

Dad laughed. Not really a laugh. Evelyn's face froze. I hadn't noticed how tired she looked, with the lines and dark circles under her eyes and red blotches on her cheeks. And by what impulse had Allan lost his reservoir of politeness on behalf of Dad? Oh, I knew what it was because politeness wasn't really there to begin with: because what was I dealing with in the Brookline Hebrew Day School case but this, the scoffing, entitled attitude of all so-called enlightened, educated people toward matters of religion? As if . . . as if we weren't all souls in this world together.

After dinner, Susan at least had an excuse for Steve. He had to get to work. Allan just didn't get it, and, when I pushed him, all he could talk about was how he hated the endowment. For all Allan's disdain, it was Steve who let it all out. (It was Susan's job to shush him. She didn't.) I tried. *"Steve . . . ,"* I said.

He ignored me. Then, even though we'd made our permissible list clear and our impermissible list even clearer, Steve began to describe the Planning Board meeting, the whole problem with the school, my involvement, the good, the bad, and the ugly.

Dad listened quietly until Steve was done and then slugged back another shot. Allan slapped him on the back.

Dad was stone silent. By now we were clearing the table. "If I've learned nothing else, it's that action requires action," Dad said. "When is the Zoning Board of Appeals meeting?"

"Thursday night. Always Thursday night." I ground out the words.

"I should have remembered that. I'll be there," Dad said.

For the first time I noticed that Susan was wearing a skirt for the occasion of this dinner. She uncrossed and then recrossed her legs, defensive. Offensive. Defensive. Offensive. "Dad, you don't want to be there."

"Why not?" Dad asked. "I've been to those meetings in years past. Don't forget that I've been in the building trade."

Susan's eyes turned cartoony and flat, but oddly undismayed.

I don't know which husband did more damage, but I remember thinking that, whichever one it was, it clearly mattered more to me.

twenty-three

THE NEXT FEW DAYS HAPPENED FAST. DAD CALLED JOAN at Town Hall. He might have been gone six months, but the way he threw himself around the town, you'd have thought he'd been away for an hour. He met with Rabbi Mandelbaum several times. Susan said that Rae said she saw him drive up to the school, and when Dad got back to his car he found an over-two-hour parking ticket tucked under his windshield wiper. Dad moved into the Holiday Inn down Beacon Street, and every time I called him he was busy, Evelyn said; he couldn't come to the phone.

This school battle would be the most significant I'd ever fought, especially with the publicity that STREPP was drumming up. When Dad did call me, he was brief and to the point. It wasn't as if he'd disown me, but, when I said that the endowment did just that, then he thought he might have to agree. Susan persisted: He will come around when he sees that, culturally, we can be Jewish without all the rigid religious stuff. After all, she was turning half of Beacon Seafood into a Middle East oasis. But what if all that religious stuff, besides making some visceral sense, gave me closure on Mom? And what about Allan and the way he folded his arms across his chest every time I tried to speak to him about the endowment? I felt as if I

were a contestant on a game show and the results were rigged and I
knew what door I had to pick but I couldn't make my mouth work.

The best I could explain to Susan was that I didn't want to be an
orphan of Dad. Period. And I didn't want an antireligion law in the
State House with my name on it. And, while I was making a list, I
wished once and for all Susan would stop thinking that renovation
was life's means and goal, which on the surface appeared to be a
sidebar distracting type thought, but it really wasn't. I thought so
hard, lost so much sleep, I thought my head would explode. And it
did explode, in its own way. Though, what I did to stop it all wasn't
as spontaneous as it might have seemed. I mean, I wanted to pursue
the truth as much as anyone, and I wanted to get comfort from Dad
and get some closure on Mom as much as anyone, him at least, and
I wanted to live my life in a meaningful way. If only there was a way
to silence the neighborhood association without alienating the other
parts of my family. Or maybe convincing the family that Dad wasn't
so off the wall. What was I going to do? Could I do anything?

TWO NIGHTS BEFORE the Zoning Board of Appeals meeting I had a
dream about Mom. In my dream I was running down Beacon Street
in the breast cancer walk, except in my dream it wasn't a walk. More
like a road race, like the Boston Marathon, but I wasn't wearing
shoes. Mom grabbed my arm and pulled me out of the crowd in front
of the restaurant at the Powerade stand. She handed me her shoes. I
didn't want to take them. Here, there're more where these came from,
she said. As soon as she'd taken off her pair, another pair grew right
in. "The gift that keeps on giving," she said. She meant the shoes.

"The loss that keeps on losing," I said. I meant, the loss that kept
me losing, but I was already a half block past her when I realized I
had to correct myself.

That's when the seed of my idea took place. I mean, what if it wasn't a dream? Dad and all his eternal soul business had jiggered loose my psyche or else I wouldn't have thought of what I thought of. What if, instead of a dream, Mom in her eternal soul form had come from some soul place in the sky—and I had a visitation?

The perfect opportunity clicked into place. Susan phoned that morning just as I'd gone into Ronnie's room to toss his empty medicine bottles. No more anti-inflammatory pills. No refills left, no refills needed. A real milestone, I told her.

"How about if I make a celebratory dinner at Beacon Seafood?" Susan said. I heard something new in her voice: The way she intoned *Beacon Seafood* sounded exactly like the way her mother-in-law sang the radio ads to the tune from *Fiddler on the Roof*. I didn't know what it meant, but it was the final push I needed.

The seeds of a lie, already planted, sprouted right then and there. The school case challenged what people—Susan, Steve, Rae—think we know, but what if it challenged the gray area of the place that people know they *don't* know but probably do want to know. I mean, look at the history of séances and the popularity of psychics: The storefronts in Mission Hill projects appeal to the same thing as the parlor rooms on Newbury Street with hemp and bead curtains and rocking tables and chills down the spine. I mean, there was truth and there was truth, and preserving one while forgoing the other—well, who knows? Maybe neither truth is what it's made out to be.

SUSAN'S STAFF HAD pushed together two tables at the back of Beacon Seafood and set them generously with three avocado wine holders with bottles, bread sticks and garlic knots, antipasti salads in three long white plates. We settled around the tables: Steve, Susan. Allan, Richard, Ronnie, and me. Carnie Goldstein. Rae Stark and her husband. With two empty spots left for Dad and Evelyn; we'd invited them, but I knew they wouldn't come to squirm and drink their glasses of water while we ate forbidden foods. What were we supposed to do, have this dinner in the kosher pizza shop?

I couldn't exude my thoughts with Susan. She'd come to the table sulky and struggling to smile. I knew why. I'd walked in the door at the loading dock and interrupted a smarmy, private exchange between Susan and Steve. His mother had e-mailed from Florida, simple and insidious: Every restaurant decision became a banner of family name. Since Mom had gotten back to Florida, she'd been thinking: What was the bed of origin of all the seafood inventory?

"She thinks I buy Boston harbor?" Susan said. "Dark skin, the loose scales are bad enough. But the rumor of mutant fish, that's true."

"The crab?" Steve asked.

"Alaska, Northern Canada."

"Oysters?"

"Seattle."

"Lobsters?"

Here, Susan rolled her yes. "Maine, Maine, Maine. Why do you pay attention to those e-mails?" she asked Steve. "Makes the after-life an easy one," she said as she slid into her seat next to Rae.

She didn't look up at Steve when he made the first toast. "Ronnie's special day, better than a birthday party."

"A rebirth party," Allan said.

As long as I kept my eyes off Allan, I could do this. The time was now; it wasn't as if I hadn't weighed plan after plan, any other solution. I'd already imagined the stir if I fainted in the middle of the ZBA meeting. But, worse come to worse, the meeting would be postponed—or go on anyway. I'd imagined a series of anonymous phone calls to Rae and Susan, but the phone calls would have had to be threats to be taken seriously, and I'd watched enough *Law & Order* in my day to figure I couldn't outsmart all the police techies.

There was only one perfect way to poke a hole in this case, deflate it and pull my family back together, and that was by coming full circle to get them where they already hurt the most and where they couldn't prove me wrong—or right. I mean, after all, what was this reaction to the school, to the religion really, anyhow? Something visceral, something inside. I mean, what it came down to was that you had the eternal-soul people going head-to-head with the antieternal-soul people, but there had to be a place where they weren't so far apart.

I'd hit on the perfect right thing. What a brainstorm. And I'm not sure what it ultimately says about me, but when the truth and the lie rubbed up against each other, the words came out of my mouth smooth as smoke.

Not before a couple of false starts. I'd intended to begin after the antipasti, except Nava the waitress butted into the family scene like a Greek chorus with her take on events. She read the push of the garlic knot basket as a gesture of hunger, that is, the kind of hunger you could feed. And for a flickering moment, I was hoping Nava was right. No sooner was the antipasti cleared than she appeared beside the table, a row of quiche plates across each forearm. She dealt the quiche around the table: crab, sun-dried tomato, scallop, and she began to chatter: All those years it turned out her name was Maria and so were all her sisters in Brazil named Maria and seeing Susan and me made her miss the companionship of her own. She pronounced the word *companionship* without the *m*, which made copanionship sound like a cooperative event.

Susan froze Nava out with downcast eyes and no direct response.

There was something to be learned from Nava's persistence, the straight-backed way she walked away from the table, through the kitchen door, and out again to the dining room, and her cheery re-appearance tableside to assemble the salad, that day a taro chip event with peppers, spinach, and avocado. With a stroke of luck, the con-versation had turned to Daughters of Rachel.

Steve and Allan matched snorty laughs. Allan repeated what was so funny. HOTDOR. Allan laughed out loud this time. They were the husbands of the Daughters of Rachel.

That was so stupid and so vapid I had no choice but to begin. "I saw her." The words glided out of my mouth, like I said, smooth as a smoke ring. In my ears only was the pit-pat of accelerated breath-ing. Mine. I unbuttoned the top button of my shirt. I wasn't sure who heard me; I had to speak louder. "I had this dream last night." At the other end of the table, even though I'd heard Susan loud and clear, she wasn't listening to me. "Take, take," Susan was saying, as she slid wedges of crab quiche onto small plates and passed them around the table.

"No, no," I said. "I have plenty." Very loud this time. I didn't want the crab. I didn't want to eat crab. Allan gave me a look when I took a wedge of sun-dried tomato. He knew I hated sun-dried to-mato. Oh, the crab was a complicating antiprop. I had to stay fo-cused. On the other hand, I didn't want Allan or Susan to ask me why I didn't take crab if it was always my favorite. So I pulled the crab quiche back and slid a wedge on my plate anyhow. I wouldn't have to eat it.

"This wasn't any old dream. It was more like a visitation."

Susan stopped serving. Allan, Steve, and Rae looked up. The boys were busy boating forkfuls of quiche through seas of ketchup on their plates. I panged with guilt; I didn't like lies from myself or from them. But this wasn't conversation I was making. I was saving the Town of Brookline and making us into a family again. "A visitation," I said again.

Susan snorted this time. "You must have eaten cheese before you went to bed. I heard this discussion on NPR. There's this British study about eating cheese before you go to bed, and it depends on what kind of cheese—"

"You're not listening to me," I said, in my best deposition voice. "Mom. I saw Mom. I thought I was sleeping, but I guess I wasn't."

"You need to have an exorcism or something?" Allan said. "Where was I, anyhow? Don't we share a bedroom? Wouldn't I have seen her too?" Oh, I hadn't thought of him. If I'd had a dream or a visitation, I would have woken him and told him.

"I don't know," I bunted, but just as quickly I remembered he'd left for work at 7:00 a.m. "It happened this morning. You were already up and out of the house."

Okay, so one by one I knocked the obstacles out of the way and it was time to click in. You would think that I lie or distort all the time, but it's just that the pathways of "seeing" Mom were already in my brain. I mean, how different was this from all the by-my-side scenarios where Mom tells me what to wear on the first day of ninth grade, and the way I imagined Mom watching me as I walked up to get my law degree and laughing that at least she wasn't as bored at the graduation as Dad?

I could tell from the o-mouth looks on the faces around the table, and the tapping but frozen fingertips and laid-back-down silverware, that I had entered the world of possibility. There was something, somewhere in most people—call it the soul, call it anything—where they might want to have just this little belief that the entire non-physical world where souls live just might be true.

"What happened?" Rae asked.

"I'll tell you, from the beginning. We were standing by a water well—"

"Water, that's symbolic. A woman's fertility, her home—" Carnie waxed.

"Don't get me impatient. Listen. It was some kind of public meeting, something going on in a room with Palladian windows with pastel decorations, eggs and bunnies and baskets and a video camera setup, these ponytailed guys in jeans barking orders. That's when Mom appeared."

"Are you sure it was Mom?" Susan said.

I have to say, the feedback grew the story for me. Rae's face froze the same moment Susan asked me to supply a detail. It was working. "Yes, I would recognize Mom anywhere. Anytime. Mom was wearing something white—"

"A shroud?" Susan said.

Steve came back into the room. I hadn't realized he'd slipped out. Carnie Goldstein emitted mouse sounds, nothing more or less.

"How did she look? Was she young, old?" Susan said.

"She looked, well, kind of luminescent in a way you'd never think about age."

Then I hit on the perfect right detail. "What she was wearing . . . was a dress, like one of these Diane Von Furstenberg wrap dresses. Remember those?" Was I confusing contemporary fashion with something from the way past? Had I blundered? I forged on.

"'Honey,' Mom said to me. She put her hand on my arm, but I didn't feel anything. She called my name again and she said, 'I'm so pleased to hear that you dropped the Brookline Hebrew Day School case.'"

"'Dropped the school case?' I said. 'Mom, you must have heard wrong or something. We're absolutely head-to-head right now, right in the thick of things, there's going to be a blowout meeting, and we're determined to make sure the school doesn't take over the neighborhood.'

"'No. *You've* got it wrong,' Mom said."

Rae guffawed and slapped her husband on the shoulder. I still can't believe I said what I did.

"Then Molly Stark came up behind Mom. She didn't come up like she was walking up, but she suddenly appeared at her side. 'Yes, you've got it wrong,' she said. 'Tell my daughter. Tell Rae I said so.'"

"Tell me what?" Rae asked. Now her hand froze just above her husband's shoulder.

"She didn't say exactly, but I knew she meant the school case. So I said, 'Mom, what do you expect me to do with the neighborhood association? I've given my time, my word.'

"'Honey, that's *your* problem. But once you stop this harassment, the neighborhood association will back off and you'll find a way to live together properly. And you and your sister, perhaps more properly. You are, after all, daughters of Rachel.' She said the name Rachel in a Hebrew way—with a guttural and a twirly *R*. And then she disappeared, and Molly Stark stood for a minute in her dress and full makeup. Did I tell you she was wearing makeup, looking as if she hadn't aged a bit, and she said, "You tell my daughter, you tell my daughter . . . '"

"Tell me what?"

"She didn't get to finish before she whooshed out of sight. And then I woke up. But it was all so real; if the snowplows hadn't woken me up, I wouldn't have known I'd been asleep."

Ronnie and Richard hit high fives, whatever that meant. Had they been listening? Steve and Allan smiled that pinchy-mouth half smile, the way men look when they're afraid they'll be called insensitive. On the table, the quiches were cold and congealed, reminding me of colored Jell-O, and someone had hand-hacked the crusts of the sun-dried tomato. In the human silence, I heard music from the kitchen, the kind of plinking mood strings and bells you hear when you're getting a massage. But the intake moment lasted no longer than my sucked-in breath. Rae and Susan and Carnie, pale and buzzing, burst into speech at the same time, which had the effect of white noise, all blurred and blended. I picked out their comments, one by one.

"Come on. Could that have been real?" Rae asked, but I could tell from her tone that she was considering. Her eyes moved in toward the bridge of her nose, and her lips peeled back off her teeth as if what she was going to say would kill her. Even then I saw the genius of the plan. Once I brought the other world and dead mothers to the table, even if you thought it had only a 1 percent chance of being true, wasn't that what we all wanted all those years anyhow? Given a chance to ferment, that desire could be as strong as any in our lives.

"Did you see her feet?" Carnie asked.

"Huh?" Three of us turned to her at once.

"If you see the dead person's feet, then it's real. There's something about the feet—"

"Where'd you hear that?" Steve said.

"Everyone knows that. There's this Jewish thing about throwing out the shoes of a dead person and not giving them away."

"I never heard of that," Allan said. I hadn't either. But . . .

"I saw the feet," I said. Call me an opportunist when it comes to the truth. "Mom was wearing running shoes, the kind with this colored webbing on the side."

"You mean she was running? Not walking to the nearest corridor?" Allan asked.

"That's mean," I said. "Now you're making fun of eternity."

"I'm not making fun of eternity—" Allan began.

Rae rolled her eyes, a generic exasperated gesture, though this time I wasn't sure what she was for or against.

Allan and Steve made puppy eyes that said, "A woman's thing?"

"Let's say there's a remote possibility—" Rae began.

"Excuse me," Steve said, sliding out from the table, sliding out of the discussion. Easy for him to do. His brush with mortality had fins, scales, and claws.

"A remote possibility it's true? Absolutely." Allan cleared his throat. "The truth is, no one could know it wasn't true. You would have to know everything in the world to know that it's not possible, not true. And we don't know that."

I've thought many times about Allan saying, in so many words, that souls and afterlife could be true; it's what allows me to hope.

"I'm going to have to think about this," Rae said.

"Me too," Susan said.

"Don't think too long," I said.

RAE CALLED ME to talk later that evening. Susan too. The next morning, on Rae's behalf, I called Rabbi Mandelbaum myself, and by the afternoon I'd called Joan at Town Hall to cancel our appearance at the ZBA. We neighborhood folks were ready to share the sandbox.

twenty-four

SINCE THE DREAM AND THE LIE AND THE TRUTH AND THE back down of the *Neighborhood Association vs. Brookline Hebrew Day School*, I still can't figure out how it was that this soul business, so slow in coming for me, was so easy to prick inside of Rae—and everyone else. Not that Rae is dancing out in the street with a hallelujah chorus. Not that she's invited the school teachers to park in her driveway or that she's pledged a classroom in honor of recently departed Moe. But I am the one who's foundering: I, who stared down eternity, I, who did something good on eternity's behalf. What do I do now? Dad confessed that he asked the same question after his maiden voyage to the Kosel. When he and Evelyn got up to receive their plaque at the Torah Lights dinner, he leaned into the microphone intimately. It was the first time I'd heard it from his point of view, how he had to push past the warmest, best-meaning obstacles of family and love (us), how his rabbis at Torah Lights shepherded his transition with sage advice: The family, sooner or later, would "come around." We heard him loud and clear, and we managed to clap with the rest of the crowd when he sat down, we—the pinched-faced, chastened, air-kissing daughters.

. . .

"DID YOU KNOW chocolate chip cookies, surgical anesthesia, and traffic circles were invented in Boston?" Dad asks. He's tailored his trivia for the sake of my fatigue and my tolerance for religious conversations. He stands at the kitchen island, trying to get me to eat, mixing ice cream with stuff he gets at the kosher store, stuff with Hebrew writing on the labels, like halvah and waffle cookies, and then plain old American junk, M&M's, Heath bars, Reese's Peanut Butter Cups. Busywork, since Dad, the same man who knew all the endings to the *Brady Bunch* before they were in reruns, admits he doesn't know the ending to this one and he didn't expect me to "come around" this way: I have breast cancer. Now that treatment's full force, I'm too tired to eat and it's hard for me to finish writing this down with the same regularity.

Dad speaks in worry-free modulated tones, but his eyes, as they say, the windows to the soul, are circled with lines like those a cartoonist uses to show anxiety in a black-and-white character drawing. He's got some answers if I want to ask the questions. I don't want to ask, I say. So he asks them for me: Why breast cancer? Why now? The rabbis and the books agree on one thing: My suffering is the very strong and obvious proof that there's an eternal soul, because we can't possibly fit what we see into our own idea of justice and there has to be more to the story.

Meanwhile, Dad has a lot of organizing to do. He's arranging for a lift crate to be sent over to Jerusalem, the bulky things, like their own bedding and a small makeup table belonging to Evelyn. Her dishes, too. She's been clamoring for her own dishes and her American pots and pans. But, after all is said and done, he's grateful that they were in town. The week after the dinner, Evelyn went with me for my annual mammogram because she accompanied women all the time. Strangers. She did it here, did it in Jerusalem. We drove down Beacon Street talking about the dream. About ghosts wearing shoes or not wearing shoes. At Schrafft Radiology they served up hot-off-the-press gossip magazines and lukewarm coffee. Evelyn followed me to the second waiting room, where I read and waited in my johnny gown to make sure everything was okay before they sent me home. Imagine my surprise, I who was an orphan, I who didn't have the nasty gene, I who fought the inheritance of Rachel but who maybe saved it in the end, imagine my surprise when the technician came back out and, instead of telling me I could get dressed, said, "Ms. Black, can we take another picture?"

What Dad knows and what I know is that sometimes you circle back to the beginning of an idea. Last December I was the one who thought Dad was sick and religion was weakness. Just because my mortality and my soul are on the line and just because I can walk side by side with him and his yarmulke, does it mean that now I really have to change? Isn't knowing all this stuff enough?

"Don't let your stubbornness and your rebellion get in the way. You're allowed to grow into religion when you feel threatened," he says.

"What makes you think something's getting in my way?" I say.

In the end, Susan has been the most helpful.

Last week Dad came home with a flyer from the synagogue bulletin board. Chavie, the Brooklyn wig maker, was coming to town. Actually, Chavie the Brooklyn wig maker had a daughter, Poppy (short for what?), who'd moved to town and opened a business. One of those businesses that cater to religious women who cover their hair for religious reasons. Maybe, Evelyn said, she'd get a wig instead of wearing those Red Sox hats and berets all the time. I was too tired to ask all the right questions about things on top of the head, but not too tired to catch the implications (getting thematic by now); the head covering has to do with the idea that our brains have limits, that it's not our ability to understand reality that creates or defines it.

Evelyn, Susan, and I found the little street in Brighton, ten minutes down the road from Brookline Hebrew Day School, but a world away. Poppy's studio was a basement walk-in. If I'd had the energy, I would have asked her about the zoning, but the first thing I saw shut me up anyhow: a wig stand with, instead of a lush wavy do, a man's head of hair, cropped short, with sideburns attached to a beard. A full head and face of hair for someone who'd lost his. That picture said more than a thousand words! What a funny place this was, the funny confluence of suffering and enlightened souls who needed hair.

"Honey's got breast cancer lite," Evelyn said to Poppy. I'm not sure where she got that one.

"Well, I have the wigs," Poppy said.

There were dabblers in wigs, Evelyn whispered, but this Poppy was the cream of the crop. I wasn't sure how Evelyn got all this information. She'd been religious, what, eight months?

I sat down on a salon chair and watched in the mirror as Susan moved behind me, flitting from wig to wig. I was surprised she'd wanted to come wig shopping altogether, but since the school case sealed over, she wasn't partnering up with Carnie Goldstein every minute, even if her renovations weren't quite done. And—of all things, her little team effort she told me just today, that she stopped eating the nonkosher shellfish. When she's at work, all she's eating is onion rings. I remind her that the onion rings at Beacon Seafood are not remotely kosher; they're fried with the seafood in the same deep fryer as the seafood. But she says it's only symbolic. And symbolic is real enough. Oh, it's comforting how Susan steers steady through all this, how even her internal commitments are external.

Meanwhile, this Poppy was willowy and stylish, wearing a tight-waisted dress with a back zipper, though apparently she had seven children. Her own wig draped over her neck like a waterfall, then past her shoulders; it fell down her back in natural waves. "I can make you one like mine," she said. "It's thirty inches long; it's called a custom wig and it takes, minimum, six weeks if I have my mother's people make it in New York."

I hadn't lost all my hair yet, but if I could look as good as Poppy, did I want to?

Susan was delighted. "Look at all the colors and styles."

Poppy grabbed a ring of hair swatches off of the counter. They looked like mini–pony tails. "Think of them like paint swatches. Or granite samples."

I had to admire her business sense, and her cultural interpretation was on target.

Poppy looked at my thinning wisps of hair and pulled me over to the light, talking in the present tense. "You are black with pink, some purple."

Susan laughed. "You sound like a decorating book. The language of color."

"What I learned at my mother's knees," Poppy said.

Evelyn sat herself on a small divan in front of a table of sensible brown wigs. Behind me, Susan rewalked the wig display, this time slowly and methodically. Chestnut, blond, ash, strawberry, red. Somewhere there had to be some in my black with the pinks and the purples. There were ponytails, swing bobs, bangs, layered long, layered short. Razor cut. Curly short, curly long, curly Afro. She held up the Afro without putting it on.

"That's the *Angela*," Poppy said.

Susan pointed to a tight pixie with a swoop over one eye.

"The *Posh*," Poppy said.

"This—this is what I was hoping to find. Mom—" Susan said. With quick hands, she lifted an old fashioned pageboy off a faceless wig head. The wig was red, not red-red but a nice auburn like our moms.

"It's called the *Nancy*," Poppy said. "For Nancy Drew; you know, the titian-haired beauty." This Poppy was full of surprises, of piety and vanity, in culture and outside culture.

Susan leaned over me and stuck her face in the mirror. Then she pulled her hair back into a ponytail; Poppy got to work. Clipping Susan's ponytail to the top of her head, she helped Susan slip the wig on, taking some expert fit measure by adjusting symmetry around the ears. I didn't want to tell Susan that she didn't look a bit like Mom, if that's what she was thinking, that she looked exactly like Susan with a red mop on her head.

"You try it." She straightened her back and turned to me.

The conversation went like this: "No, no, no. I don't like dress up."

"No, you try it. More than me, you'll look exactly like Mom."

As soon as she invoked Mom to me, I swiveled to face Evelyn and the divan. "I want to try the wig that's most like my hair. Chin length, black purple pink, and straight."

"Where's your adventure?" Susan spoke to my back.

"Radiated out." I saw the pain flare up on Evelyn's face.

"Try it."

I didn't want to. I swiveled back to Susan, who'd pulled off the wig, and now her hair was muffed up and Mohawky. Then what Susan said, coming from her mouth, was double edged. I know she didn't mean harm, nor did she intend truth. It's just that sometimes you can see very clearly what another person's problem is, especially if it's something that's the opposite of yours. She said, "Honey, even when you see the good perfect right thing in front of your eyes, you will always be afraid of change."